Dead In
Dublin

Dead In Dublin

CATIE MURPHY

KENSINGTON BOOKS
www.kensingtonbooks.com

KENSINGTON BOOKS are published by

Kensington Publishing Corp.
119 West 40th Street
New York, NY 10018

All Kensington titles, imprints, and distributed lines are available at special quantity discounts for bulk purchases for sales promotion, premiums, fund-raising, educational, or institutional use.

Special book excerpts or customized printings can also be created to fit specific needs. For details, write or phone the office of the Kensington Sales Manager: Attn.: Sales Department. Kensington Publishing Corp., 119 West 40th Street, New York, NY 10018. Phone: 1-800-221-2647.

Kensington and the K logo Reg. U.S. Pat. & TM Off.

First Printing: January 2020
ISBN-13: 978-1-4967-2418-2
ISBN-10: 1-4967-2418-6

ISBN-13: 978-1-4967-2419-9 (ebook)
ISBN-10: 1-4967-2419-4 (ebook)

10 9 8 7 6 5 4 3 2 1

Printed in the United States of America

For Rachel Caine, in thanks for all your
friendship and support. You're an amazing
lady and I'm so glad I know you.

Acknowledgments

There is never a situation where an author doesn't have a list of people as long as their arm to thank for getting a book out into the world. (Well, maybe not *never*, but rarely!) This one owes two particular epic debts: one to my husband, Ted, who thought a series about a limo driver who kept driving in and out of murder mysteries would be a lot of fun. He was right. :)

The other is to Mary-Theresa Hussey, my editor for about fifteen novels written under my other by-line, C. E. Murphy, who asked one day if I had any ideas for cozy murder mysteries. I said, "Boy howdy do I!" and she got me pointed in the right direction to get this series out to the world. I'm completely indebted to both of them, and equally delighted to have those conversations pay off in these books.

I'd also like to tip my hat to my editor, Tara Gavin, who thought the idea was fun enough to let me dip my toe into writing a genre I've loved reading my whole life. Also, OMG, all the props to the Kensington art department, art director, Lou Malcangi and cover illustrator, Anne Wertheim, for the most wonderful, charming cover a writer could want for her first cozy mystery.

I literally could not have gotten this book written without my dad helping out by keeping an eye on my son while I worked. (Said child kept kicking me out the door to get work done. "I'm only thinking of you, Mommy!" Uh-huh. Right. It's definitely not that you're waiting to get screen time from Grandpa, kiddo . . . :))

I'd like to thank the War Room—my online writing group whose sole purpose is to get words on the page—for always being there to make me write. A thousand blessings are to be heaped upon Ruth Long, Sarah Rees Brennan, and Susan Connolly for helping me get the idioms right in this book. You're all stars.

Pronunciation Guide

Irish names will often trip up English-speaking readers because we try to map English letter sounds and combinations onto a language never intended to use them. The trickier names in *Dead in Dublin* are pronounced as followed:

Ciara = Keera
Cillian = Kill-ee-an
Fionnuala / Fionn = Finn-OO-luh / Finn
Micheál = Mee-hall
Niamh = Neev
Ní Shuilleabháin = Nee Sullivan

Molly Malone **Lyrics**

In Dublin's fair city,
Where the girls are so pretty,
I first set my eyes on sweet Molly Malone,
As she wheeled her wheel-barrow,
Through streets broad and narrow,
Crying, "Cockles and mussels, alive, alive, oh!"

"Alive, alive, oh,
Alive, alive, oh,"
Crying, "Cockles and mussels, alive, alive, oh."

She was a fishmonger,
But sure 'twas no wonder,
For so were her father and mother before her,
And they each wheel'd their barrow,
Through streets broad and narrow,
Crying, "Cockles and mussels, alive, alive, oh!"

(chorus)

She died of a fever,
And sure no one could save her,
So that was the end of sweet Molly Malone.
Now her ghost wheels her barrow,
Through streets broad and narrow,
Crying, "Cockles and mussels, alive, alive, oh!"

CHAPTER ONE

Elizabeth Darr died at Molly Malone's feet.
Molly—bronze, buxom, her fixed gaze distant and serene—gave no notice to cries of concern that became screams of alarm echoing off centuries-old stone walls.

Megan, a few meters away, lurched from her car toward the fallen woman. Toward her *client*: toward Liz Darr, renowned restaurant critic, food blogger, and explorer of international cuisines. She'd been visiting and blogging in Ireland for months, and Megan had been her driver whenever she was in Dublin.

Megan had been a lot of people's driver since she'd moved to Ireland. None of them had ever died before, much less died spectacularly, in public, at the feet of Dublin's most famous fishmonger.

People crowded around the Molly statue, trying to see Elizabeth more clearly. Megan lifted her voice, roaring, "Move it! Let me through!" in her broadest Texan accent.

Like the Red Sea, the crowd parted, and Megan scrambled through to collapse on her knees at Liz's side. Her husband, Simon, knelt beside her, his usually pale face red with fear and exertion as he administered CPR with professional expertise. Literally professional: he was a doctor, though Megan didn't think he worked in resuscitation wards as a matter of course. She said, "Let me," as he broke from breathing for Elizabeth to begin the chest thrusts again. He gave Megan a wild look that she answered with, "Combat medic."

Understanding tightened the skin around his eyes and mouth. He nodded once and let Megan take over thrusting as he bent to breathe for his wife again. She centered her hands on Elizabeth's breastbone, pushing, counting, holding her *own* breath with the hope that somehow the woman would be revived.

Elizabeth Darr's temples were wet with sweat, the light hair there curling tightly. Her golden skin rapidly became sallow beneath a flush that looked hot even as death settled in place. Megan knew when Simon gave up: a helpless sound broke from him, almost inaudible beneath the sudden scream of ambulance sirens.

They'd been on approach for a few minutes, she realized; she just hadn't heard them until they were there, on top of them. Someone shouted, "Get that car out of the way."

Paramedics arrived as unexpectedly as the ambulance, pushing Megan from Elizabeth. She caught the kerb under one foot and slipped to a knee as the paramedics brushed Simon Darr aside, too. Megan lifted her voice, repeating, "That's her husband. That's her *husband*!" until one of the paramedics registered it. They started handling Simon more gently. A distraught young woman with bushels of corkscrew blonde curls offered Megan a hand up. She took it, nodding her thanks, and finally *heard* what someone had been demanding.

Get the car out of the way. They meant *her* car. Well, her company's car: Megan drove limousines and town cars for Leprechaun Limos, who catered mostly to tourists like the Darrs, and to Irish teens who thought the leprechaun-logo limos were gas for their debs—a term that loosely translated to *funny for prom.* She pushed her way back through the crowd toward the town car, which somebody was *in*, because she'd left the door open. Megan jerked her thumb at the kid. "Out! It's mine, I'll move it."

The kid sullenly mumbled, "Says who?" but crawled out in a mess of high heels, short skirts, and heavy eyebrows, unwilling to argue with the crisp, black-and-white driving uniform that indicated Megan belonged with the car. A couple of other opportunistic youths looked disappointed, but they'd have had a hard time stealing the vehicle anyway, given the congregation mashed into the Suffolk Street pedestrian area.

Megan edged the car into a quasilegal parking space around the corner, where the ambulance would be able to pass it easily, and hoofed it back the forty or fifty feet to Elizabeth Darr.

The crowd had thinned in the two minutes it took her to move the car, though there were still plenty of onlookers. Mostly young white Irish, watching disaster with the same impunity white Americans did: as a spectacle, nothing to do with them except to say they were there. A tall man with the thick build of a weight lifter sniggered into his phone about the whole display.

Gardaí appeared, clad in shades of blue, several of them wearing high-vis safety jackets over their uniforms. Itinerants, sun-scarred and too thin from living on the street or from drug use, disappeared even before the guards formed a perimeter, pushing gawkers back from the body. Hordes of others wandered off then, no longer caring, or reckoning they'd get a better view of the proceedings on the next evening's news.

A fair few stayed, though, dozens at least, including the bodybuilder. Megan elbowed her way past him, leaning on an insistent, "Excuse me, I know her," delivered in her strongest American accent. Three years hadn't done much to erase her stateside origins, and Americans got away with a lot in Ireland. She didn't like using it to her advantage most of the time, but these were extraordinary circumstances.

Grim-faced paramedics loaded Elizabeth's body onto a gurney as Megan made her way up to the yellow police line being stretched around sweet Molly Malone. A tall, slimly built detective garda with the pink-gold undertones to his pale skin that so many redheads had, and pale-blue eyes, had taken Simon Darr a few feet away from his wife to ask him questions, although Simon didn't appear to be in any condition to answer them. The detective nodded at a uniformed guard approaching them, and the woman took Mr. Darr to the ambulance.

Megan's phone rang, a quick, insistent buzz in her hip pocket. She took it out, saw the caller was her boss, and decided she hadn't noticed it. It went back in her pocket, but the detective's gaze lighted on her. A few long steps took him to the police cordon in front of her, which he lifted and gestured her under. "Megan Malone?"

Neither of them could help it: They both glanced at the bronze statue just behind them. Megan, mouth crooked wryly, said, "No relation," and the detective, with an affable charm, said, "I expect you get that a lot. American?"

"Living here almost three years now." Megan reached for identification, though the guard didn't ask for it. She would probably never adapt to that: everyone in the US, especially everyone military-related, asked for identification, but one of the delightful—or weird, depending on her mood—things about Ireland was that ID was rarely requested.

"Detective Paul Bourke." Bourke had sharp features beneath the sandy red hair and exceptionally pale eyebrows, blond against sun-flushed skin. A boy-next-door face, Megan decided: pleasant but forgettable. It probably stood him well as a cop. "Mr. Darr said you're their driver?"

Megan nodded. "I work for Leprechaun Limos."

"I've seen their cars around town. How long have you known the Darrs?"

"Three months, on and off. They've spent a lot of time out of the city, but when they're in Dublin, I drive them."

"Even though you're American."

"Ah, sure and I can turn on the accent if I need to, to make the clients happy. It's all part of the authentic experience so." Megan cringed halfway through her lilting reply, remembering that a woman had died and humor was uncalled for. A smile ghosted over Detective Bourke's thin lips anyway.

"Not bad, for a Yank. I suppose you sing."

"Mostly in the shower." Megan knew, she *knew*, the detective was using small talk to make her comfortable for the other questions he had to ask her. It worked anyway, and she was half-piqued and half-admiring at his skill. "Some people, especially Americans, like having an American driver. They like the familiarity, and not having to wrestle with an unfamiliar accent." As soon as she said it, it sounded xenophobic.

Bourke only nodded. "Were the Darrs like that?"

"No. Elizabeth—Mrs. Darr—loved the Irish accent, especially. Her grandmother was born here. But they've been traveling for over a year, and she said it was nice to hear a voice from home, too, so they requested me when they came back from the West."

"They were in Galway?"

"Mayo, I think. Westport. I don't know for sure. They've been all over."

"So your relationship with them was merely professional?"

Megan's eyebrows went up. "Friendly, but professional. I was waiting to pick them up from dinner."

Paul Bourke looked toward the restaurant,

housed impressively in the old church. Officially simply "Canan's," it was colloquially called "Canan's at St. Andrew's," while the nightclub upstairs, wholly owned by Fionnuala's business partner, was nominally "Club Heaven" and generally called "The Church." Both establishments had done well since their grand opening just before Megan moved to Ireland, and Canan's had established itself as a popular new Irish cuisine spot in the wake of the tourist office moving out of the church and leaving it up for lease. "It's got a fine reputation."

"It's good. I eat there pretty regularly."

Bourke, faintly surprised, turned his attention back to Megan. "Are limo drivers well paid, then? Maybe I should look into a career change."

"The hours are not good," she warned him. "No, a friend of mine owns the place."

The detective flipped a notepad she was sure he didn't need open, consulting it. "Martin Rafferty?"

"No. I mean, I know him, but Fionn's my friend. Rafferty's her partner."

"Fionnuala Canan? What can you tell me about her?"

Megan made a face. "What do you mean? She's a great chef and she bakes my birthday cakes for me as a present."

"Not prone to food poisoning guests, then?"

"What? No!" Megan jerked a horrified look after the ambulance, long since gone with Simon Darr and his dead wife in it. "Oh, no, she couldn't have had food poisoning, could she? It takes longer to set in. It doesn't usually kill people, does it?"

"I suppose we'll find out." Bourke closed his notebook. "Do you have a card, Ms. Malone? I might like to talk to you more later, although I imagine we'll find this to be an open-and-shut case, in so far as minor celebrity deaths can be."

"Who uses cards in this modern age?" Megan had one, though, with her name and the car company's contact information, tucked into a pewter carrying case embossed with Irish knotwork. She offered it to Bourke, who gave her one in exchange. She put it in the back of her case without looking at it.

He glanced over hers, tucked it into his wallet, and nodded in the direction of her car. "You might want to drive over to St. James's Hospital. That's where Mr. Darr will be, and he'll probably need a lift home sometime tonight."

"God, he probably will, the poor guy. Yeah, I'll do that." Megan forbore to mention she'd known which hospital: it had been blazoned on the paramedics' uniforms as well as the ambulance. Bourke waved her under the police barrier again, and she took several steps back toward the car before hesitating and glancing toward Canan's.

If Elizabeth Darr had died of food poisoning, there would be inspectors and food safety and health officials crawling over the place soon, but for the moment, it hadn't even been cordoned off. Meg slipped back through what remained of the crowd—the girl with the short skirt and heavy eyebrows hadn't left yet, and neither had her cadre of hopeful young men. The corkscrew blonde who had helped Megan up earlier still hung around, her face furrowed with unhappy empathy as Megan entered the restaurant.

An open area with a handful of tables sat just inside the door, and behind it a narrow stretch with a bar before the back two-thirds of the restaurant spread out to hold most of the tables. Stained-glass windows lined the exterior wall, with a few modern windows inserted at the tops and open to encourage a little breeze.

The walls were done in creams and golden browns that caught the coloured light from the windows, and the inner wall had numerous well-placed mirrors that reflected light, making the place seem larger than it really was.

It smelled good enough to make Megan's stomach rumble. A few diners still took up tables or places at the bar, but an awful lot of them had cleared out, with all the excitement outside. Meg hoped most of them had at least paid their bills before leaving, but caught a glimpse of Fionnuala, sitting dejectedly at the far end of the bar, and her hopes sank. "Fionn?"

Fionnuala Canan blurted, "Meg," in relief and flung herself out of her seat and into Meg's arms. Meg grunted, catching her—Fionn stood a good four inches taller than Meg, and was strongly built to boot—and she squeezed hard.

"I'd ask how you are, but I assume everything's awful."

"Oh, God, Meg, you've no idea." Fionn stood back a bit, her usually clear green gaze muddy and worn. Normally, Meg would call her striking, even after an evening sweating over cooktops in the kitchen, but right now the other woman's coppery hair hung limply around her heart-shaped face, dragging its lines down. Blotches of heat shone on her cheeks, and she'd abandoned her chef's coat for the olive-green vest—what Americans called a tank top—she wore beneath it. Even it looked bedraggled, and at odds with Fionn's black-and-white-checked chef's trousers. "I've sent most of the staff home. Syzmon and Julian are good lads and stayed to clean up what we can, mostly the front of the house—" she gestured at the tables— "but we can't clean the kitchen until the health inspectors arrive, to see if we're at fault." Her jaw tensed. "We've passed every inspection we've ever had with flying colours, Meg, and that seafood was still flopping when it came in this afternoon. We can't have poisoned that poor woman. We can't have."

"I'm sure you didn't," Meg said, meaning it sincerely, but Fionnuala shook her head.

"No, you don't understand. Do you know who's liable in Ireland, if someone comes down with food poisoning?"

Megan turned up her hands, indicating bewilderment. Fionn's lips tightened. "The chef. Not even the restaurant, but the *chef* is liable. And I was cooking tonight. I know it's not the food." Frustration glimmered in her eyes, one blink away from tears. Her voice rose in pitch, though she kept it low enough as she spoke more and more quickly. "I know it's not, but I'm still going spare. If it *is* the food, and if they prove it is, it'll ruin me. It'll ruin the *restaurant*. Even if it's not the food here, even if it's not the restaurant, Elizabeth Darr was one of the most popular food bloggers in the States. Do you know how many tourists follow her restaurant recommendations for dining out just here in Ireland alone? Thousands, every year. She could make a restaurant, or break one, did you know that? So no matter what, that she walked out my front door and *died* is going to be almost impossible to recover from. If it's actually food poisoning? We're finished. Canan's is done. We might be able to reopen as Rafferty's, but it was my business, my dream, and having someone else's name on it—"

"Fionn. *Fionn.*" Megan put her arms around the other woman again, holding her until her shaking subsided. "Look, I can't actually help, but I've got to go to St. James's to get Mr. Darr tonight anyway. Maybe I can see if there's any news about Liz's death yet. Maybe it'll be really easy to tell that it wasn't food poisoning and you can get ahead of the news cycle somehow. You guys do social media, right?"

Fionnuala sagged with gratitude. "You'd do that? That would be—that'd be deadly, Meg. And yeh, we do social—oh, feck, I'd better get on that, I'd better—I don't know what to say."

"Condolences for the tragedy, admiration for Elizabeth's blog, restaurant will be closed a few days, I don't know, something like that. Look, I'll text you if I get any news from the hospital, okay? I probably won't, but I'll try." Megan hugged Fionn again. "Where's Martin?"

"On his way. He wasn't supposed to be in tonight, but obviously I called—There he is." Fionnuala jumped up and ran to hug her business partner, a big man who always looked worried, as he came through the door. Unsurprisingly, he looked more worried than usual, deep lines furrowed into his forehead and around his mouth. He shook Meg's hand absently and spoke over Fionnuala as she began to explain what had happened.

"That ginger detective caught me up and cross-examined me outside. Jesus, Fionn, this is desperate altogether. How long will we be closed?"

"At least three days."

"And at the weekend?" Rafferty asked, horrified.

Megan ducked her head and pressed her lips together so she wouldn't let herself *say* that given that it was Thursday night now, yes, three days would definitely mean they'd be closed at the weekend. Martin Rafferty brought out that impulse in her, but she worked to keep it muted because she liked Fionn, and Fionn had been business partners with Martin far longer than she'd known Megan.

"And in this weather?" He looked worriedly toward the fading light, tinting gold through the stained glass, the last vestiges of what had been one of an unusually glorious run of summer days. The weather had been good for every business in town except maybe tanning booths, with cheerful, sunburned Dubs happy to be out and spending money. "There must be some way to open up again. If I talk to my local councillor or get a TD down from the Dáil to have a—"

Megan shook her head at the reliance on an old-boys-network that made so many people—men especially—think they could lean on the government to bypass regulations and laws. Fionn obviously felt the same way, her voice rising as she said, "Martin, they've got to do a health inspection, they have to run tests on the food, they have to do an *autopsy*, for God's sake. The Taoiseach himself couldn't change that. We're going to have to—"

"The club, at least," Martin said with increasing strain. "Surely they can't close Heaven because of what's gone on in Canan's—"

Megan touched Fionn's arm, murmuring, "I'm going to go over to the hospital to see what I can learn," under her frustrated explanations to her partner. "You hang tight, and call if you need anything, okay?"

Fionnuala gave her a distracted nod and Megan headed for the door just as Detective Bourke strode in. He looked bigger in the restaurant than he had outdoors, broader of shoulder, though Megan would bet he'd never worn a suit that wasn't skinny cut in his life. Well, maybe he had: he was at least her age, forty, maybe older, and clothes had been large and floppy when they were young. Still, she bet he'd been pleased about the advent of skinny suits. He noted her presence without much change of expression but paused to look between the women when Fionnuala, suddenly, said, "Megan."

Megan looked back, surprised at the fervor in Fionn's voice, and then the brightness in her eyes. "Thank you, Meg. It's me life you're saving."

CHAPTER TWO

It's me life you're saving.
Fionnuala's words kept playing in Megan's mind as she drove up to St. James's Hospital, barely a mile—a couple of kilometres—up from where Liz had fallen. If only she *had* saved a life. If only she'd somehow—but she couldn't even finish that thought. Moving faster wouldn't have saved Liz. Warning her not to—not to what, eat the shellfish? Megan shook her head, watching the street corner for a traffic light to change.

A few years of driving in Dublin had mostly accustomed her to the lights being on corners instead of above the streets, though she would never really adapt to street names being posted on the sides of buildings. It made navigating hard, for Americans. Maybe for everybody; Megan had had an Irish cousin visit once, and he'd exclaimed over how easy it was to read the American street signs. She hadn't understood until she'd come to Ireland and discovered the signs there were all on the corners of buildings, and mostly grime-covered so they were hard to read even if she knew where they were.

It's me life you're saving.

The cadence of it sang in her head again, soft and generous as a tune. Megan didn't believe for a minute that dodgy shellfish had been the culprit in Elizabeth's death, and not just because that laid the consequences at Fionn's feet. The light changed, traffic rolling forward quickly enough at this hour: just before ten now, with the sun dropping behind the horizon to bring twilight to the long summer evenings. Dublin Castle's grey stones were cooled by blue shadows, touched by the last drips of sunset gold at the top.

Megan hadn't saved Liz's life, wasn't really saving Fionnuala's either. Helping, at best, although if the restaurant dinner wasn't at fault . . . a strain of song slipped through her mind: *She died of a fever, and no one could save her, singing cockles and mussels, sweet Molly Malone.*

Elizabeth had seemed fine when Megan dropped the Darrs off for dinner, and no fever Megan knew about settled on somebody and killed them in three hours. Neither did food poisoning, though, at least, not typically. Allergies, maybe, but Elizabeth Darr had been a food critic. She wouldn't have eaten something that would make her sick.

Not deliberately, anyway.

She beat her fingertips against the steering wheel, then reached out to touch the leprechaun figurine on the dashboard, as if he could lend her some luck. *Not deliberately* skirted too near a thought she was trying to stay away from: that maybe someone had murdered Elizabeth Darr. Every food critic had industry enemies, although Megan didn't think they generally resorted to killing one another. Now that she'd let the thought loose, it seemed preposterous.

And if it wasn't, Detective Paul Bourke would figure it out, because unlike Megan, he had been trained and got paid to determine whether there had been foul play. Megan only liked to talk to people and find out their stories, which meant driving a limo was about the perfect job for her. It also made her adore the Irish query "what's the story?" which meant anything from "how are you" to "what's going on?" She always wanted the answer to that question, and listened well enough that people often told her.

Her phone buzzed in her pocket again. Megan didn't even take it out this time: getting caught driving while on the phone meant points off your license and whoever it was could wait.

The underground car park at St. James's smelled faintly of hops, courtesy of the Guinness brewery just down the road. Some days the malty odor could be smelled all over the city centre, but she hadn't noticed it earlier. The wind had probably been wrong. She wrinkled her nose, got out of the car, and hurried toward the hospital's main entrance.

The stainless-steel border between the sliding doors offered just enough reflective surface to surprise Megan with her own appearance. Someone she knew, however casually, had just died in a public display. She felt like she ought to look frazzled, stressed out, coming apart at the seams. Instead, the brief reflection showed a woman with her dark hair in a tidy French twist, her black-and-white driver's uniform crisp, her light makeup still in place. She didn't even look tired.

The doors swooshed open and Megan entered, tucking her chauffeur's cap under her arm. Maybe looking sharp and professional would encourage someone to tell her that Fionnuala's restaurant was off the hook, although realistically, she couldn't imagine why anybody would share that information with her. Perhaps her sparkling gaze and winning smile would do the trick, but even if they wouldn't, she still had a responsibility—albeit only a self-assumed one—to Simon Darr. Getting him home, and seeing whether she could find anything out for Fionn, were the only two things Megan *could* do right now, so she wanted to. Being able to take *some* kind of useful action in a crisis was always better than being helpless. That was part of why she'd become an Army medic.

There were no receptionists at the desk this late. Megan tapped a tattoo on the desk for a few seconds, looked around, then found an older man in a custodial staff jacket and asked for directions to the A&E—Accidents & Emergencies, what would be the ER in the States—and he smiled, a light South Asian accent was sympathetic as he asked, "Is everything all right, miss?"

Megan shook her head, smiling awkwardly. "No, but it's not my loss. Thank you."

Her guide nodded and told her it would be easier to get to the A&E by leaving the building and going around the outside. Megan hurried outside and down the sidewalks until she reached the pedestrian entrance and took a breath upon seeing the crowd inside as she pushed the door open.

At a glance, it was clear that the fifty or so seats held people suffering mostly from contusions and various degrees of intoxication, but the dim fluorescent lights made everyone look sicker than they were. Crowded as it seemed on a Thursday night, she knew it would be worse on a weekend.

Simon Darr wasn't amongst those sitting there. Megan patiently waited in line until she reached the admitting nurse, who snapped, "Details?"

"I'm looking for a friend or her husband. Elizabeth Darr. She would have come in around nine or nine fifteen. Her husband is Simon. Elizabeth may have been dead on arrival. I'm here to drive Simon home when he's ready."

Not even a hint of sympathy flickered in the nurse's eyes. "The mortuary is by the James Street entrance."

Megan nodded. "Thank you for your time." She stepped aside, making way for a lumbering man holding a flap of his forehead in place. The nurse, as unsympathetic to the blood caking his face as she'd been to Megan's tale, barked, "Details?" at him, and Megan slipped away to the mortuary.

Simon Darr sat alone in a corridor that could have been purposely built for a grim film scene: both ends were swinging double doors and a series of plastic chairs sat beside another single door in the hallway. Even the chairs seemed sad, like they'd held the weight of too many broken hearts, and Simon's was only one more in a long and unhappy line. Only hours earlier, Megan would have described him as a runner, fit and athletic. Now his thinning hair was limp and his shoulders bowed beneath clothing as rumpled and unkempt as Megan had expected hers to be. She'd noticed when they'd first met that his nails were beautifully manicured, but they were rough and ragged now, his reddened knuckles swollen as his hands encased his face.

A nurse or mortuary assistant—a professional dressed in hospital blues at least—exited the double doors beyond Simon, opposite the ones Megan had just entered. She gave him a brief, compassionate glance that became guarded with inquiry as she met Megan's eyes. Megan indicated Simon with a twitch of her fingers, and the nurse, relieved of that duty, strode past her with no further communication.

Megan sat on the edge of the chair beside Simon's, putting her hand on the arm of his seat. He shifted, then lifted a dull gaze to her without a shred of recognition in it. "Megan Malone," she said quietly. "Your driver. I thought I'd come take you back to the hotel when you were ready."

The man's eyes cleared and he shuddered. "Megan. Right, of course. I'm sorry, I should have recognized you."

"No, it's okay. Are you—" Megan stopped herself from asking the obviously stupid question, but a terrible, broken smile darted across Simon's face.

"All right? No, but—" He drew a shuddering breath and passed his hands over his face. "I'm probably in shock. I don't quite believe she's dead. I'm expecting her to—" He made a sharp, clumsy motion toward the mortuary doors beside them.

"To walk through and laugh at me for believing this was real, or to yell for me to come hold her hair while she pukes because she drank a little too much. Or to hear her singing that god-awful song again. She hasn't stopped singing it since we got here." His face spasmed. "Hadn't."

"'Molly Malone?'" Meg asked softly. "I saw her singing it on the *RTÉ Lifestyle Show*. She had a lovely voice."

"She studied opera at college, but she got nodes." Simon gestured loosely at his throat. "They healed, but she lost some of her upper range. Then she got involved with a chef and decided she liked writing about food more than singing for her supper." The same terrible slash of a smile creased his face, cutting deep lines around his mouth and nose. "That's what she always said when her parents complained about not having a prima donna daughter. I think they forgave her when her first foodie book came out, though. It was something they could . . ." He gave a short, harsh laugh, a sound of grief barely disguised by humor. "Something they could dine out on. I have to call them. I don't know what to say."

"What did the paramedics say? Was it food poisoning?"

"It can't be ruled out until the autopsy is done, but I tried some of her dinner and I'm fine." His expression crumpled again, this time beyond salvation. Megan, uncertain but not wanting to leave him entirely alone in his grief, put a careful hand on his shoulder. If Leprechaun Limos didn't have procedures for comforting a bereaved client, Megan's boss would no doubt have them in place by morning, along with an itemized list of how Megan had handled it wrong.

After a minute, Simon put his hand on top of hers, acknowledging her effort. Her fingers were short and blunt compared to his.

"Do you want to stay?" she asked when the worst of his sobs had passed. "I don't know what their rules are, but I'm sure they'd let you sit with her if you want to."

"I won't do her any good," came his bleak reply. "They promised they'd hurry up the autopsy, but even if I could stand it, they won't let me be there for it, and it won't get done before morning anyway."

"Do you have any friends here?" Megan asked. "Someone who could come to your hotel, or whose house you could go to?"

Simon laughed hoarsely. "I'm supposed to say 'Elizabeth didn't make friends' now, right? Except she did. People—fans—wanted to meet her. They'd feel like they already knew her, from her blog and reviews, but then they'd learn how funny and kind she was and they'd become friends. Most of them. There were people who didn't like her, people whose restaurants she'd reviewed badly, but . . . I don't know who I would call. We've been traveling around too much. God, we loved it, though. She was always ready to get back home after a long trip, but this time she—we—thought we might want to stay. I even interviewed at several of the Dublin hospitals, looking for work. But we hadn't made any close friends yet." Another of the terrible, anguished smiles slashed his face. "I'm afraid you might be the closest thing we have to a friend here right now. We've seen you more regularly than almost anyone else."

Megan's hand found its way to her mouth, pressing against her lips. She knew from experience how isolating moving to a new country could be, but she'd had the military structure as support for most of her life. Being a lone civilian, facing the death of a loved one in a foreign country would daunt even her. She grasped Simon's shoulder in consolation. "Then I'll stay with you."

Surprised gratitude, then discomfort, washed across Simon's face. "No, I can't put you out. I'll be all right. I have to call her parents. My sister. Her publisher. I'm going to have to post on her blog. . . ."

"Not tonight." Megan squeezed his shoulder. "You don't have to post tonight. Or call her publisher."

"She died in public. It's probably already all over social media. I have to do something." A thread of angry strength came into Simon's voice and Megan fell silent, not wanting to diminish whatever consolation he could draw from having something to do. "I'll call her family first. If you can drive me back to the hotel . . . ?"

Megan rose, nodding, and opened the single door beside the chairs. A young woman looked up from a desk in the room beyond and Megan said, "I'm bringing Dr. Darr back to his hotel. You have his contact details?"

The girl moved papers around before finding the one she wanted at the top of the pile. "We'll call as soon as we know anything."

"Thank you." Megan let the door close behind

her and caught up with Simon, who strode through the double doors leading to the exit. He had his phone in hand, his jaw set as he lifted it to his ear. Megan moved a few steps ahead of him, unobtrusively leading the way with a purposeful set to her shoulders that spoke of professionalism and an uncanny inability to hear his phone call.

Her phone gave the specific pattern that meant a call had gone to voice mail while she'd been in the depths of the hospital. Eventually she would have to answer it, but it could wait.

Walking and the prospect of an audience—not Megan; she'd become a position, The Driver, rather than a person, but there were people in the hospital corridors even this late—helped Simon Darr hold himself in emotional check as he spoke with his in-laws, but the facade disintegrated as Megan closed the car door behind him in the garage. The town car didn't have a privacy window or she'd have rolled it up to allow him to be alone in his grief. Without it, she could hear Elizabeth's mother's high, keening wails, and the deeper, rougher sobs from her father through the speaker on Simon's phone. Her vision blurred with tears and she wiped them away with the heel of her hand, trying to breathe steadily enough to keep more from falling.

Midnight traffic meant a short drive through Dublin's thousand-year-old heart, past the Guinness Storehouse, still smelling strongly of hops, and St Patrick's Cathedral, its spire piercing the blue-black night sky as a darker shadow. Even hours after sunset, the greenery surrounding the cathedral gave off cooler air than the bricks and concrete of the city around it. Megan adored St Pat's, partly for its beauty but mostly for the fact that it wasn't meant to exist: Dublin had two cathedrals, the second, Christ Church, being barely a stone's throw away from St Pat's. She didn't pretend to understand the depths of the eight-hundred-year-old religious and political mess that had resulted in the both of them being cathedrals, but she loved the resulting buildings.

The streets beyond that were just as memorable, medieval arches here and there creating pedestrian by-ways that led toward a tangle of streets meant for carts and horses, and newer—which meant two or three hundred years old, rather than a thousand—streets lined with the tall, Georgian manor houses that were part of the city's pride.

Simon's hotel, the Shelbourne, dated from that era, overlooking the north end of St Stephen's Green, a park that had been there, more or less in its current form, for over a hundred and fifty years. The Alamo was older, but not much else built by Europeans in Texas was. Megan hoped she'd never get over being awed and delighted by that.

She parked illegally outside the hotel, reckoning the odds of a ticket were slim and she'd pay it without complaint if she got caught, and walked Simon up to his room. He paused his phone call and pulled himself together again in the public space but couldn't muster the coordination to open the key card lock on his room door. Megan took the card silently, opened the door, ushered him in, and waited until he gave her a tremulous nod of dismissal to leave again. On the way out, she stopped at reception and told them what had happened, causing the already pale desk attendant to whiten until his freckles stood out like a disease.

Feeling vaguely guilty, Megan left the poor kid to figure out how to deal with a bereaved guest and slipped back outside into the comparative quiet of the Dublin night to find she had not, in fact, been ticketed. Nor would she be, once she was in the car, so she sat behind the wheel, opted to ignore the three missed calls and voice mail from her boss, and texted Fionnuala: **Husband ate some of her dinner, he's fine, so probably not food poisoning. Hope that helps you get ahead of the story. <3 <3 <3**

A response came back almost instantly: **OMG TYSM you're a star**, followed by **how's the poor man doing?**

Pretty crappy, Megan texted back. **You?**

Better now. Thanks a million, Megan.

No worries.

She sat for a moment in the silence of the car, letting the phone's screen go dark. It lit up again a moment later, playing the three-note tune that said another text message had come in. Her boss, Orla. Again.

Rather than answer it, or even look at it, Megan made a face and tossed the phone into the passenger's seat. "All right, all right, I'm on my way to face the music. . . ."

CHAPTER THREE

Orla Keegan reminded Megan of a rattlesnake: small, leathery, and full of poison. Megan believed that buried somewhere in her depths—very, very deeply in her depths—lay a woman of compassion and kindness, but working for her had led Megan to conclude that her compassion might only extend as far as vehicles. It had no apparent time for actual human beings.

Not even at half twelve on a Thursday night—Friday morning, now—with a dead client in the morgue and a local restaurant at risk. She'd swept out to the garage upon Megan's arrival, investigated the car's soundness with what Megan knew from experience was not a cursory glance, even if it looked like it, and turned a deadly glare of expectation on the American woman.

Megan raised her hands in peremptory defeat and retreated to the office attached to the garage before even trying to explain. She turned on the overhead lights, avoiding the reception counter and the low desk that sat in front of a couple of expensive, soft, leather chairs under a curtained picture window that overlooked the street.

Orla came in behind her, switching off the main lights and opening the blinds so the street-lamps and passing cars could throw some degree of illumination into the room. Megan made a what-the-hell face—she often felt like her expressions regressed to teenager-dealing-with-impossible-mother around Orla—and dropped into one of the leather chairs. "There's no point spending up the electric bill when there's plenty of light from the street," Orla said to Megan's look.

Megan gestured expansively at the reception desk. "There are lamps!"

"What, and have people thinking we're open at this hour, like no decent business would be?"

Military life had taught Megan there were hills worth dying on, both literally and figuratively. Office lights in the middle of the night weren't one of those hills, so she only rolled her eyes and explained the events of the evening to her boss.

Nobody received any sympathy, not for herself—who least needed it—not for Elizabeth, and certainly not for Fionnuala. What garnered Orla's concern was that the guards now had a reason to be aware of Leprechaun Limos, though Megan spluttered, "It wasn't like I had a choice about saying who I worked for, Orla, the car was right there—!"

"The woman was after dying already," Orla complained. "Why didn't you bugger out while you could?"

"The Darrs were our clients," Megan said incredulously. "They were paying me to be there."

"And they'd best be paying for the three hours you were there after your shift ended!"

"Oh, come on. You can't bill them for that."

"Can I not?" Orla possessed a ferocious stare, coldly blue and calculating beneath a mess of hair that waged a continuous battle with its natural grey-brown and the bleached blonde regularly applied to it. None of the colours were done any favors by the orange streetlights, or even the occasional bright white flashes from passing cars. Megan guessed Orla to be in her mid-sixties, though truthfully, she could as easily have been a hard fifty. She'd never once said anything that dated her past about thirty years ago, but if she was ten years Megan's junior, Megan would eat her chauffeur's hat.

Regardless, whether she'd seen thirty years or seventy, Orla Keegan had clearly never met an hour of the day she couldn't wring an extra few quid from. Megan didn't doubt she would charge the Darrs—Simon Darr—for the hours Megan had waited for him at the hospital.

She sighed. "Of course you can, but it's unethical. Take it out of my paycheck instead of slapping a surcharge on a man who's just lost his wife."

The gleam in Orla's eyes said she'd do both and pocket the profits. Megan sighed again. "You're a terrible person, Orla."

"It's a free country. Go find another job if you dislike this one so much. Rich Americans, swanning in and talking about money like it grows on trees. Not all of us grew up as privileged as you did, lass, and I'll thank you not to forget it."

"If I find another job, you'll make me find somewhere else to live," Megan replied dryly. It had seemed like the perfect situation when she'd arrived in Ireland: a job driving and an apartment just up the street from the garage, all in a package deal. Orla had been outrageously charming then, laying on the kind of lilting accent Americans thought of as most Irish. Megan had since learned there was practically an accent for every street, and that the one Orla came by naturally was a thick inner-city cadence that Megan hadn't understood clearly for months. By then, though, she'd agreed to a job and a three-year-lease on the apartment and had found out Orla only charmed when she wanted something, like a driver who—by dint of being American—could probably be trusted to show up on time.

"Sure I should anyway so," Orla snapped. "You've got that apartment at half of market value."

"I've got it at *barely* below market value, and the only reason you haven't doubled my rent is because I signed a three-year-lease. And because if I sign another one, they've enacted that law saying you can only raise it by ten percent. Which you'll do."

Orla's shrug challenged Megan to do something about it, though they both knew she wouldn't, mostly because she liked the job as much as she found her boss exasperating. Satisfied with Megan's silence, Orla said, "Fine so. I expect you to get it sorted out before the company gets a bad name around town. I can't have the competition saying 'oh, Leprechaun Limos, they're the ones who lost a client last year,' now can I?"

Megan allowed herself a long blink as her eyebrows crawled up her forehead and thought about just leaving her eyes closed and going to sleep in the cozy leather chair. Only the thought of being rousted by Orla made her reject the plan, and when she opened her eyes again, it was to find her boss staring at her expectantly. "Get what sorted out?"

"This mess! You weren't thinking, getting us involved in it at all, but now you'd better start, and get it sorted."

Megan's face crinkled on its own, like if she wrinkled her nose and bared her teeth it would reflect Orla's ridiculousness back at her. "The guards are looking into it, Orla. That's their job."

"And what do they care about us? It's your own self who'll be *out* of a job if the company folds under this nonsense!"

"Okay! All right." Megan raised her hands in a gesture of defeat again, trying not to think about how many times a day she did that with her boss. "All right. I'll do my darnedest to prevent the besmirching of Leprechaun Limos' good name, ma'am. I'll go get this sorted." She meant it about as far as she could throw Orla, but at pushing one a.m., that didn't seem to matter much. As a caveat, she added, "In the morning. I can't do anything about it at this hour," and, upon Orla's grudging nod, fled home.

Habit rolled Megan out of bed at five thirty, got her into workout gear, and out the door before her brain could put together a coherent objection. It couldn't get her across the street without a cheerfully *bipping* crosswalk telling her it was okay, though, even if traffic was scant at half five in the morning. That was true in most places, but Dublin seemed to take it to an art form: the Irish were not, generally speaking, early risers.

Megan leaned on the crosswalk post, idly pushing its big silver button, and stared blearily at the little red man on the other side of the road. Eventually the once-a-second *bip* exploded into an enthusiastic, rapid-fire twitter of beeps and the man switched to a little green one.

Megan lurched into motion, smiling as the beeps slowed down. She sort of loved the noisy signal, which was just as well, because the thin panes of her apartment's windows didn't block it very well. That was the trouble with—or the charm of—living in what had been student housing a hundred years earlier. To be fair, though, if it hadn't been student housing in Rathmines, it would have been Victorian factory housing somewhere else, and double-paned glass was as hit-and-miss there as it was in her flat.

Heating bills could be ridiculous, although she'd become Irish enough to turn off the heat entirely when she left the apartment and had lined the windows with thin weathering film meant to keep the warmth in.

She was too early for the gym, which didn't open until six, but she'd learned the hard way that if she so much as stopped for coffee, she somehow never quite made it to her workout. The staff were used to her hanging around in the doorway, stretching and doing jumping jacks—stars, they called them—to warm up. Just before six, another woman arrived, and they exchanged a friendly nod and a couple

of inanities about the fine weather before somebody opened the door and let them in.

The gym, like her apartment, gave her a view of
the gorgeous church down the street, with its massive copper-green dome. Megan ran on the treadmill, her phone strapped to her biceps and playing
upbeat music in her headphones, watching the
dome brighten with summer dawn. It stood high
enough to be *the* landmark for the entire area,
though Meg thought it was a little like the Cheshire
cat, disappearing from view when she most needed
to orient herself by it. On the other end of the
road, well past the church, was the Stella Theatre,
which brought a little glamour back to going to
the movies. Everything in between—including
Meg's little apartment—was the heart of Rathmines, a village that still existed inside the greater
city of Dublin. Meg loved it. Her hometown of
Austin, belovedly weird as it might be, didn't have
anything with quite the same feeling to it. Of
course, her hometown hadn't had people dropping dead in front of her either, so that balanced
something out. Meg made a face and stepped off
the treadmill, mopping sweat and popping her
earphones out to dangle around her neck.

"Got a minute to spot me?"

A smile blossomed on Meg's face before she
even turned around. "Sure." The sky had brightened too much to show Jelena Kowalski's reflection in the window, but Meg knew the woman's
tight, curly hair and heart-shaped face as clearly as
if she saw it. She turned, still smiling, to see the
other woman—a few inches taller than Meg, pale
olive skin, sparkling dark eyes, and wonderfully

broad shoulders—setting up the weights on a barbell. "You're here early."

"I have to get here early if I want the best spotter at the gym."

Jelena smiled over her shoulder at Meg. "You Americans," Jelena went on. "Always up early."

"What time do people get up in Warsaw?"

"Not as early as you do." Jelena swung onto the bench, flexed her wrists, then took a firm hold on the barbell as Megan came around to spot her. Jelena had biceps to die for. Meg's were pretty good, but watching Jelena lift always reduced her to an admiring mental *daaaang*. She wanted to be in same fit form. "We switch out?" she asked as she finished her first set.

"You lift more than I do," Megan said but switched places, exhaling a couple of times before pushing the barbell into the air under Jelena's supervision.

"That's why I watch," the other woman said approvingly. "Good job, nice form. Breathe." By the start of the third set, Megan's arms were wobbling, but Jelena had finished her own set so smoothly she was determined to match her. Later, when she couldn't pick up a cup of coffee, Fionnuala would tease her about trying to impress Jelena again and Megan wouldn't be able to argue.

An image of Detective Bourke's angular, expressive face flashed through Megan's mind. She wouldn't mind impressing him, too. The thought made her laugh and she almost dropped the barbell as her breathing changed. Jelena caught a little of its weight and gave Meg a scolding look that made her laugh again. "Okay, okay, sorry." She steadied her breathing and finished the set with more strength than she'd thought she had left and earned a pat on the shoulder for her efforts. They continued to work their way through the rest of the weights, spotting each other and occasionally pausing for a breather. Jelena muttered about the unusually warm summer, earning a grin from Megan. "This is cold in Texas."

"And Irish winters are warm if you're from Poland," Jelena said, not really sourly, "but we're not in Texas or Poland, and it's hot."

"I'll bring you homemade lemonade on Monday."

"Lemonade. At seven in the morning?"

"*American* lemonade," Megan stressed. "It's not fizzy. We have it at barbecues and stuff."

Megan's phone buzzed, then began ringing, on her arm. Jelena waved and trotted off to the changing rooms, letting Megan untangle her phone, see who was calling, and fumble it to her still-sweaty ear. "Niamh. Kill me now. Also, what are you doing up at this hour?"

"Fionn texted and told me everything, but I couldn't call her back, I knew she'd be asleep, so I called you because you never sleep. Why am I killing you?"

"Oh, because I'm a moron who can't talk to people after a gym workout." Megan grabbed a towel and wiped down both the weight benches and herself before trotting out the door and jogging toward home.

"Hmph," said Niamh. "Anyway, what's the story, tell me what you know about Fionn and it all. Over coffee."

Megan squished her phone between her ear

and her shoulder, a location that no one had ever intended a mobile phone to sit, and unlocked the street-level door that led up to her apartment. "Someday I'm going to get a headset that works as a mic for my phone, too."

"You still don't have one? You do know we're well into the twenty-first century, like? Where are you?"

"At home, now." Megan climbed the stairs two at a time, opened her own front door, and threw her gym bag under the kitchen table as she came in. It was a nice little flat, with an unusual-for-Ireland open-plan kitchen/dining room/living room. A table for one sat beneath the kitchen window, a tiny kitchen with a half-size fridge nestled beside an under-counter washing machine, comfy chairs and stacks of books dominated the living room, and an en suite bedroom overlooked an alley. "You don't want to have coffee with me until I've showered." She'd stripped off most of her gym gear by the time she reached the bathroom—the advantage of living alone was nobody cared if she left sweaty clothes on the floor—and put the phone on the bathroom sink, set to speaker.

"Are you showering in my ear?"

"I am so." Megan lifted her voice over the sound of water and used the Irish phrase on purpose.

Niamh laughed. "You're mental. Look, I'm in city centre, will you meet me at Accents at nine?"

"Are you *trying* to make me eat peanut butter cake for breakfast? Yeah, I'll see you there." Meg let Niamh end the connection and scrubbed her fingers through her hair, feeling the sweat of her workout loosening and washing out. She didn't even have to hurry; Dublin's city centre was a twenty-minute walk from her apartment, and Niamh's favourite cafe was on the near side of it to her. And how the mighty had fallen, that she even considered distances in terms of what could be walked: Meg had never walked as much in her life as she did in Dublin, with a job as a limo driver. But Dublin's core was only a few miles across, and most days it was easier, faster, and cheaper to either walk or take public transportation than it was to drive and find parking.

Forty minutes later, clad in sandals, flowing linen trousers, and a crop top to try to eradicate the tan lines on her shoulders, Megan swooped into the little cafe near Grafton Street that Niamh liked so much. It had two kinds of seating: enormous, squishy, faux-leather couches and bean bags, although the latter were downstairs and usually only in use by people under the age of thirty.

Usually: Niamh, already downstairs, had dragged a beanbag from the corner where they were stored and collapsed across it, her feet propped on the comfy chair she was saving for Megan. When Megan appeared, Niamh unwound—it was a production with her, although she wasn't tall, just long-limbed and ballet-dancer-fit—and swayed across the wooden floors to embrace Megan. "You look gorgeous, darling."

"*I* look passable. *You* look gorgeous." Megan air-kissed Niamh's round cheeks and fell into the chair beside her beanbag, smiling. Niamh was all dramatic features: large brown eyes and a slightly crooked nose, full lips and a strong jaw that belied the delicacy of her bones. She wore bright colours almost all the time, setting off the warmth of her light brown skin, and looked as at home in highly tailored outfits as flowing sundresses, one of which she wore now, in red.

"I am gorgeous," Niamh conceded immodestly, "but you're more than passable, my sweet. Now, tell me everything about last night."

"I thought Fionn already told you." Megan looked up to thank the waiter who brought her a latte with a bear face as the foam art, then summarized the previous evening's events a bit more juicily than she'd related them to Orla. Niamh, clasping a cup of herbal tea, listened with the air of a child hearing a particularly good bedtime story, then settled back into her beanbag with a contented air.

"That's desperate, every word of it. But you don't even know the best part, Megan. Elizabeth Darr was having an affair."

CHAPTER FOUR

"*What?*" Megan set her coffee aside and sat up straight, staring at Niamh. "Are you sure?"

"Sure as I can be," Niamh said easily. "A load of friends have said they've seen her around with some young thing, a girl no less. Sneaking off to dinners and shows and the like. One girl—you wouldn't know her—said she saw them together at the protest last weekend, and one of the lads saw them at the Gate when he was working the box office."

"Niamh—" Megan, trying not to offend, swallowed the first few things she wanted to say. Sometimes it seemed that Niamh knew everyone in Dublin, from actors to politicians and everybody in between, including protesters and itinerants and people who were a little of both. It often meant she had insights those with fewer friends, across narrower spectrums, couldn't lay claim to.

It also often meant that no one wanted to let the truth get in the way of a good story. Megan had seen an exasperated look reach operatic proportions in the retelling, making mountains of molehills. "Niamh, if you're *sure*, you need to tell the guards."

The actress shifted her shoulders backward, nonplussed. "Well, I'm not as sure as all *that*."

"Two seconds ago you were!"

"That was a bit of craic, Megan. I don't want to get involved with the guards. They already know my name."

A sliver of humor cracked Megan's surprise. "Power to the people, babe. Besides, everybody knows your name. It's what happens when you're famous."

Niamh lifted a hand in the Mockingjay salute. "I don't mind being a troublemaker, love, but I don't need the press coming forward with information about a suspicious death. They already look for my face in a crowd."

"That's because it's usually at the front," Megan said wryly. "Everybody knows you're politically active, Nee. It hasn't exactly hurt your career. But okay, look, I'll . . . I don't know, I'll tell them I heard a rumour. Or I'll go ask . . . I don't know. I can't exactly ask Simon if it's true, can I? I dunno, though. I've been driving them on and off for months, and they seemed happy. I didn't see her sneaking around."

"Well, you wouldn't, would you? She wouldn't call up the driver who knows her and her husband and say 'me and my bit on the side want to go down to the shore for the day,' would she now?"

"She's American. I don't think she'd say 'bit on the side' at all."

"Oh, ffsh." Niamh waved a hand, and this time Megan smiled more readily. "You know what I mean."

"Yeah." Meg scrunched her eyes shut a moment, considering what an affair might mean. Nothing good, probably, but the gardaí would want to know. As if they wouldn't find out themselves, but it wouldn't hurt to check into it a little. She yawned suddenly and popped her eyes back open. "Holy moly. I need more coffee and to stop sitting in a warm, dimly lit cafe after only four hours of sleep."

"Oh! I should have stayed upstairs, then. I thought you'd gotten in earlier, somehow, although I don't know why. Fionn texted late enough. How is she? How's Martin taking it?"

"He said 'Closed? For three days? At the weekend?'" Megan did her best impression of the restaurateur's voice, and Niamh laughed.

"Did you tell him that's how it works?"

"I refrained. No, and honestly, it's not even fair of me to be snide. The poor man—"

"Martin Rafferty is not a poor man," Niamh said dryly. "He's worked long and hard to make sure of that."

Megan made a face. "All right, the *unfortunate* man. The unfortunate man *had* just learned an internationally renowned food critic had died on his restaurant's doorstep, and that would rattle even the best of people."

"Which Rafferty is not." Niamh's eyebrows rose, leading Megan on.

"Nee, you've barely even met him."

"Ah, sure, no, but I know *of* him. The self-made

man from Bray, a proper Irish success story, and if there's one thing we resent, it's someone who's gotten above themselves and made good." The deprecating humor in Niamh's voice faltered almost inaudibly, and she added, "I should know," in a mutter.

"I'll never understand that," Meg said, honestly. "Pulling yourself up by your bootstraps, building a successful business, it's the American ideal."

"Sure it's one thing to go to America and do well," Niamh acknowledged. "You'd best come home again the same person you were, though, without any notions. We're a contrary lot, we Irish."

"I hadn't noticed. But anyway, I know I don't like him very much, but that's different from him not being a good person. I read somewhere that sometimes we instantly dislike somebody because our brains actually work on slightly different wavelengths and it causes antipathy."

Niamh, who didn't wear glasses, mimed pulling down a pair and looking over their top edges so expertly that Megan half-doubted her own eyes and felt maybe Niamh *did* have glasses on, and she just couldn't see them properly. "And here I thought *I* was the mad actress who's supposed to have neohippie shite ideas."

"Well, I don't know, it might not be true, I just read it somewhere. Regardless, I know restaurants usually run on a really narrow margin, so I'm sure being closed for days on end is going to be a near disaster for them. I'd probably be asking kind of stupid questions, too."

"But you weren't. You were asking if it was food

poisoning and finding out Liz Darr was having an affair."

"It's easier to be clear-headed about somebody else's disaster. And I wasn't *finding out* that she was having an affair, I mean, not like I was sleuthing and hunting for clues. I just have gossipy friends." Megan yawned again. "Oh, man. I really do need another coffee."

"And to not be in the windowless basement where the beanbags are."

"But you love the beanbags." Megan shook herself and stood, offering Niamh a hand up. She took it and sprang upward, pushing through her toes to leap straight up instead of just standing. Megan, used to that kind of behavior by now, took enough of a step back that Niamh didn't land on her toes—not that Niamh would—and pulled her into a laughing hug when she was earthbound again. "And that's why you love them. I think you're six, at heart."

"Six is a fine age to be. Look, Meg, if you do mention the affair . . ."

"I won't bring your name into it," Megan promised, and gratitude lowered Niamh's shoulders a centimeter or two. "I'll see you later, all right? With all the gossip."

"You'll raise my social credit to the stars," Niamh said happily. They parted ways on the street outside, Niamh striking north toward her dance studio and Megan heading east toward Simon's hotel, only a few minutes' walk from the cafe. The city had woken up while they were inside, parents and businesspeople mixing with tourists and disaffected youth along the streets.

There were an awful lot of sunburns on pale shoulders and exposed chests, and even more Irish brogues moaning about the appalling heat as they sweated their way through town. "Twenty-three degrees," she heard someone say grimly, "and it's meant to climb to twenty-eight today. I'm dying, I am."

Twenty-eight was about eighty-three degrees in American terms. Megan, grinning at the gasps and misery around her, gloried in the warmth on the short walk to the Shelbourne.

Simon Darr opened his hotel room door almost before Megan knocked, like he'd been watching through the peephole since she'd called from the front desk to make sure it was all right to visit. He obviously hadn't slept, or had only collapsed in the heavy, deep fog of grief and awakened some-time later, still harrowed. He wore the previous night's clothes, his hair a wrecked spiderweb drift-ing from his scalp, and exhausted, crust-lined, red-dened eyes. "Her parents will be here in a few hours," he said hoarsely. "Can you get them from the airport for me?"

"Of course. I'll set it up with the car service." Megan came in at his gesture, taking in the still-made, king-size bed with its covers barely rumpled, the writing desk scattered with papers, and an enormous, heavily framed mirror doubling the ap-parent size of the already generous room. The television on the desk was on but muted. Over-stuffed chairs sat across a small table beneath the window, and a door led to the bathroom. Everything coordinated, all in shades of sage and moss, though at least the room's floor didn't have the slightly dizzying triangles-and-waves pattern of the blue-and-green hall carpeting.

Megan took one of the chairs, hoping that if she sat, Simon would, too. He did, dropping bonelessly into the other chair as if his strings had been cut, and rubbed his hands over his face and through his hair, making the spiderweb effect worse. "Have you eaten?"

"I don't think I can. Coffee is turning my stomach."

"Coffee is acidic." Megan rose, moved papers around on the desk until she'd unburied the room phone and called room service for plain toast and cold water. Simon's face creased with the weary expression of someone who didn't want favors done for him but recognized they were probably necessary and slumped deeper in his chair. Megan glanced at the TV—commercials—and sat again. "What else can I do for you?"

"Make them stop talking about it." Simon nodded at the television. "It's all over the news. No," he said sharply as Megan reached for the remote. "Leave it on. I wrote a blog post for her last night," he added. "After I'd called the family and our closest friends, so they wouldn't find out from a news story. I don't know if I said it right. Liz was the people person, not me." He flickered his fingers at a closed laptop on the desk. Megan took it as an invitation and got up to open it.

Elizabeth Darr's website had a slick, modern design that somehow also managed to be friendly and welcoming. Photographs, some professional and others candid, but all of them curated to give a sense of approachability, surrounded the main text of the blog. A fierce, shocking pang of loss cut through Megan's chest, taking her breath, and she had to brace herself, fingertips against the desk, before she could read Simon's post.

It was simple, saying only that Elizabeth had died suddenly in Ireland a few hours earlier, the cause of death was unknown, and that he would post more when he could. He asked if people might be willing to share their stories about Liz and take comfort in seeing how many lives she had touched.

The post had over four thousand comments.

Megan sat at the desk, not daring to open the comments page. She hadn't known Elizabeth Darr well, but just seeing photos of the food critic vibrant and alive had caught her off guard with grief. Odds were that stories from thousands of fans would leave her sobbing, and she didn't think she had the emotional wherewithal to deal with that just then. Simon, wearily, said, "Comments began coming in the moment I posted it. I started reading them, but it was too much."

"They'll be there later." Megan left the computer open, watching the page refresh itself and update the number of comments on Simon's post for a moment before she turned away. "I have a . . ." Halfway through the sentence, she wondered just what she thought she would accomplish by asking Simon if Elizabeth had been having an affair. It would break his heart if he didn't know. It might break it even if he *did* know. He looked at her expectantly, if an expression so defeated could even be expectant. "I have a pickup to do in a little while," Megan lied. "What time is your in-laws' flight in, so I can get them?"

"Four o'clock. Aer Lingus. Their names are Peter and Ellen Dempsey." A pained smile pulled his lips. "Liz's first name was Dana. Her mom used to say she married me just to keep the alliteration going, but then she used Elizabeth professionally. She said it was less bouncy, easier to take seriously."

"As an alliteration myself, I understand. I always wanted to be a Samantha, but I got named after a grandmother instead. And then there was a while there when being Sam Malone wouldn't have been great either, because everybody would have expected me to know their name."

Simon's blank look told her an eight-year age gap could be insurmountable at times. Megan waved it off with a smile. "I'll get the Dempseys at four, then. Will I bring them back here?"

"Please."

"All right." Megan rose, then startled as a knock sounded at the door. "Oh, the toast. I'll get it for you." She collected the food, which had a pot of tea she hadn't ordered but which she imagined the kitchen offered in sympathetic hope that it would cure all ills. "Try to eat it, okay? And try to rest, maybe." She put the tray on the table beside his chair, but he leaned around her, anguished horror drawing his face long.

Behind her, Elizabeth Darr spoke.

CHAPTER FIVE

"I'm in Galway today," she said cheerfully. "There's a terrific Saturday market that's been going on for *centuries*, I'm standing in the middle of a *centuries-old tradition*, and it doesn't matter how many old markets I go to around the world, this never ceases to amaze me. It's a vibrant, exciting space, and oh, man, I cannot *tell* you how good it smells—"

Elizabeth Darr was, in life, a tall, big-boned presence in whatever space she entered, even the bustle of Galway City's Saturday market. She'd never been sharply thin, the way some food critics were, like they didn't dare indulge in the very thing from which they made their livelihoods. Instead, she carried her weight in soft-padded muscle, and often brought her viewers on the hikes up mountains and scuba-diving explorations she pursued to maintain that muscle. She wore her brown hair in a flattering and easy-to-maintain pixie cut, and had more pairs of glasses than anyone Megan had

ever met. She'd been wearing her purple ones on
Saturday, matching a lilac sundress that showed off
golden shoulders gleaming just a little with sun-
screen. Liz, at least, had not gotten burned during
the unusual heatwave.

She worked her way through the market, stopping at stalls to talk about food, asking about ingre-
dients and traditions. Her phone camera swooped
from selfies with the vendors to steady, well-framed
shots of her interviewees talking about the family
traditions that kept them running a stall at the
market generation after generation, or imploring
her to try something new they'd recently come up
with. Indistinguishable music played in the background, mostly drowned beneath the general
noise of the market and Liz's New England accent
narrating as she explored.

The video had come up on its own. Or not, obviously. Elizabeth had clearly set it in advance to
post, and one of the website's automatic refreshes
had caught it going live. Simon had thrown himself past Meg, slapping his hands on the keyboard
as if he'd prevent the world from seeing the video
if he moved fast enough. Then he'd fallen back
into his chair, tears streaming down his cheeks as
Liz did her job like she'd returned from the dead
to haunt him.

Comments were already piling up as the video
ended. Meg, slowly, wrote a short blog saying that
the announcement about Liz's death hadn't been
a mistake or a joke, and that she had, unbeknownst
to the family, prescheduled the last video for that
morning. Simon, weeping, nodded his consent for
her to post it, and after it went live, Megan pinned

his original death notice to the top of Elizabeth's page. There were other half-finished posts waiting, but nothing in the queue ready to go. Megan closed the computer and gazed helplessly at the grieving widower.

"You have a job to get to," he finally said as his tears slowed. Megan stared at him blankly a moment, then remembered the lie she'd told.

"Right. Yeah. I almost forgot. I don't know, I don't know if you should be left alone . . ."

He gave her a miserable, watery smile. "Maybe not, but your life can't be put on hold." Pain streaked his face again. "Even mine can't, it seems. Why doesn't everything just . . . stop?"

"I don't know. It never does." Not as many people died in the American military as might be supposed—though injuries were a different story, and training fatalities something else again—but when those deaths happened, and it was someone Megan knew, she always had the same question. How could the world go on, how could *she* go on, when everything had changed? She always did; people usually did. Knowing that, experiencing it, didn't help it make any more sense. "Stop all the clocks," she whispered, and a sob, almost a bitter, broken laugh, burst from Simon.

"Did you know that was written as satire? But yes. Yes. Stop them all. The world can't go on." He put his face in his hands and Megan, quietly, left him to his grief.

A half-familiar voice said, "There's a sombre face," as she came down the stairs into the Shelbourne's lobby. Megan, who'd been paying attention to not tripping on the steps if she'd been paying attention at all, looked up to find Detective Paul Bourke coming through the main doors, which were held open by a trim blonde woman in a Shelbourne uniform. Megan exhaled heavily, shaking off a little of her gloom, and found a half-hearted smile for him.

"I was just visiting Simon. They, um, there was a video, one of Liz's blogs, that she'd set to post this morning, and he didn't know. He's a wreck."

The detective stepped to the side, beckoning Megan with him to stand in front of the stone fireplace that fronted most of one wall and hid the hotel's breakfast room, rather grandly called The Lord Mayor's Lounge. "You don't look well yourself."

"Gee, thanks." Megan shrugged. "Not enough sleep, and it's no fun intruding on somebody's grief. Otherwise I'm okay. What are you here for? Did the autopsy report come back? Was it food poisoning?"

"I have a few questions for Dr. Darr, that's all. How's your friend, Fionnuala, is it?"

The way he said it made Megan certain he knew perfectly well it was Fionn, and that he knew her last name and probably her shoe size as well. "Well, Simon said last night he'd eaten some of Liz's dinner, so it didn't seem likely she'd gotten food poisoning. I told Fionn, and I hope she at least got some sleep after that, although I don't know, because apparently she was texting our friend Niamh at one in the morning. Or maybe that's just when Niamh saw it after her show." Niamh, who, like

Orla, hadn't wanted her name mentioned to the police. Megan smashed her mouth shut, too late.

"Niamh? O'Sullivan? The actress?"

"There are hundreds of Niamhs in Ireland," Megan said testily. "Why would my friend be Niamh O'Sullivan?" Then, more sullenly, she muttered, "Yeah, Niamh O'Sullivan."

"She's deadly," Bourke said in admiration. "A pain in the arse, but deadly. The woman's all up in everybody's business, politics and protests left, right, and centre, but I saw her at the Abbey last season and she walked away with the show. Mad props to her for coming back to do stage work when her film career is on the rise." He said it the way so many Irish people did, *fill-uhm*.

"I'll tell her you're a fan."

"You can give her my number," Bourke said, sounding more cheerful than a man investigating a suspicious death should be.

Then again, Megan supposed he was always involved in that sort of business, and she, after all, wasn't all that closely associated with the victim. He presumably wouldn't ask Simon Darr to give someone his number, under the circumstances. "Even if I went around giving her fan phone numbers, I don't have yours."

Bourke's nearly invisible eyebrows rose to make wrinkles in his forehead. "You threw away my card?"

"Oh!" Megan clapped her right hand to her chest, although her crop top certainly didn't have an inside pocket like her chauffeur's jacket did, and she supposed that she looked as though she'd been taken by the overwhelming urge to feel herself up. Curdling red, she dropped her hand. "I forgot."

Paul Bourke turned out to have a movie star grin, a bright white flash that changed middling good looks to a breathtaking attractiveness. The spark lasted after the smile disappeared, a lingering charisma that made Meg suddenly suspect he closed a lot of cases that left the guilty parties not entirely sure why they'd confessed. Maybe she should give Niamh his number after all. Amused, she smiled back, but the expression fell away just as fast. "Did anybody you talked to mention Elizabeth might have been having an affair?"

The detective's expression snapped straight back into pure professional. "No. Where'd you hear that?" Without giving her a chance to answer, he said, "Niamh O'Sullivan," as if the connection had already been made clear. Maybe it had, since detecting things was his job. Megan nodded, guilt surging through her at betraying Niamh's confidence. Bourke glanced upward, like he could see through three hotel floors into Simon Darr's room. "Did you ask him about it?"

"No. I was going to, but then it just seemed like an awful thing to do."

"Good. It's better for me if he's not prepared for it." The corner of Bourke's mouth twitched, a kind of shrug, as he acknowledged, "And you're right. It is an awful thing to do."

"Do you get used to it? In your line of work?"

His pale eyebrows drew down and he examined her for a moment, like the question was unexpected and she'd become more interesting for asking it. "It's uncomfortable, pressing people, especially grieving people, for things they don't want to talk about, but it's necessary. I suppose I'm after getting used to it, but it's easier sometimes than others."

"Like if you're sure somebody's guilty?"

"Or if they're just an unlikeable bastard." Bourke's grin flashed again, less intense than before. "Darr's a nice enough lad. Don't go asking him about affairs, though. That's my job, not yours."

Megan shook her head. "All I want is to make sure my friend doesn't lose her restaurant. You can solve the mysteries." She hesitated. "Is there a mystery?"

"There's always a mystery when a healthy young person dies unexpectedly. Most of the time, it's easily solved. A heart defect or a brain aneurysm. Sometimes undetected cancer."

"Those don't usually kill somebody over dinner, though, do they?"

"Not unless there's an impassioned argument going on, no." Bourke gave her another smile, this one professional and without the startling effect of the grin. "Text me Niamh O'Sullivan's number, will you? I'll want to talk to her about what she saw. Nice to see you again, Miss Malone."

He left her at the fireplace, taking the stairs up in long strides and showing the young man at their head his police identification, which, like Megan's own chauffeur's outfit, got him past the barrier the boy presented between the world and the Shelbourne's guests.

Megan meandered to the middle of the lobby, watching Bourke disappear around the corner of the stairs, taking the same path she'd just come from, then took out her phone and called Fionn as she left the hotel. "Hey, babe. How are you doing?"

"Shattered." Fionn sounded it, as if she hadn't slept all night, or possibly all week. "Our social media has blown up. Half of them are calling for a boycott of the restaurant, another half are horrified and sympathetic, and the last half are the kind of gobshite trolls you get mixed in with any tragedy. That's too many halves, isn't it? How are you? Martin spent the whole night going over the books and muttering. He tried not to let me see it, but he's scared, Meg. I know we're doing all right, but I haven't a head for numbers and I'm afraid we're doing less well than I thought. But how *are* you?"

"I'm okay. I just ran into Detective Bourke. Were Simon and Liz fighting last night over dinner?" Meg crossed the street into St Stephen's Green, where traffic sounds were replaced by birdsong and children shrieking happily in the distance.

"He asked me that, too. I don't know, Meg, I was in the kitchen. Cíara was their waitress, and she said they were grand, all smiles and laughter. God, the poor girl is in bits. She's only new and she spent the whole evening in tears, wondering if she'd done something wrong. Look, Meg, do you think it would be wrong for the restaurant to open up for a vigil tonight? You should see Molly. She's knee deep in flowers and consolation notes and her cart's full of them."

"Oh really?" Megan turned north, looking in the direction of both the statue and Fionnuala's restaurant. "I'm only a couple of blocks away. Maybe I could come see. And if you're going to do a vigil, you, uh, you might not want to cater it. . . ."

Fionn gave a deep, bitter snort right in Megan's ear. "I don't think I'd even be allowed to. I just feel like I ought to do something. There are people out there weeping on Molly's skirts."

"It's okay, she's bronze. She can handle a little saltwater."

"Megan!"

"All right, all right, sorry. Okay, look, are you at the restaurant? I'll come over. Ten minutes or so."

"Bring ice cream," Fionn said miserably and hung up.

Meg tucked her phone in her pocket and left the park through the magnificent granite arch that led to Dublin's main touristy shopping area, Grafton Street. It lay wide and open and packed full of pedestrians, giving it a completely different feel from the warren of medieval-to-Georgian streets and alleys that lay literally just beside it.

Meg stopped at one of the gelato shops—almost as ubiquitous as Starbucks—and got chocolate, honeycomb, and wild berry gelato in more-or-less pint-sized boxes. Around the corner, she cut through the excessively high-end Westbury shopping mall, holding her breath because she always had the sense that even the air there was too rarefied and expensive for her to breathe. The mall let out in what Megan thought of as Jewelers' Row, an alley lined on one side by tiny jewelry shops and on the other by the high wall of one of Dublin's many, many churches.

Across the street lay the Powerscourt shopping centre, which, two centuries earlier, had been somebody's very fancy house and was now as high-end a shopping centre as the Westbury Mall. On the other hand, just inside its doors lay a jewelry shop called Gollum's Precious, and Megan figured anywhere that allowed shops to make Tolkien references wasn't so exclusive that she had to hold her breath to walk through it. Which was good, because it made the shortest route down to Suffolk Street and Molly Malone.

The buxom statue stood awash in flowers, photographs, and handwritten notes, just as Fionnuala had claimed. Someone had even braided a crown of blue-eyed grass flowers and put it on Molly's head, although the delicate blooms were already wilting in the morning heat. Almost all the wreaths and bouquets had at least some native Irish flowers in them—purple thistles, bright pink wild roses, even sprigs of the heavy, gorgeously scented yellow gorse that grew in wild hedges all over the country.

Megan crouched, brushing her fingers over some of the tributes, and supposed that Liz Darr had mentioned being fond of local plants at some point. It seemed like such a little thing not to have known, and such a big one all at once.

Most of the notes had simple expressions of sympathy, but a handful spoke of how Elizabeth Darr had changed the writer's life. One note, written in the fat, loopy handwriting of a teenage girl, told of how the writer had started her own food blog and planned to make a career of it. Others talked about how Liz had inspired them to travel and try new things, and one held a picture of a shy-looking, older woman with Liz, both of them smiling broadly. The woman had never met a celebrity before, and it had taken all her nerve to attend the book signing the picture was from, but since then, she had met dozens of writers and had begun writing herself. Megan wiped her eyes and ran a hand under her nose, not even trying to be surreptitious.

"Is that my ice cream you're melting all over the ground?"

Megan, still sniffling, stood up and gave Fionnuala a watery smile before looking in to the carrying bag. "It's not melted yet. It should be soft enough to eat, though."

"Aw, chicken." Fionn hugged her. "You all right?"

"Ah, sure, I'm grand so." Megan sniffled again as she gave the common Irish answer, and Fionnuala looked at her suspiciously. "No, really, I'm okay. I just keep getting taken by surprise at feeling sad. I didn't know her very well."

"I cry over total strangers' cats dying on the internet, so I can't say that I blame you. Come, we'll eat the ice cream and you'll tell me what you know."

"I don't know much. What do *you* know?" Megan put her arm around Fionn's waist as they went into the restaurant, strangely quiet and hollow with no patrons in it. Fionn got down bowls and spoons, making Meg sniff again, this time with disbelief. "Are we that fancy? I was going to eat out of the cartons."

"I don't want wild berry mixed in my cho . . . actually, that sounds really nice." Fionn scooped ice cream into the bowls anyway, chocolate and wild berry together, and left the honeycomb to melt some more upon the unspoken agreement that it wouldn't go well with the wild berry. "I texted Niamh last night to wail at her, but she must have been onstage. I know that Martin's in absolute bits. The club is closed and he's in a dead panic about finances. The restaurant is on fine financial footing, though." She sounded determined, if not certain, as she handed Meg a bowl and dug into her own ice cream, eyelids drooping with bliss at the first bite. "So what's the story?"

"Well," Meg said around a spoonful of ice cream, "the good news is, I think you probably *are* off the hook for food poisoning."

"Oh thank God. I mean, I thought so, but—how do you know?"

Meg put down the spoon and took a deep breath. "Because Niamh says Elizabeth was having an affair, which might mean she ended up with a bad case of murder."

CHAPTER SIX

"Elizabeth Darr was having an *affair*? Jesus, and I thought she had everything. She was rich, she was smart, she was pretty—what hope have the rest of us if *she* couldn't have a happy marriage? Who was sh—what the *hell*?" A metallic bang from the kitchen preceded a thunderous, teeth-jarring crash, like every pot in the building was crashing to the floor. A high-pitched yelp of fear rang through the other noise.

Both women shot to their feet, with Meg just a step behind Fionn as they ran into the kitchen.

A rack lay against the counters at an angle, all of its pots and pans scattered across the tile floor. A lid, still rattling, spun a few more times and clattered to a standstill. A torn paper bag spilled a sandwich over the counter, just in front of the fallen rack. The silence echoed and rang in Megan's ears after the enormous noise. Fionnuala gripped the doorknob with one hand and a counter with the other, cords standing out in her neck and her whole body swaying slightly. "What the hell."

"Did you leave the door open?" Megan ducked under her arm and edged forward into the chaos. At least the pans were all empty; there could have been food spilled everywhere as well as pots.

"Of course not! And I came in through the front this morning, because I wanted to see Mol . . ." Fionnuala trailed off uncertainly. "I didn't lock up last night, though. Syzmon was the last one out. I suppose he could have . . . but he's never not locked up before."

"Last night wasn't exactly your usual night at the shop," Megan breathed. Something ahead of her squeaked and she froze, then crouched slowly to pick up a frying pan by the handle.

Fionn's voice shot sky-high. "If that's a rat, I'm *dead*."

"If it's a rat, I'll tell you to look away until it's dealt with so you'll have plausible deniability." Megan inched forward, transferring the frying pan to her left hand, and reached out to haul the kitchen rack aside in one tremendous heave.

It weighed a ton and moved about three inches, rather than flying across the room like she'd imagined it would. Megan yowled as its weight pulled at her shoulder socket. A series of squeaks and whimpers in front of her were half-drowned by Fionn's semi-frantic laughter. "That looks a lot cooler in the movies."

"I guess they have wires in the movies." Megan rotated her shoulder, trying to get it feeling normal again, and this time shoved the rack back on its wheels like a normal person, using her own weight as counterbalance and flinching when the whole thing slammed and rattled back to the floor. More whimpering, and a growl, came from under the counter. "That's not a rat."

"A rat would have run by now," Fionn agreed. She edged forward, peering over Megan's head as she crouched, the frying pan still held aloft as a weapon.

Brown eyes and bared teeth looked out at her from deep under the counter, as far into the shadows as a small dog could get. She was dirty white with a brown patch over her eyes like a mask, and although she growled again, low and menacing, her tail thumped frantically on what had, probably as recently as the night before, been a chef's jacket.

Megan lowered the frying pan. "Congratulations, Fionn. You've got puppies."

"What?" Fionnuala elbowed Megan aside, sticking her own head beneath the counter. "*What?* I can't have puppies! This is a professional kitchen! I'll—they'll—how'd they get here?"

"The usual way, I suppose." Megan caught herself as Fionn pushed her over, then pushed a few pots out of the way, put the frying pan on top of them, and sat, cross-legged, to peer at the mama dog and her puppies. Two of them, barely big enough to fill Meg's hand, lay obliviously behind their mama.

Fionn, exasperated, said, "I know how they *got* here. I meant, how did they get *here*?" She gestured wildly at her kitchen, then rose and went to test the back door, which was locked. She unlocked it and opened it to stare down the alley outside.

"God, there's a dozen places out here a dog could have been hiding."

"She must have slipped in during the ruckus last night. Even with people in and out, it's warmer than the street, and she found herself a nice little hidey-hole. I want to know how she knocked over that rack; it weighs a ton. And whose sandwich is that?"

"Syzmon's. He doesn't like eating while he's cooking, so he saves a sandwich for after his shift ends. She must have climbed up and caught the balance just right somehow. Or just wrong." Fionn knelt up to gaze at her counters in dismay. "I'm going to have to scrub everything with bleach."

"Don't you kind of do that anyway?"

Fionnuala gave Megan a look that said she wasn't helping and sat back down to stare at the puppies. "I can't have *dogs* in here, Megan."

"Well, call Dogs Trust or the SPCA." Megan took the meat out of the sandwich and crouched, offering it to the mama dog. Her tail thumped harder, though she stayed where she was. After a few seconds, Meg tossed the meat toward her. She lurched forward, snapped it up, and gobbled it down, her tail wagging harder still. "Is there something in the fridge I could give her?"

"You can't feed a *dog* in my *restaurant*!"

"It's not like I'm setting her a place at your best table." Megan went to the fridge, which, being nearly as large as her apartment, had plenty of food she could feed to a hungry dog. She took some cold grilled chicken and chopped it into smaller pieces, then stuck it in the microwave for a few seconds to take the chill off, all while Fionn watched in dismay. A minute later, the little dog wolfed it down and, more trusting, edged toward Megan and Fionnuala. "There's a good girl," Megan cooed. "Can we see your puppies, huh? What a good job you did. Such big, strong pups. And all by yourself, huh? It's hard work, isn't it? I'm glad you found somewhere safe to have them."

"My *kitchen* isn't *sa*—"

"Well, yeah, it is. It's not ideal for you, maybe, but it's terrific for her and them." Megan offered the back of her hand and the mama dog sniffed it carefully, then gave it a tentative lick. "There's a good girl. Fionn, call the SPCA, see if they can get somebody to come take these sweeties away. Yes, you're a good girl, aren't you? Smart mama, finding somewhere warm and safe to have your babies. Can I see them? Hm?" She petted the little dog— she was a Jack Russell, short-furred and clever— and offered some more of the chicken. Fionnuala, face still disbelieving, got up to call animal rescue. By the time she'd returned, Megan had a lapful of mama and puppies, the latter of which were squirming with warm, happy puppy delight while Megan chortled over them.

"The pounds and animal rescue places say they're overflowing," Fionn said grimly. "Apparently it's been an especially good summer for kittens and puppies. One of them said they could take them, but only for twenty-four hours, and they'd have to put them down after that. A couple of others say if I can just hold on to them for three days, maybe a week, they'll have room. I can't have dogs in my restaurant for a week, Megan!" Her voice rose until it broke.

"Seriously?" Megan held up one of the puppies, a girl, whose fat pink tummy had only the faintest blur of fur over it. "Seriously, you can't have this darling in your restaurant for a week?"

"Megan!"

Megan cackled. "I know, I know, but she's adorable, isn't she? Look at her head." The baby's white muzzle led up to a streak through the rusty-brown patches over her eyes and ended with a heart-shaped spot between her ears. "Maybe her name should be Amor."

"That's a terrible name." Fionn reluctantly rubbed the puppy's tummy and started to smile as her tail wagged. "She's an Irish dog. She should be Agra. That means love."

"I can't give them Irish names. I don't know any. I'd have to call this fat wee fellow Cúchullainn. It's the only dog-related name I know." Megan picked up the other puppy, distinctly fuzzier than his sister, and with only a halo of white around his nose; otherwise, his face was dark brown and the rest of him entirely white. "Maybe he should be Dip. He looks like he's been dipped in chocolate."

"Cúchullainn was the Hound of *Ulster*," Fionnuala half-roared. "We're in Leinster! Just call him Cú; it means dog, you can have Dog and Love and . . . you could take them."

"What? Orla would skin me alive. There's a clause longer than my arm about pets in my rental contract."

"She won't either. She needs you to drive. Besides, it's just until the dog rescue people can take them."

"You could be Thong," Megan said to the girl puppy. "Then we'd have Dip Thong."

Fionnuala said, "*Megan*," in a perfectly horrified tone, and Megan laughed until tears came. The mama dog sat up and licked her face in concern, making Megan laugh harder. Finally, she petted the mama into lying back down, wiped her face, and giggled at the appalled expression Fionn had maintained.

"No? I thought it was good. Yes, all right, of course I'll take them home, Fionn. You can't have dogs staying in your restaurant, and you don't need the extra stress of babies at home either. Just text me the information on who can take them and I'll deal with the rest of it. Orla *will* skin me," she warned the chef, but Fionn bent over and hugged her, puppies and all.

"You're a star, Meg. I don't know what I'd do without you."

"You'd eat all that melting gelato by yourself. Bring it in here, I want to finish it, but I can't get up."

"Pinned down beneath the terrible half-kilo weight of puppies. I know how it is." Fionn nodded solemnly and went to get the ice cream.

She came back barely a minute later, a young woman trailing behind her. The girl had thick, sandy blonde curls pulled back in a bushy pony-tail, and a face red and swollen from crying. "Meg, this is Cíara. She needs ice cream, too. And maybe puppies."

"Oh, they're darling." Cíara knelt beside Megan to brush a tentative finger over the male puppy's back, but her eyes filled with tears as she looked up at Fionn. "Ms. Canan, I don't know how they could have sneaked in here. I'm sure they weren't in here during dinner last night."

"I'm sure not," Fionn said wearily. "There were a lot of people in and out. I expect their ma took advantage of it and slipped in. Ciara was the Darrs' server last night, Meg."

Meg nodded. "I remember her. You helped me up off the flagstones yesterday evening," she reminded Ciara. She hadn't recognized the girl's black slacks and white shirt as part of the standard server's uniform the evening before—the blouse had been fashionable enough to pass for ordinary wear—but now that she knew Ciara had been working at the restaurant, it seemed obvious.

"You were being so helpful," Ciara whispered. She sounded like she'd been crying for hours. Megan bet she needed water more than ice cream but didn't say anything as Fionn handed her a bowl of gelato. "I saw you talking to that police detective last night. You made it look easy. I thought it was terrifying." Tears welled in her eyes again. Storm-blue eyes, a pretty shade with a lot of grey, though at the moment they also were bloodshot, salt-rimmed, and watery. "I'm afraid I killed her somehow. I'm afraid her husband will die. I didn't sleep at all." The tears spilled into her ice cream.

"I probably would have been more frightened talking to a cop if I'd thought I might have accidentally had something to do with somebody's death, too." Fionnuala made a horrified face at Megan and she made a pained one back. "That sounded better in my head. I just meant . . ."

To her surprise and relief, Cíara blurted a wet laugh. "No, I understand."

"You almost certainly didn't, you know," Megan said as reassuringly as she could. "I just saw Simon and he's fine, so whatever happened to Liz probably isn't going to happen to him. I mean, it doesn't seem likely to have been food poisoning—"

"It couldn't have been anyway," Fionnuala said ferociously. "Everything's off at the lab for tests now, but it couldn't have been. All that fish was fresh. I bought it myself from Wrights out in Howth at half eleven yesterday morning, and they'd only just come in off the trawlers themselves." She sounded like she'd said the same words a thousand times in the past fifteen hours.

Meg, firmly, said, "It's going to be okay. Listen, Fionn, it's going to be okay. We're going to finish the ice cream, I'll take the puppies to my place, and we'll get this sorted out. All right?"

Fionnuala slumped, caught Cíara's expression of dread, and pulled herself together. "Okay." She hesitated, then offered a lopsided smile. "But I think you should have brought more ice cream."

She *should* have brought more ice cream. Enough to justify sitting there all day eating it, instead of furtively sneaking a dog and two puppies, still wrapped in the somewhat gross chef's jacket, into her apartment. They had to be snuck; otherwise, Orla would lay her out in lavender. But if Orla simply never knew there were dogs in the flat, she couldn't object. And she'd never see the new dog bed, one that Megan had stopped to buy on the way home. Or the dog food, a food dish, a water dish, some weird smelly pads the puppies were supposed to want to pee on, a couple of chew toys . . .

"This is a lot of stuff for a week," she told the three of them, puppies and mama alike, as the mama rooted around in the jacket-on-the-bed and made it comfortable enough for her babies. "I guess I can donate it to the rescue people when they collect you."

One set of soulful brown eyes and two squinty-eyed baby faces turned toward her mournfully. Megan waggled a finger at them. "Stop that. I'm anthropomorphizing. You are not sad. Go to sleep."

She filled the bowls and put them down near the bed while the mama dog did just as she'd said, curling up with her babies for a rest.

"Well, it's been a big day for you," Megan murmured and rubbed the mama's head as she drifted off. She'd need a bath, but not just then. The same could probably be said for Megan herself, after having a lap full of newborn puppies, but that would have to wait, too.

She threw herself onto the couch, decided she was in real danger of falling asleep if she stayed there, and stood again to call the office, hoping to catch anybody but Orla answering the phone. But it was her boss's affected, RTÉ-Irish voice that answered. "Leprechaun Limos, Orla Keegan speaking."

"Hey, Orla, this is Megan. Simon Darr wants me to collect his in-laws at the airport at four. Is that a problem?"

The RTÉ accent dropped instantly in favor of

Orla's natural brassy tones. "Jesus, haven't you cut us loose of that mess yet? What're you doing with your time?"

Megan could think of no acceptable answer in the few seconds Orla gave her before speaking again in the tone of a long-suffering maiden aunt. "Far be it from me to turn down money in the bank. Get them if you have to, but I've got a half seven pickup tomorrow for you, to go out to Howth."

"Can you give it to Cillian? I'd like to be on call if Dr. Darr needs anything."

"I will not." Orla gave a good impression of outrage at having even been asked. "You'll drive as little for those people as you can. I don't like our name being dragged through the mud. We could be on television!"

"There's no such thing as bad publicity?"

Orla barked derisively and hung up. A few seconds later, a text with the who-when-and-where came through for the next morning's client. Megan sighed, glanced at the clock, and went to wash up thoroughly before pulling on her chauffeur's uniform. She clunked her knuckles on her business card case and, reminded, took Detective Bourke's card from it. It carried his scent, just faintly: warm and a little spicy, not like the vague, sickly sweet smell of most deodorants. Megan, smiling, tapped the edge of the card to her lips, then decided she'd better call Niamh to make her confession, rather than just text.

"Darling!" the actress proclaimed. "How did your talk with our bereaved doctor go?"

"Remember when people answered the phone

with 'Hello' and 'Hi, this is Megan' because our phones didn't tell us who was calling?" Megan wondered idly.

"I refuse to answer on the grounds it may incriminate me," Niamh said. "And you *are* older than I am, darling. We young people use vone apps now."

"Vone? Video phone? That's a stupid word."

"If we can have vlogs, we can have vones. I'm going to make it happen. Next time you can vone me."

Megan rolled her eyes so hard it hurt. "Anyway, I didn't bring up the affair. At least, not with Simon. I ran into that detective I told you about, Paul Bourke? He's a fan of yours."

Niamh airily said, "Who isn't," but sounded pleased. Then, the implication of Megan knowing Bourke was a fan caught up with her, and the pleasure changed to an *aw-maaaan* dismay. "Wait. You mentioned me?"

"Only in passing, and then when I mentioned Elizabeth might have been having an affair, he put who I heard it from together. He wants to talk to you. I'm supposed to text you his number."

Niamh's tone changed to slyly teasing. "You got his number? Fast work there, Major. Is he cute?"

"I—yes? No? Kind of? He's the type that grows on you."

"So does mold," Niamh said dryly. "All right, give me his number. You're sure this is legit, he's not just trying to get an actress's number to impress the lads?"

"He's a cop, Nee. I'm sure. I'll text it in a minute. Look, if you get a chance, drop by the restaurant? Fionn's in bits. A dog had puppies in her kitchen this morning."

Niamh's pealing laughter soared, a rich, delightful sound. Megan had thought for years—long before they'd met, back when Meg herself had been just a fan—that Niamh O'Sullivan might have made it in the movies on the basis of that laugh alone. It ended with a wheezing giggle, like Niamh was wiping her eyes and recombobulating herself. "I shouldn't laugh. That probably violates all kinds of safety and cleanliness laws."

"I think it violates *all* of them. Anyway, I've got the puppies—"

"OmyGod," Niamh said breathlessly, "you're adopting puppies? How many?"

"I am *not* adopting them. I'm keeping them until the rescue people can pick them up. Two. A boy and a girl. Dip and Thong."

Niamh burst out laughing again. "You can't do that to defenseless puppies!"

"Thus proving I'm an unfit dog mother and won't be keeping them. Anyway, do go over if you can, okay? She needs some moral support. And there's honeycomb gelato in the freezer."

"Well, why didn't you say so? I'm on my way already. Any other social activities you've arranged for me today?"

Megan smirked at her phone. "I'll let you know."

"Good woman." Niamh hung up and Megan, amused, went to collect Simon's in-laws from the airport.

CHAPTER SEVEN

The Dempseys, a kind-looking but clearly devastated couple in their late fifties, had little to say to Megan. She greeted them with sympathies and drove them to the Shelbourne in silence, foregoing the genial patter about the route through the city that she often gave to new visitors. They looked bleakly out the windows, not speaking to one another, though they held hands tightly and once Mr. Dempsey pressed a kiss into his wife's hair. Losing a child had to be the worst kind of grief, so encompassing Megan couldn't really imagine it, though she'd known enough parents who had faced that loss within the military.

She opened the car door for them outside the hotel and, to her surprise, Mrs. Dempsey took her hand in a crushing grip as Megan helped her from the car. "Simon told us how kind you've been to him in the past twenty-four hours, and how much our daughter liked you. Thank you. Thank you so much."

"I'm glad to have been a little help. I liked Liz very much, too. She favored you."

Mrs. Dempsey's eyes filled with tears, but she managed a tremulous smile. "She did, didn't she? She called me her mini-me, once she outgrew me. She got all that height from Peter." Her husband stepped out of the car to put his arm around her waist, and she turned against his chest, muffling sobs. Mr. Dempsey met Megan's eyes over his wife's head and nodded, a quiet but important benediction. Megan smiled a little, returned the nod, and got their baggage from the car's boot. Mr. Dempsey looked torn, but she shook her head, waving off his impulse to assist her, and he walked his wife into the hotel with Megan taking up the rear.

They were in the room beside Simon's. Megan took one of their room keys and put away their luggage as they knocked on, and were admitted to, Simon's room. On the way out, she slid their key under his door, but the door opened and he called after her as she headed for the stairs. She waited, and he almost stumbled approaching her, like he'd been coming in with a hug and thought better of it at the last moment. Instead, he opened and clasped his hands together several times, saying, "I don't know what I would have done without you, Megan. Thank you."

"I'm glad I could help," Megan said again. "My boss is a complete jerk, by the way, and she plans to charge you for the hours last night. I'll cover them."

"What? No. No." Simon's hands opened and closed again until he noticed and frowned at them briefly, like they belonged to someone else. He folded them together firmly, in front of his stomach, and shook his head. "No, we can aff—" He blanched. "I. I can afford to pay the few extra hours. I don't want you put out, not after what you've done for us."

"It'd be fine, really. It's—"

"No, I insist. Thank you for letting me know, but I wouldn't have imagined otherwise." A smile crept around the corners of his mouth. "Ms. Keegan seems like a stickler for the rules."

Megan ducked her head. "Especially when it comes to her bottom line. All right, look, you have my number, right? Just . . . give me a call if you need anything, a lift around town, a semi-local guide . . ."

"I will. Thank you." Simon went back to his room and Megan, taking the stairs down to the ground floor, sighed. She'd been gone from home a couple of hours. Mama dog probably needed to go out, and the car would be on Simon's clock until Megan got it back to the garage, so, with an even more dramatic sigh—one which no one at all was around to appreciate—she headed back to Rathmines in 6 p.m. Dublin traffic. The three-kilometre drive took forty minutes, longer than it would have to walk, which was why they said cycling was the best way to get around Dublin, and that walking was often second-best.

Still, Megan didn't mind creeping along, start-and-stop, watching pedestrians pass her, fall behind, and catch up again. The cyclists she rarely saw again, proving the conventional wisdom's point, but there were familiar strangers whose faces she knew, sometimes whose dogs' names she knew, although their own names were mysteries to her. She would lift a hand in greeting to those people, exchanging smiles, or roll down her window to listen to an argument as she drifted slowly by. Some people carried open umbrellas, keeping the sun off themselves without daring the panache of parasols, though, to be fair, Megan thought, it was a lot easier to find an umbrella than a parasol in Dublin.

She pulled into the garage just before seven and tossed her keys to Tymon, a round-faced blond who spoke Irish, English, and Polish so interchangeably that Megan had started to understand bits of the two languages she didn't already speak.

He waved a handheld hoover and dove into the car, vacuuming it clean for the night. He was one of Orla's two on-staff mechanics, an expense Megan was always surprised she laid out for. It meant someone on call in emergencies, though, without the exorbitant rates an unaffiliated garage would charge, and the lads otherwise mostly got to set their own schedules, satisfying everyone.

Ten minutes later, she discovered the puppies snuggled so deeply inside the old chef's jacket that they wouldn't even miss their mama being gone. She took Mama for a walk, then back to the apartment for a bath, an abuse she took with stoic misery, her ears and tail clamped down and a betrayed look in her eyes.

"Yeah," Megan said, toweling her off, "but you smell a *lot* better, and you're so pretty now!"

Mama, balefully, shook herself hard, spraying dog water over Megan, and then licked herself all over, just to show Megan who was boss. "You're not getting any drier that way, Mama. You should let me use the hairdryer on you." She doubted the little dog *would* let her but took it out anyway, and to her surprise found Mama more than willing to lean happily into the hot, noisy breeze of the dryer until she was no more than damp- and fresh-dog smelling. She gave herself another businesslike shake, and Megan unrolled the puppies from the stinky chef's jacket, nestling them into the bed instead, before letting Mama back in. Everyone looked satisfied with the arrangement, especially Megan, *especially* after she'd thrown the jacket in the wash. She kind of doubted it could be salvaged, but at least it would smell better when she threw it out.

After that, by the time she'd eaten dinner, the clock read nearly 9 p.m. Hot young things would just be getting ready to go out for the night, but Megan, somewhat defensively, said, "I'm old and boring and have to get up in the morning," to Mama Dog, who didn't even bother to cock an ear at the sound of her voice. Megan harrumphed, muttered, "See, why would I keep dogs who don't even care," and went to bed.

Choosing to wake up at half five and go to the gym was one thing. Being awakened at two in the morning by a whiny mama dog and two wriggling puppies who had decided the middle of the night was an excellent time to spend some time awake was something else entirely. Meg, vowing to never own a dog in her life, took Mama for the shortest walk in dog-owning history and, to her relief, discovered that brand-new puppies apparently couldn't stay awake more than twenty minutes at a time. As soon as Mama returned, they had a greedy go at her milk and fell asleep again.

Megan's alarm went off at five thirty, as usual, and for once she shut it off instead of getting up for the gym. By half six she'd had almost a reasonable amount of sleep—"See," she yawned at the dogs, "this is why it was smart to go to bed early"—and after bringing Mama for another walk, she got to the garage in good time to get the car and make it to her 7:30 a.m. pickup.

The clients were an American couple, goodlooking, sporty men in their late twenties too involved with each other—or the fact that it was half seven in the morning—to talk much with Megan. She collected them in Drumcondra, another of the village-within-a-city centres that lay north of the river. Their B&B was a five-minute walk from the DART—Dublin Area Rapid Transit—station that connected north and south county Dublin, and Megan was tempted to tell them they could have taken the train out to Howth for an insignificant fraction of the cost of hiring her car. She didn't, because first, Orla would kill her, and second, they had the power of the internet and had still clearly decided on a hired car. Besides, Megan loved the drive along the water out to the little peninsula and the fishing town that it supported.

They arrived well before nine, which meant absolutely nothing was open but the fishmongers. Her clients headed for the cliff walk, giving Meg at least a couple of hours to herself in the pretty seaside town. She parked the car and walked out along the north pier, distinguishable as the working pier from the sturdy, two-toned, and often rust-streaked fishing boats with their heavy equipment soldered on and their multicoloured plastic fish totes stacked on the decks. The southern pier, in contrast, bristled with masts stemming from lower, sleeker, white-hulled sailing vessels, and ne'er the twain shall meet, thought Megan.

Men and women—mostly men—in chest-high waders over sturdy, warm shirts with the sleeves rolled up to display powerful forearms brought the fishing boats in from early excursions, unloading their catch into totes and hauling them to the dock.

Half a dozen harbourside restaurants, a fish processing plant, wholesale fish marketers, and restaurateurs up from Dublin proper shouted and chatted back and forth at one another, exchanging stories and wares with equal ease. Megan worked her way through them, stopping to talk without really acknowledging to herself that she had a plan until she'd already chatted with one of the fishmongers and had stopped in to a second. By the third she couldn't fool herself anymore, but fortunately for her, everybody wanted to talk about Elizabeth Darr's shocking death, and most of them were eager to point fingers at one another.

"Nah," said a big lad at the third shop, "we know Fionn, sure, but she didn't buy from us that day. Me da's got the receipts, if you're like that guard and want to have a look like."

"Guard?" As if Megan had been unique in the impulse to talk to fishmongers. Of course the police would have been out here already.

"Sure, a tall, ginger fella, like me." The lad gestured at his own short-cropped hair, which was brighter red and thicker than Detective Paul Bourke's had ever thought of being. "I told him like I'll tell you, I don't think for two minutes that yer wan got food poisoning from anybody's catch, no matter if it was ours or the Wrights or anybody's. We don't sell bad fish, and a chef like Fionnuala Canan's too smart to buy it if we did. Now, if she'd gotten it down on Moore Street, I couldn't say, but—"

"Oh, come on, that's not fair, is it?" Megan loved Moore Street as much as Liz Darr had loved the Galway market. Around two hundred years of age, it laid claim to being Dublin's oldest market, and still had green grocers, butchers, fishmongers, and people braying *tobacco!* along its cobbled length, as well as innumerable shops run by immigrants from Africa to China and everywhere in between. It lay on Dublin's north side and had a problematic reputation, but the vendors took their jobs and their wares as seriously as any posher location in the city.

She could see the fisherman bump up against his own prejudices, consider his audience, and choose to back off with a noncommittal roll of his big shoulders. "I'd best get back to it."

"Thanks for your time." Megan left him loading fish for processing and meandered down the dock, watching people at work and early fishermen with their rods and reels out to climb the granite bulwark that held back the sea and made Howth's harbour safe. A tour boat proprietor asked if she'd like to go out on the harbour and she took a pamphlet, having never done it and thinking she might wrangle Niamh or Fionn into joining her. A troop of scuba divers made their way from a scuba shop toward their boat, all fresh-faced and cheerful in the morning sun. Megan climbed the five steps up the bulwark and stood watching the sea for a few minutes, her cap keeping the wind from blowing her hair into her face.

After a while, someone came up to fish next to her, and in the name of not getting caught on a hook, Megan scooted back down to the wretchedly uneven cobblestones—flagstones, maybe; she thought they were too big to be cobbles—and headed back toward the main stretch of the pier. Up ahead, she caught a glimpse of familiar sandy red hair and waved as she came closer to Detective Bourke.

A complicated dance of emotions flickered over his face when he noticed her. "Ms. Malone."

"Detective Bourke. Any luck with the case so far?"

He made a noncommittal sound and, with a twist of his lips, said, "You?"

Megan laughed. "Strangely enough, not much. The lads down there—" she pointed at the fish-mongers she'd visited "—say they wouldn't believe it for a moment that Fionnuala Canan bought and served unsafe fish, but I bet you got that out of them already. One of them said he'd talked to you, but then I annoyed him by being too egalitarian and he sent me packing." Bourke's fair eyebrows rose and she said, "I had the nerve to suggest the mongers on Moore Street cared as much about the quality of their product as they do on the pier here."

Amusement brightened Bourke's eyes to summer-sea blue. "Sure and how dare you, coming in here a foreigner and all, and still having opinions."

"I know, right? What a lot of nerve I've got. Did you get ahold of Niamh?"

"She rang me—no, what did she call it? *Voned.* She voned me." Bourke's thin lips curved upward again as Megan spread a hand over her face and shook her head.

"She says she's determined to make that word happen."

"She might yet. She must practice holding the phone at the right angle to flatter. She looked—" He broke off, looking for the words, and Megan supplied them.

"Like Niamh O'Sullivan?"

"Yes, now that you mention it. And I looked like an orangutan."

"You're not nearly that hairy," Megan offered consolingly. Somehow the detective failed to look consoled. "Did she say anything helpful?"

"Unsubstantiated rumour, though she was sure enough of herself. I'll be looking into it. Rumors don't usually start out of nowhere."

"Anything on the autopsy yet?"

"Are you always this gruesome, Ms. Malone, or are these special circumstances?"

"Oh, definitely special circumstances. I met poor Cíara O'Donnell yesterday after I saw you. She's in pieces. Fionn told me restaurants—the chef, in fact—is responsible if someone gets food poisoning here. That poor kid isn't going to get blamed for anything, is she?"

They were gathering sea gulls around them, big

ones that nearly came up to Megan's knee and who sidled closer without a hint of fear. Megan said, "We don't have any food" to them, and one hopped nearer, as if it thought she was trying to get it to leave by lying to it.

Bourke murmured, "Bold bird" but shook his head. "It seems unlikely she's in any sort of trouble, but at this stage of an investigation, I'd be unwise to dismiss anything entirely."

"How not reassuring of you."

"If you want reassurance, Ms. Malone, go to a priest. If you want answers, stick with me."

"Why, Detective Bourke, are you inviting me along on your investigation?"

"No."

Megan laughed at the finality of the single word. "Fair enough, then. I'm—oh, God. . . ." Her phone, situated in her hip pocket, buzzed. She pulled it out, saying, "Please tell me nobody's fallen off the side of the cliff into the Irish Sea. Orla will kill me if I get the company mixed up in another scandal. . . . Oh, no, it's just Niamh. Never mind, then."

"Would she come to you first with gossip?"

Megan tried to look affronted. "Do I look like someone who gossips?"

"You look like a human being, and in my experience, that generally means yes."

"I can't really argue with that." Meg swiped the screen open, reading, then smiled at Niamh's text, which she read aloud. **"'Your detective's quite fit, isn't he? I might consider a mutual admiration society with that one. Do ye's know if he's married?'"**

Megan, her gaze as open and innocent as she could make it, looked enquiringly at Bourke. "Are you?"

The detective's fair skin flushed bright pink, a genuinely disastrous combination with his sandy red hair. "Em, no."

"Gay?"

He blushed even more furiously. "Em, no again."

"Brilliant. Any skeletons in the closet? Wives in the attic? Secret babies?" Megan squinted, first at the sun sparkling off the blue harbour waters, then at Bourke. "I think I'm getting close to romance novel tropes now. Any mysterious connections to sheiks or secretaries?"

She thought Detective Paul Bourke might never return to his natural colour again. Even when the worst of the blush faded, he still looked pinker than before, like the blush had reminded a sunburn that it could settle in. "No skeletons or relatives in either closets or attics, no secret babies, and if I've missed out on a sheik, my bank account is the sadder for it."

Megan grinned, typing back to Niamh as she said, "Deadly. Are you busy a week Monday?" to Bourke.

"You're never setting me up with Niamh O'Sullivan." Bourke sounded somewhere between aghast and anticipatory.

"I'm certainly trying to." Megan, chortling, sent the text and burst out laughing a few seconds later when her phone rang.

"You need a vone app, darling," Niamh said chidingly. Megan put the phone on speaker and held it out so Bourke could hear the actress as well. "When did you interview our fit detective for dating suitability, and for whose benefit?"

"Well, I didn't get his life history," Meg said, grinning. "You can do that your own self."

"I *am* available Monday week." Niamh's light teasing tone fell away into a note of hesitance. "Does he really want to go out with me? With me, you know. Not with Gilda."

Meg lifted her eyebrows challengingly at Bourke, whose expression softened to a surprising, unexpected sympathy. He made a small motion that managed to coordinate every part of the body that could shrug: open hands, a tiny lift of his shoulders, an equally minute tilt of his head, an upward twitch of his eyebrows, and, most importantly, an oddly shy half-smile that brought the whole action together into agreement. "I'd say he does," Megan said with confidence. "Will you ring him?"

"Well, I'm meant to anyway," Niamh said. "I got a description of Liz Darr's lover."

CHAPTER EIGHT

Bourke's affable, regular-guy charm fell away in a heartbeat and he took Megan's phone without asking. "Miss O'Sullivan? This is Detective Bourke—"

Niamh O'Sullivan, award-winning stage and film actress, darling of the Irish media, known for her quips and clever one-liners, yelped, "*Shite!*" and howled, "Why weren't you after telling me he was *with* you, Megan, you utter langer! *Jay*sus, you can't trust anybody these days, what the absolute fuck, Meg, you manky wagon—"

Megan's shoulders hunched with laughter as Bourke stared at the phone in horror. "Stop, stop, Nee, you're giving Detective Bourke a heart attack."

"Well, he didn't want Gilda!" Niamh shrieked. "*Je*sus, Megan—"

"She's not really mad, just surprised," Megan informed Bourke beneath Niamh's outraged rant. "Enjoy the performance."

"How can you tell?"

"You remember a couple years ago when that reporter asked a couple of nasty questions on the red carpet?" Bourke nodded, and Megan, remembering, felt her cheeks turn red in angry solidarity with her friend. It hadn't been the first time, and probably wouldn't be the last, that Niamh, whose Afro-Caribbean heritage made her stand out in the pantheon of successful Irish film and stage stars, had been questioned about the authenticity of her Irish roots, but the tone had been particularly condescending. Niamh had eviscerated him with a smile, and while the embarrassed broadcast networks had cut away during her speech, more than one company—and several individuals—had caught it in full. She'd gone viral, upstaging the awards show, and her ascending star had suddenly risen in meteoric fire. Megan had been driving her that night; it was how they'd met.

"That's what Nee is like when she's really angry," Meg said. "Absolutely calm and brutal and able to undercut every stupid thing anybody within a three-mile radius says. This—" she gestured at the phone "—is showboating."

"—setting me up like that, I can't believe you, Meg," Niamh was saying in still full-fledged outrage that disappeared with the next word. "Anyway, Adam says herself is only in her early twenties, young enough to be impressed by fame—"

"Almost everybody is that young," Megan pointed out.

Niamh made a generally agreeable sound without otherwise stopping. "—and that she's quite pretty, with gobs of browny-blonde curls and pale blue eyes. He didn't have a clue what her name was, but he says he'd swear to it in court, that he's seen them skulking around together."

"I'll want to talk to him." Bourke turned the phone off speaker and put it to his ear, meeting Megan's eyes as he did so. "That's very helpful, Miss O'Sullivan. Thank you for your efforts. As for next Monday . . . it might be better to wait until this case is wrapped up before we meet. Fewer complications that way, even if you're only tangentially involved."

She said something, and Bourke shook his head. "It's only being treated as suspicious right now, but yes, that's the rule of thumb. The first forty-eight hours are critical. That doesn't mean we all throw in the towel at the end of two days, though." He smiled briefly, nodded, and said, "Don't think I won't," before handing the phone back to Megan.

Niamh, grimly, said, "Did he actually *hear* the Gilda comment? No, don't answer that right now, I don't want him to know I asked. He won't ring."

"I wouldn't count on that. Look, I'll ring you later, okay? Thanks for calling." They hung up, and Meg met Bourke's eyes. "Liz's lover sounds like she looks an awful lot like Cíara O'Donnell."

"She does at that." Bourke gave her a direct look. "And I'll be the one looking into it, Ms. Malone, not your own self."

Megan raised her hands defensively. "I'd never dream of it."

Bourke hmphed, a sound of doubt and acceptance and, with a nod, left Meg on the dockside. She waited until he was a silhouette in the distance, slim black shape outlined by glittering blue water, then called Fionnuala. "How are you holding up?"

"I've had more inspectors than I can shake a stick at come through," Fionn said. "I had to explain about the damn dog—how are the puppies?—because I wasn't *allowed* to clean up, because they had to inspect the place, but—you know the Reddit cow poem?"

Megan pulled the phone away to stare at it, thinking that Niamh might be on to something with using video calls all the time. It certainly would be more satisfying to gape at Fionn rather than her own faint reflection in the glassy black background. "The *cow* poem?"

A brief silence in which she could all but hear Fionn trying to decide if it was worth it came over the phone and ended with, "It's a health inspector story involving cows. Never mind. The point is, I explained about the dog, and that obviously that kind of thing never happens, and the restaurant's passed the health inspection. Now I've got to wait for the report on the food, but so far so good. How *are* the puppies?"

"Boring. Apparently puppies sleep twenty hours a day for the first week or so of their lives. I thought they were supposed to be wiggly and adorable. Can you go over to my apartment and take Mama Dog out for a walk?"

"I can't," Fionnuala said unhappily. "They're sending more people to talk to me, even though they say the place is clean. This is going to haunt me forever. Martin came over this morning with the books. Honestly, Meg, I thought we were safer than the numbers say we are. Two more days of this and we might never open our doors again."

"We are not going to let that happen, Fionn. We'll figure it out. I don't know how, but we will, okay? How's Martin doing?"

"Worse than me. Sweating bullets. I think he's sunk more into Canan's than he'll tell me, Meg. It's not just Canan's, of course. It's Club Heaven upstairs, and the bar with it that makes so much money—"

"But they're not closed, are they? Oh, no, wait, you said they were, but not why?"

"They are, though, because there are stairs up and down that are only blocked off with the gates, like. Waitstaff go up and down them with key cards, and people might be able to get over them, or throw things through them, so to keep the whole scene clean—" Fionnuala's voice broke and she took a breath so deep and shaky that Megan could hear its rattle over the phone. "The club will probably be able to reopen, maybe sooner than the restaurant. But right now, Martin's just watching his investment money drain into the River Liffey."

Megan, mostly to herself, breathed, "I thought the Poddle ran under Temple Bar," and Fionnuala's baffled silence filled the phone line momentarily before she gave a sharp, hard laugh.

"It doesn't come this far east, I don't think. I'm not being literal, you eejit—"

"No, I know. I'm sorry, I shouldn't make stupid jokes when you're so stressed. I just like the idea of underground rivers."

"Ah, you're grand." A little of the strain went

out of Fionn's voice. "You know that big, ugly grate you can see on the south side of the river when the tide is low, just past the Millennium Bridge? The one that looks like a hellmouth? That's where the Poddle meets the Liffey."

"Oh. Yeah, that's farther west than Canan's. There, I learned something today." Trying to keep her tone nonchalant and feeling like a total failure, Meg asked, "What about Cíara? How's she?"

Fionn didn't seem to notice the awkward note in Meg's voice and only sighed explosively, her tone much less stressed than it had been. "I don't know. I haven't seen her since she finished the ice cream yesterday. I'd go check on her, but I can't be in two places at once. Or five. I need a clone, Meg."

"Look," Megan said, as false-brightly as before, "I can go check on Cíara for you, if you know where she lives?"

"Um, it's on her employment file, but I probably shouldn't just tell you, you know? It's probably illegal."

Meg wrinkled her nose at the soft sea horizon. "I guess it probably is. Maybe I could just go be in the neighbourhood, coincidental-like." Like a stalker, she thought, and bit her tongue on the idea.

"Right. Hang on." A few minutes of silence ensued before Fionn came back and said, "If you were coincidentally in the area of—oh, you actually could be, she lives near you. I'm just saying, if you wanted to take in a movie at the Stella later today and happened to walk by the apartments behind it . . ."

"Oh, brilliant. I'll go see what's playing after I get done with this job."

Fionn said, "Thank you," sincerely enough to make Megan feel guilty. "I'm worried about the poor creature. She's taking it all very hard." A tired laugh followed. "Unlike me, of course."

"You both have reason to," Megan said. "I'll let you know if I catch her and how she's doing."

"Thanks, Meg. You're a star." Fionnuala hung up, leaving Megan alone to stew in her own guilt about knowing things and not sharing them with friends. Not that mentioning the possible affair angle to Fionn would have helped anything at *all*. It would almost certainly have made things worse, because Fionn wouldn't just let it lie, any more than Megan wanted to. And she hadn't *lied* to Fionn. Checking up on Cíara, a distraught young woman of her recent acquaintance, was a perfectly legitimate thing to do. And she *had* distracted Fionn for a moment with the idiocy about the rivers, and that had to make up for something.

She snorted and headed back for the car. She could jump through all the mental hoops she wanted to; it wouldn't fool anybody, least of all herself. Clearly, she wasn't cut out to be a criminal, since presumably actual bad guys didn't go through mental turmoil trying to justify their behavior to their friends. Or maybe genuine bad guys didn't have any friends, which would solve the whole problem but seemed unlikely.

Out loud, the better to silence her hamster wheel of thoughts, she said, "Oh my *God*, Meg," and climbed into the car to await her clients.

* * *

Somewhat to Meg's surprise, her clients finished the hike in good time and were content to return to their B&B rather than spend the day exploring Howth's other touristy activities. She'd been rather looking forward to trailing along on a tour of the still-lived-in Howth Castle, which had stood overlooking the Irish Sea for eight centuries, or to climbing the lighthouse, which she'd actually never done, or any of the other half-dozen things her clients could have stuffed into the day. Instead, they arrived back at the car only minutes after she did, and by 10 a.m. she had the car back in the garage and had gone home to rub the puppies' tummies. Mama Dog managed to convey that she deigned, rather than desired, to go for a walk, and Megan said, "I've got to bring you to a vet" as they headed out the door. "Maybe you've been chipped and somebody is looking for you." She doubted it, though: Mama seemed like she'd been on the street a while, and Meg was afraid someone had abandoned her when she got pregnant.

They were on the way home, actually at the lower apartment door, Megan fumbling with her keys, when from up the street came Orla's deeply offended voice: "And what is *that* I see?"

Megan flinched like she'd been caught breaking in, then looked down at Mama with a sigh. "I'm just keeping her for a few days for a friend, Orla."

"Is the lease not very clear?" Orla demanded. "Does it not say *no pets* and outline the costs of a deposit for so much as bringing one into the house?"

"It's a *week*, Orla," Megan said wearily. "I'm not keeping th—*her*—forever."

"I'll have three hundred euro from you straight-away or it's out you go," Orla snapped. Mama Dog's ears flattened, though she had the good grace not to bare her teeth at Megan's boss and landlord.

"Strangely enough, Orla, I'm not carrying three hundred euro around with me right now, and if you throw me out, you'll have a driver who smells of whatever gutter she slept in the night before. That'll be grand, won't it?"

"Or I won't have a driver at all," Orla said with a threatening gleam in her eye.

Megan's eyebrows slowly rose. "You can take that tack if you want to, but I'm not the one always complaining of how hard it is to turn away clients because you haven't enough drivers to begin with. And we both know I'm your best driver for early morning clients because I don't stay up as late as the lads. It's a *week*, Orla. Give it a rest, okay?"

"I'll want to inspect the place the moment that little bitch is gone," Orla warned. That time, Mama did growl. Megan couldn't blame her, though she did bend to pet the dog soothingly.

"Fine. You can inspect it next week. Come on, pup." Just inside the door, with a fuming Orla left outside, Megan muttered, "Her bark's worse than her bite, Mama, but I admit she's got an awful bark." Upstairs in her apartment, she lay down on her stomach next to the puppies and gave them her fingers to nibble on. "You're going to cost me three hundred euro plus all this stuff I bought to feed you guys for just a *week*. I am *definitely* not keeping you."

The boy wiggled toward her on his belly, more like a baby seal than a dog, and plopped his tiny head on her hand. A little pink tongue emerged to give her one small lick, and then, exhausted by his efforts, the puppy went straight to sleep.

Megan, smiling, extracted her hand so she could find an early lunch—it was only half ten, but she'd been up a long time already—and had almost finished eating when the phone rang and Simon Darr's broken voice said, "Megan? Megan, it happened again. Liz uploaded another video."

CHAPTER NINE

Megan ran for the Luas, the Dublin tram system that would get her nearest to the Shelbourne, and got to the hotel in under half an hour. She jogged upstairs and Simon's room door opened before she even had a chance to knock. She came in quietly, bottom lip between her teeth as she saw Liz's father, Peter, with his head huddled in his wife's lap to muffle his sobs. Mrs. Dempsey, stroking her husband's temple with a mechanical gesture, looked decades older than she had a day earlier.

Simon Darr, slim to begin with, had lost weight since Megan had last seen him. His cheekbones were gaunt, his eyes hollowed, and his thin hands leaped with nervous energy one moment and fell listless the next. He gestured at his computer. Megan squeezed his shoulder, then, making sure to mute the speakers and turn the screen away from the devastated family, sat down to watch a few seconds of the video. There were hundreds of comments beneath it, many of them angry and even more of them confused. A few were agonizingly sympathetic, guessing that Liz had left more vlogs unexpectedly prepped.

"She hadn't, though," Meg murmured, mostly to herself.

Simon sat heavily beside her, shoulders slumped and face in his hands, as if his head simply weighed too much to hold up anymore. "I didn't think so," he said, muffled. "You checked. I didn't remember how, but I knew you'd checked. Someone else posted it. How could someone else have posted it? It was on this computer, Megan. I found the folder with the rest of her prepped vlogs, but no one has been in here to use the computer except me. Us," he said with a short, whole-body lean toward Liz's parents.

"Did anyone else have access to her files? Through cloud sharing, maybe? Did she lose her phone?" Megan checked the location the latest vlog had been uploaded from, macabrely wondering if it would claim to have been posted from the morgue. An IP address came up, the same as the last post, and she picked up the phone to call the front desk. "Yes, hello, I'm wondering if you can tell me what the hotel's IP address is? No, not just the Wi-Fi network name, but the—yes, thank you." She waited while they transferred her to the business centre, where a young-sounding man read off a four-part number that identified the hotel's permanent internet location. It matched the last several posts on Liz's blog, including the two vlogs and the posts both Simon and Megan herself had made. She thanked the youth and fell back in her chair as she hung up, frowning at the screen.

Simon remained silent while she did all that, only answering her questions once she'd hung up. "She never lost her phone, and as far as I know, no one had cloud access—could she have been hacked?" His voice broke, but Megan thought he sounded relieved rather than distressed. "That would explain—"

"It would, but these were all posted from here. A hacker could have come here to post them, or spoofed it, but why? It—"

"I don't even know what you're saying," Mrs. Dempsey broke in shrilly. Her husband sat up, pulling her into his arms now, but she continued in the too-sharp voice. "Why would someone hack Dana's blog? What's spoofing? Why do you know this? I thought you drove cars, not—" Her imagination failed her and she fell silent.

"I got online before it was cool, much less normal." Megan thought, but didn't say, *how very hipster of me.* "Long enough ago that learning some of the backbone information about how the internet works was just kind of something you did in order to use it. I'm hopelessly out of date now, but I still know just enough to look where not everybody would think to. Spoofing is making the internet think you're posting from one place when you're really somewhere else. Kind of like in the movies, where you see somebody trying to trace a phone call that's been routed all around the world to hide the caller's location."

Mrs. Dempsey nodded tightly and turned her face against her husband's shoulder, clearly understanding well enough and not caring for any more in-depth explanation. Just as well; Megan didn't think she could have provided one.

"So probably someone hacked her and spoofed this?" Simon asked. "But why? I didn't think Liz *had* any enemies."

"How many restaurants closed down because of her reviews?" Megan asked.

Mrs. Dempsey cried, "That's not fair!" as Simon flinched.

"Some. I didn't keep track. Nobody closes on the weight of one bad review, though, Megan. There has to be something more already wrong. There's no such thing as bad publicity."

"That's not what the owner of Canan's says," Megan told him with a sigh. "The point is, Mrs. Darr probably did have some enemies. But I don't know what value an enemy would get in posting vlogs after her death. It's not a restaurant review. It's not even a market review, like the last one. She's just hiking."

"We were hunting for stone circles," Simon whispered. "Down on the Ring of Kerry. She just wanted to share it with everyone. That's what her vlogs were, personal stuff, things she was excited about, not reviews. She left that to text. Easier to compile into a book." He tried for a thin smile and almost succeeded. Megan returned it sadly, then took a deep breath.

"You're sure no one else had access to the computer?"

"I was the only one in my room at ten thirty." Simon gave a short, hard laugh. "Of course, I don't have an alibi because my *wife*, who would have provided one, is *dead*."

Mrs. Dempsey gave a terrible choking sound that turned into harsh sobs. Simon paled, his anger evaporating as he spun toward his in-laws. Mr. Dempsey's unforgiving gaze met Simon's and held for a long moment until a sudden weariness swept him and he bent his head over his wife's. Simon sagged, drained.

Megan's skin prickled from the raw breaking of emotion around her. She moved her hands stiffly, wishing she knew what to do with them—or herself—then made herself hold still. After what felt like forever, Simon, much more dully, said to her, "And you were with me when the first one went live. You're my alibi."

Megan blinked, then let out a breath of faint surprise. "I am, aren't I? It's something." More than something maybe. If Liz had been having an affair with Cíara O'Donnell, Cíara might have had access—for no reason that Meg could think of—to post from Liz's computer. But Megan had been with Simon when the first vlog went live after Liz's death, and Cíara certainly hadn't been there then. She had no idea what all that proved, if anything, except that Simon probably hadn't posted the vlogs himself. There were new comments rolling up on the vlog, accusing him of pulling a publicity stunt, but he didn't look or sound to Megan like a man engaged in that kind of behaviour. "You should probably tell Detective Bourke about this."

"What? Why?" Mr. Dempsey looked up from comforting his wife. "What could this possibly have to do with her death? It's a computer glitch. Some kind of horrible error."

"Well, I don't know, but that's his job, isn't it? Figuring out if it's related? It's kind of too weird to be totally unrelated, right?"

"I think there's plenty of police activity around Dana's death already," Mr. Dempsey said shortly. "I don't think we should complicate it any more. It really can't be any more complex than food poisoning, and I'll be glad when that horrible restaurant is shut down."

Megan bit her lip hard, stopping herself from defending Canan's. "Well, maybe I'll look into it," she said instead. "At least so we can figure out who's posting those things and get it to stop. I wonder if there's a setting to block new posts."

She went back into the blogging software, searching for something of that nature as Mrs. Dempsey said, "Yes. Yes, please. You obviously understand this internet thing—" a gross overstatement, in Megan's opinion, but she didn't argue—"and I want this to *stop*. Our poor girl, being dragged around like this after her death. All of *us* being taunted this way. It's like being haunted by a ghost."

Megan, almost guiltily, thought *now her ghost wheels her barrow through streets broad and narrow*, and bit the inside of her cheek to keep from breathing the lyrics aloud. It took a few seconds to promise, "I'll try to stop the posts. I don't see anything to just, like, archive the whole thing and set it, so it can't have any more updates, but I'll keep looking."

"You have to do more than keep looking," Mrs. Dempsey pleaded. "You have to figure out what's happening. This can't be related to her death, so I don't want the police involved any more than they must be. I just want someone I trust to figure out what's going on."

How she had gone from car-driving stranger to someone the Dempseys trusted—it should have been an impossible leap, but really, Megan recognized that she must seem like a lifeline to the Dempseys, and maybe to Simon Darr as well. They were all Americans, but the mourning family were strangers in a strange land, one that Megan had been navigating for a while now. She understood how they'd latched on and could neither blame them nor, she knew, turn her back on them. If she had been Liz, she would have wanted someone there to help take care of her family in the worst moments of their lives. Maybe if she were a little wiser, or a little colder of heart, it would be against her better judgement to say, "I'll do everything I can to figure out what's happened, Mrs. Dempsey," but she didn't have it in her to turn her back on Liz's bereaved parents.

Grateful tears seeped from the older woman's eyes. "Thank you, Megan. Thank you."

Megan nodded, but in spite of the woman's gratitude, she steeled herself for the likely backlash of what she had to say next. "If I'm going to figure out what's happened—what's really happened here—I need to ask some questions you might not like. Maybe—" She glanced at Liz's parents. "Maybe one at a time or, at least, Simon alone."

Colour made dark streaks along Mrs. Dempsey's cheekbones and her nostrils flared, but just as swiftly, she seemed to accept the wisdom of Megan's suggestion. She stood without speaking, took her husband's hand, and led him from the room.

As soon as they left, Simon collapsed, though he'd never sat up straight since Megan's arrival. "Detective Bourke asked me everything anybody could ever need to know."

"I'm sure he did, but I wasn't there for that." Megan sighed. "Do you want me to do this? Poke into Liz's death and whatever's going on with these vlogs?"

"Ellen does. I . . ." Simon lifted his face, gaze going to the ceiling. His throat, stretched long, showed the Adam's apple prominently, and when he swallowed, it looked painful. "I can't imagine what the vlogs might have to do with her death. Galway, Kerry . . . nothing *happened* there. We talked to fans at the market, but we didn't even see anyone while we were out hiking. I want them to stop." He lowered his head again, eyes fixed on the carpet's diamond fleur-de-lis patterns. "If you have to look into her death to figure out how to make them stop, I guess that's okay with me. If you want to, I mean." He finally met Megan's eyes. "I realize we've been asking a lot of you. This isn't your problem."

"No, but I feel—" Megan made a small, useless motion with her hands. "I feel responsible, in a way. Like you were in my squad and . . . even if I didn't slip up myself, something went wrong, and I want to know what. I want to—" She pulled a lopsided smile. "I want to be able to prevent it from happening again. I know that doesn't exactly make sense."

"It does. Sometimes a patient comes in too late to do anything for them, and you know it's not your fault, that there's nothing you could have done, but you look for the answers anyway. As if next time, when someone comes in too late, that extra little bit of knowledge might somehow be enough to save them. You said you were a combat medic?" At Megan's nod, Simon nodded, too. "Then you know what I mean."

"I do. Okay, then, look. Here's the first horrible question: Were you two okay? I mean, your marriage was . . . ?"

"We were happy," Simon replied quietly. "We'd had some rough patches. Who doesn't? But we were doing well."

"Do you know a Cíara O'Donnell?"

Simon's entire face shaped itself into a question. "Detective Bourke asked that, too. I have no idea who she is. Why? Who is she?"

"Apparently Liz knew her. Did Liz go off on her own a lot?"

Simon spread his hands. "Define 'a lot.' We weren't joined at the hip. I guess there are people who can live that way, but we always had our own hobbies. And we noticed a long time ago that when we were traveling, if we did everything together, we didn't have anything new or interesting to talk about and we got kind of sick of each other. So we'd do some of what we were both interested in and some things independently. I went for interviews while she went for hikes, or I'd go to a movie she didn't want to see while she found a knitting group. That kind of thing. And I left her alone while she wrote, obviously. We weren't a single unit, but we'd talk about what we did at the end of the day. She never mentioned a Cíara."

"What does that mean to you?"

For a moment, Simon didn't look like he even understood the question. Then he blew air between his lips, almost dismissing it. "That she didn't know her very well, or she wasn't very important to her. I don't know. I suppose it could mean the opposite, that this girl was *very* important to her, but . . ." He shook his head. "As far as I know, Liz didn't have any romantic interest in other women. I mean, she said once that she'd have run off with Josephine Baker given the chance, but that's like me saying I'd have run off with David Bowie. *Anybody* would run off with Bowie or Baker."

Megan smiled. "And nobody would blame them for it. All right, look, um. How were you . . . financially? I mean . . ." She'd never had any particular inclination to be a cop. Asking Simon a load of invasive questions quenched any thought at all she might ever had had along those lines. "I mean, with her death, I suppose you're the beneficiary of any life insurance?"

Simon Darr looked so appalled Megan thought he might actually vomit. "I am, yes. I . . . Jesus. I didn't need money, if that's what you're asking. We have—we had—Jesus. A prenup. Liz didn't want one. She—I insisted. My parents—" Simon exhaled deeply, his colour deepening. "My parents had a terrible marriage and a disastrous divorce. Liz hated the idea of a prenup, but I'd seen what my parents went through—my mom especially—and I wanted to be sure neither of us would be in that condition if we eventually split up. She said it was because I was going to be a doctor; I'd have made all the money and I'd want to keep it." His laugh sounded like tears. "What a surprise for her, when her foodie career took off and she ended up being the real provider, while I had hundreds of thousands in student debt. It turned out I was protecting her from me, if it had come to that. It didn't. It hadn't. We were happy," he said, sounding lost.

Megan reached out to put her hand on his knee. "Okay. I'm sorry. Look, I don't . . . I don't think I even know what else I should ask right now. I'll try to find out what's going on with the vlogs and I'll see if I can find Cíara O'Donnell and figure out what she has to do with any of this."

"I can't believe it hasn't even been two whole days yet," Simon said tiredly. "I feel like it's been forever and no time at all and neither makes any sense. I feel like all the answers should be figured out already, and instead, nothing is."

"I know. I'll do what I can to change that."

Simon nodded. "Thank you, Megan."

Megan, quietly, said, "You're welcome," and slipped out the door.

Ellen Dempsey met Megan in the hall, standing in front of the Dempseys' room door like she'd never gone in. "Peter is resting," she said as soon as Megan emerged from Simon's room. "I just wanted to say thank you, Megan. This has all been so awful."

"No, it's okay." Megan leaned on the doorframe beside Liz's mother and folded her arms. "Can I ask you a couple of questions, while we're talking?" Mrs. Dempsey nodded unhappily, and Megan wondered which prying query to try first. She started with, "Did Liz ever date any girls, in college or high school?" and earned a genuinely astonished look in return.

"Not that I know of, and I think she would have told her mini-me." Tears filled Mrs. Dempsey's eyes again and she wiped them away without trying to stop their fall. "Why?"

"She apparently had a young female friend Simon didn't know, so I was trying to figure out what kind of relationship they might have had. Okay. I know you might not know this, but . . . were she and Simon financially stable?"

A deep sigh shuddered from Ellen's chest. "Their first few years were terribly hard. Simon's student debt was almost insurmountable and Liz wasn't making any real money as a blogger yet. But Simon had a few windfalls and they got on their feet, and then Liz's career took off. I think they were doing quite well."

"What kind of windfalls? New jobs or something? Doctors get paid a lot."

"They do, but not compared to their student loans, not for the first several years. And the interest fees are usury." Anger flashed in Mrs. Dempsey's eyes, momentarily drowning the grief, but it returned as swiftly as it had gone. "He said real estate investments; money from his mother, I think. We helped where we could, too, of course. Liz didn't have too many student loans between her scholarships and what we were able to give her, though, and Simon never wanted us to be paying off *his* loans, he said. So they relied on their own incomes and his investments. They were even able to buy a house recently, which isn't common for people their ages anymore, I understand."

"It's lucky," Megan agreed. "I don't know if I'll ever own one. Thank you, Mrs. Dempsey. If I think of any other questions, I'll drop by to ask them, okay?"

Mrs. Dempsey nodded and let herself back into her room. Megan waited until the door clicked shut and then, motivated, marched off to find Cíara O'Donnell.

CHAPTER TEN

Cíara's apartment, like her own, sat above businesses, and it took a private key to enter the stairway. Megan made a show of searching her pockets every time someone came near, until the door suddenly opened from inside and she gasped a thanks at her oblivious benefactor. The stairs went up five flights in all, and Cíara's apartment—of course—was on the fourth floor. Or the fifth, if Megan was to count it the way the Irish did, with the ground floor being zero rather than synonymous with first. The floor above it, what Americans would call the second floor, was the first, in Ireland. Almost three years living there and she still went to the wrong floor all the time if directed by a local.

No one answered when Megan knocked, which she did loudly enough to wake the dead or—more likely—hung over; in fact, she *did* wake the next-door neighbour, who opened the door with a glower that said Megan had awakened him, at least.

Megan, summarily ignoring the scowl, said, "Hi!" brightly. "Do you know if Ciara's home?"

"She's not answering the feckin door, so what do you think? I haven't seen her since Thursday."

"Do you usually?"

The youth—Megan couldn't tell from the shaggy hair, skinny frame, and loose clothes whether they subscribed to a gender binary or not—shrugged sourly. "Yeh, we get home about the same time most nights. She was a feckin wreck Thursday, all after crying over somebody dying, and that's the last I saw her."

"Did she have a boyfriend or somebody she'd go stay with? Family?"

"Nah, only yer wan she'd been hanging out with. Who the feck are you, anyway?" Suspicion finally worked its way through the haze and irritation of an abrupt awakening, their scowl sharpening into something more personal.

"A friend of her employer's," Megan said truthfully. "We were worried about her. What one she'd been hanging out with?" A "wan" in Irish parlance generally meant a woman; "yer man" and "yer wan" had, Megan suspected, some kind of basis in the same kind of institutional sexism in the Irish language that begot the question "Was it a boy or a child?" when babies were born. She hadn't quite worked up the resolution to try getting to the bottom of the linguistic matter, although it nagged at her whenever she heard it.

"I dunno, a tall wan with gobs of dark hair and a proper tan. Fit, if you like that type, and American. But not like you."

Megan said, "Okay, thanks. Look, if you see Ciara, can you tell her Fionn's worried about her?"

The neighbour shrugged and retreated into their apartment. Megan stared at the closed door a moment, then shrugged, too, and trotted back downstairs. Sleuthing had to be easier when you could wave a police badge at someone and demand answers, instead of slinking around, waking up the neighbours without ever finding out if your suspect was even home. Though it sounded like Liz had been to Cíara's apartment, which could support the affair theory. Or at least a friendship, which seemed more likely, if Simon and Ellen's beliefs about Liz's preferences were right.

She pulled out her phone on the walk home, searching for personal information about Liz Darr as she took the long way to her apartment so she wouldn't pass in front of the garage and catch Orla's attention. Odds were that her boss wouldn't try to get her to drive—Orla hated paying overtime more than most people hated liver and onions— but even entering the woman's line of sight would remind her that Megan had a prohibited dog in her apartment, and an extra ten minutes of walking seemed worth avoiding that potential confrontation.

There were loads of articles about Liz, everything from her own blogs to interviews with the *Times*, book reviews and fan encounters, pictures dating back to high school, but nothing to indicate whether she'd ever dated women or had wanted to. Which meant absolutely nothing, of course, but from Meg's perspective, Liz's mother might not have known everything, and it would have been helpful to find Liz had had a tragic love affair with a college girlfriend to establish the possibility that she and Cíara O'Donnell had been dating. Evidence was leaning heavily toward not, though, and she had to remind herself that she'd gotten the idea that there was an affair going on from Niamh, who thrived on the most dramatic possible interpretation of any circumstance.

She tucked the phone back into her pocket as she went up to the apartment and said, "What good is the power of the internet if it can't deliver relevant gossip to my fingertips when I want it?" to Mama Dog as she came in.

Mama had no answer and couldn't be bothered to rise up and go for a walk when Megan shook the leash at her, but the puppies wriggled and squirmed blindly as she petted them with a fingertip and tickled their tummies. Then, exhausted from their efforts, they fell asleep again. Megan took Mama on a walk whether she liked it or not and returned home to watch Mama poke her puppies until they woke up and started to nurse. Then she gave a great, heaving sigh like she now carried the unwanted weight of the universe on her little bony shoulders and looked tragically at Megan, who laughed and fell backward onto the couch to study the ceiling as if it might contain some answers.

"Okay. How hard can it be to find Cíara, right? Just to talk to her, you know? That's what the internet is for." After another few seconds, she said, "I'm talking to dogs. Wow. Okay, then. Up and at 'em, Meg. There must be more to your life than this." She squirmed her phone out of her pocket and did a search on the girl's name, which led her to plenty of women, none of whom—according to their photographs—were the one she wanted. A few attempts at narrowing the search—even using Cíara's apartment address—achieved nearly identical hits and engendered a faint sense of exasperation. On one hand, it was probably good she couldn't find someone armed with only their name and a vague guess at their age. On the other, it was a real bother when she wanted to be able to do that.

And on the third hand, Megan was old enough to remember the world before the internet, and how what she'd just tried would have been absolutely impossible then anyway. "How quickly we adapt," she told the puppies, who had eaten greedily and fallen asleep without warning. They weren't really so much trouble, Megan thought. Mama Dog lifted one ear, then let it flop back down without further commentary, while Megan tried to remember if she'd eaten yet today. Her phone, still in her hand, binged to announce a text message from a neighbourhood friend. It said, in its entirety, **hungry?**

Megan laughed, texting back **you must have read my mind. Starving!** and twenty minutes later, an American bearing a bag of food and a tray of coffees appeared at her door. Megan stood on her toes to kiss his scruffy cheek. "You're a man among men."

"It's true, I am," he said cheerfully. About her age, bespectacled and afflicted with the notion to wear tweed, Brian Showers had been in Ireland for pushing twenty years and ran a small-press publishing house out of his spare room, because that was a thing people did. Megan was convinced that he had been invented for the purposes of making Ireland just that little bit more surreal and delight-

ful than it could naturally lay claim to. His extrava-
gant, "Look on my works, ye mighty, and despair!"
rolled out with the soft, Transatlantic accent that
called his country of origin into question.

"I will never look on food delivery with despair."
Megan took the stack of bags and coffees from
him and put them on the table on her way to get a
couple of plates. Brian went directly for the puppies, whose milk-sotted sleep went undisturbed
even while he gave them gentle ear rubs. Mama
opened one eye and moved her head just far
enough to suggest he pay attention to someone
who would appreciate it, and he transferred the
ear scruffles to her. "I see," said Meg. "You're really
just here to visit the dogs."

"Fionnuala told me about them, and yes, you've
scored a very palpable hit, but that's why I brought
lunch, to make up for the fact that I'd be neglect-
ing conversing with you in favor of cooing over
these wee darlings."

"Mmm. I've been up since six and can't remember eating, so all is forgiven." Megan plunked down
at her kitchen table and dug through the bag to find
not only sandwiches but still-warm pains au choco-
lat, which were almost universally called chocolate
croissants in Ireland. "Breakfast first," she said to
the flaky pastries, and sank her teeth into one
while turning a remarkably good cup of coffee
from one of the local roasters around until she
could drink from the little sip hole. "I thought Two
Fifty Square didn't open until noon on weekends.
Or is it noon already?" She looked for a clock and
found it to be a quarter till.

"No, they open early, at nine. And even if they

didn't, neither can they resist my ineffable American charm or my sorrowful hungry gaze when I arrive early at their back door," which, Megan knew, lay less than a dozen steps from Brian's own front door. "Also, I told them I'd be back with all the Liz Darr gossip after they closed tonight."

"Oh, you really *are* using me." Megan caught him up on what she knew anyway and he abandoned the puppies to eat—sandwiches; he, apparently, had already had breakfast—and listen with interest. She pulled up Liz's website to show him the second video that had been posted, and he took her phone with long fingers to hold the speaker next to his ear.

"What's the music?"

"I think it's 'Molly Malone.' It was on the last video, too, but not quite as loud. But she was talking a lot more in the other one. Simon says—" She made a face. "I don't know how anybody could name their kid Simon, knowing they'd face a lifetime of that. Anyway, he said it was her favourite song. Her mother hates it, though. Or hates that these are posting." Megan sighed. "She says it's like being haunted, which I guess it is."

"You know that traditionally, the dead only haunt the living if they need vengeance."

Megan stared at Brian, who blinked mildly back at her. He looked ordinary enough, all high forehead and diffident smiles shining through a beard that came and went with the seasons. "You know, normal people don't have case files on when and why ghosts haunt people."

"Normal people don't run small presses dedicated to the gothic and supernatural either. Ergo,

I'm not normal. Did Ms. Darr leave behind reasons to haunt someone?"

"Brian, you—" Megan broke off, uncertain if what she'd been about to say was true, then charged onward anyway. "You can't really believe she's *haunting* her . . . her own blog site? Her husband? Ghosts aren't real."

"Aren't they?" Pleasure, but not necessarily teasing, sparkled behind Brian's round glasses. "I don't know, Meg. I've spent a lot of time with stories of ghosts and the fantastic. Now, most of them are fiction, I grant you, but even fiction is inspired by something, isn't it? *Did* Ms. Darr have a reason to haunt us?"

"Well, she may have been murdered, so I guess *so*, but—but you can't be serious, Brian." A chill, ridiculously, ran across Megan's nape and lifted all the hair on her arms, proving that *she* thought the idea had some slight degree of merit, no matter how preposterous it was. "What kind of ghosts would haunt blogs anyway?"

"Twenty-first-century ghosts obviously." Brian laughed as Megan rolled her eyes and finished, "All right, fine, there's probably a more mundane explanation, but it can't be coincidence that she's playing a song about a ghost after her own death. I think probably—"

Megan's phone rang, Fionnuala's number coming up. Megan held up a finger, pausing Brian's speculation. "Lemme get this."

"Megan?" Fionn's voice, high and thready with panic, made Megan pull the phone a few inches away from her ear. "Megan, you've got to get to the restaurant right away. Martin is dead."

CHAPTER ELEVEN

Brian handed Megan the key to his bike lock without a word and she sped into city centre on his bike, whipping by traffic that seemed to crawl and, despite her hurry, noticing bits of architecture she never saw while on foot or driving. She needed to explore those alleys and colourful doorways, follow the plaques that told stories of Dublin's history, now that she knew they were there—but that would wait. It took just over ten minutes to get from her flat to Molly Malone, where Megan locked up Brian's bike and ran into the old church housing Fionnuala's restaurant.

She stopped short just inside the door, quick breathing from her vigorous ride turning to a gasp of surprise. Gardaí swarmed the place, virulent yellow safety vests blinding under the house lights Megan had never seen fully on before. The fluorescent tones reflected painfully off the vests and washed out all the warmth and colour of the stained-glass windows. A young woman with a strong jaw and her hair in a severe twist beneath her blue cap stopped Megan at the door, her hand lifted. "I'm sorry, ma'am. You can't come in here."

"No, I—I mean, yes. I see that. I didn't—" Megan took a deep breath, trying to steady both her racing heart and her thoughts. "Fionnuala Canan is a friend, and she called me a few minutes ago. May I see her?"

The cop made a dubious motion with her up-lifted hand but went to check. Megan stood on the threshold, looking back and forth between the bustling, gardaí-laden restaurant and the growing crowd in Suffolk Street. Molly gazed out over the onlookers, taller than the biggest of them by a head and clearly in the way of some of the gawkers. There were a few faces Megan recognized, mostly itinerants whom she'd seen time and again on Dublin's streets who had also been there when Liz died, but a couple of others were familiar, too—the big bodybuilder type wearing now, as he hadn't been on Thursday, a white shirt and a thin black tie that said he probably worked at one of the other restaurants nearby, and a sharp-faced woman with frazzled hair whom Megan hadn't ex-actly noticed on Thursday but knew now she'd seen then. The stroppy teen girl with the heavily made-up eyebrows and the hopeful boyfriend weren't there, but then, Megan wouldn't expect kids that age to roll out of bed before 2 p.m., given their druthers.

Detective Paul Bourke came out of the restau-rant, looking vaguely resigned. "You do turn up like a bad penny, don't you, Ms. Malone?"

"I guess. Is that even a thing Irish people say? Fionn called me. What happened?"

"This Irishman says it. Martin Rafferty was found dead here at half twelve this afternoon, which I presume you know."

"Yes, but what *happened*?" Megan puffed her cheeks and lifted her hands, trying to draw back her tone. "Sorry. I just—is Fionn okay? She was pretty distraught when she called and I didn't get much out of her. I just want to know if she's all right."

"What *is* your relationship with Ms. Canan, Ms. Malone?"

"My what? We're friends; why?" Megan frowned at Bourke's gaze, which seemed paler, like sunlight had drawn the blue from his eyes.

"Because as far as I can ascertain, she called you before she even called the gardaí."

"Well, you know," Megan said under her breath, "good friends will help you move. . . ."

Bourke's white-blond eyebrows rose, digging deep wrinkles in his forehead. " 'But a great friend will help you move a body'? Ms. Malone, you may want to think about who you're speaking to."

Megan bared her teeth in an apologetic grimace. "Yeah. Sorry. It would have made Fionn laugh."

"Did Ms. Canan call you here to ask you to help her move a body?" A faint note of incredulity coloured Bourke's tone, as if he couldn't decide whether she'd made a confession or if she was just an *amadán*, which is Irish for "idiot" and often used as code to reference fools who—like Megan—had no Irish.

"Detective," Megan said somewhat wearily, "if she had, she wouldn't have called the cops right away, too, would she have? So no, I'm pretty sure she didn't call me to move a bo . . . wait, holy cheese, does that mean Martin was murdered? I mean, you don't try to hide bodies that didn't meet a foul end, do you? Not that we were going to hide him, but—"

The incredulity that had touched Bourke's tone settled very lightly on his features as Megan leaped to conclusions and tried to cover her own tracks all at once. She finally just stopped talking, then, unable to help herself, added, "I'd make a terrible criminal, wouldn't I?"

"It may not be in your blood," Bourke said gently, and that time Megan heard the thinnest shard of amusement in his voice. She ducked her head, looked up again with a grin, and was met by Bourke's own brief, gobsmacking grin. It disappeared as quickly as it had come, and he said, "Martin Rafferty was murdered, yes," in the same gentle way.

"Jesus." Megan thought she'd expected it, but hearing an authority say the words made her sway. She put a hand against the doorframe to steady herself, and Bourke finally took a step back, freeing the doorway.

"Go ahead. Your friend is just inside the door to the right."

"Which one?" Megan asked, high-pitched. "Fionn or Martin?"

Surprise creased Bourke's face. "Ms. Canan. There's no reason for you to see the body."

"Just checking." Megan squeezed past him and barely got inside the door before Fionn cried out and fell upon her with an embrace so tight it left Megan breathless.

"Megan, thank God it's you! What am I going to do? What am I going to *do?*" Her knees collapsed and Megan, startled, caught her weight.

"I don't know." Megan supported Fionn—all but walked her backward—to the table she'd been at, a table blockaded by serious-faced gardaí.

Fionn had the pale skin tones of nearly every native-born Irish person up to the turn of the century, but what Megan would usually call "milky" on her was now chalky. Bruised-looking shadows stood out beneath feverishly glittering eyes, and stress gouged lines into crevasses around her mouth and nose. Megan got her into a chair and looked around, saying, "Could we get a—" before realizing she was surrounded by, and talking to, on-duty gardaí, who couldn't be expected to run errands. "May I go into the kitchen and make her a coffee?"

The stern-faced young woman who'd stopped her at the door glanced at her compatriots, then shrugged. "Go ahead."

"Bring me one, too," someone else said, and the whole crew chuckled. Megan squeezed Fionn's hands, said, "Don't go anywhere," as if she would, and went into the kitchen.

There was a pot—nearly a vat—of coffee already brewed, which Megan had thought there might be if Fionn had gotten as far as the kitchen before finding Martin's body. Making the coffee was always her first task. The fact that Megan had been allowed in the kitchen indicated his body wasn't found there.

Megan went back out to the bar, got a bottle of

Jameson's finest, and returned to make Fionn a
stiff Irish coffee and to pour cups without the
added whiskey, cream, and sugar, for the gardaí.
She boiled a kettle while she was at it, putting together a big pot of tea, and brought a tray balanced with everything, from teacups to a carafe of
coffee and cream, out to the table, where the
guards visibly thawed at her efforts.

Fionn looked askance at the pile of teacups, and
Megan, not so quietly she couldn't be heard by the
gardaí, said, "Nobody wants to deal with tragedy
first thing on a Sunday morning. Tea isn't going to
solve anything, but it soothes the soul."

Water filled Fionnuala's eyes, but she nodded
and wrapped her hands around the tall coffee mug
Meg had made for her, bending her head over it as
the police, relaxed a little bit now, poured tea and
began murmuring amongst themselves instead of
standing in stony silence. Megan waited until
Fionn had taken the first sip of the whiskey-doc-
tored coffee and a flush of colour come into her
cheeks as her eyes widened. "This is brilliant. You
used the good stuff."

"I did, but I make a mean Irish coffee even with
cheap whiskey. Drink up." Megan didn't expect
Fionn to actually chug the thing, and she didn't,
but after a few more sips and a bit more colour in
her face, Megan took a deep breath and asked the
pressing question. "What happened?"

"I don't know." The roughness in Fionn's voice
came from more than the whiskey. "I came in
around eleven, and . . . I wanted to make the place
feel welcome again, like. The past few days, it's
been as if my own restaurant was a stranger to me,

if that makes any sense." She darted a look at Megan, clearly expecting it wouldn't make sense, but Megan nodded, and Fionn went on. "So I got coffee on and tidied up the kitchen—scrubbed down where the puppies were born—how are they?"

"Getting bigger, but not opening their eyes yet."

Fionnuala smiled weakly, took a fortifying sip of the coffee—larger than before—then focused her gaze on it as she spoke. "I got the kitchen sorted and thought I'd do a walk-through. That's when I found him, in the back. He was . . ." She stood suddenly, striding into the kitchen. Her feet, bizarrely, were bare, which had to be a health and safety violation, not that Megan thought she should bring that up just then.

Fionn returned a few seconds later with the whiskey bottle Megan had liberated from the bar. She poured a no-nonsense measure into her mug, added more sugar, and drained the lot in a few hard gulps. Only then could she say, "They'd cut his throat. I'd never seen the like. Blood was . . ." She gestured with the coffee cup, suggesting splatters everywhere, and turned a grim gaze into the emptiness of the mug. Megan took it and mixed up another Irish coffee, this one much lighter on the booze. Fionn made a face but didn't add any more whiskey. "I called you and then I called himself."

Himself, more formally known as Detective Bourke, approached as Fionnuala finished the tale. The sharp-jawed garda woman, whose jaw had unclenched a bit with the application of tea, gave him a nod so subtle, Megan imagined she hadn't been supposed to see it. Bourke looked satisfied, not surprised, and made a questioning motion toward the tea. Fionn said, "Go ahead" and he poured himself a cup, which he drank straight, no milk or sugar.

"Why did you call Ms. Malone first, Ms. Canan?"

"For God's sake, sit down," Fionn snapped. "I can't talk to you lording it over me like that, I'll get a crick in my neck." She didn't talk either, until Bourke, his expression neutral, as if he was snarled at by civilians every day—and maybe he was, Megan thought—sat across from her and put his hot tea on the table in front of him. "Megan's been rescuing me sorry arse for the past two days." She paused, staring past Bourke's shoulder, and Megan could all but see her trying to count the days.

"One and a long half," Bourke agreed. "Since Thursday night."

"Day and a half, then. She kept on top of finding out whether it'd been food poisoning that killed Elizabeth Darr and she took the puppies even though it meant trouble of her own—"

"Puppies?" Bourke's voice flickered upward in surprise.

"A pregnant dog broke into the kitchen Thursday during all the chaos and had puppies under the counter," Megan volunteered. "I took them home."

An abbreviated sound, like the start of a swallowed laugh, escaped the back of Paul Bourke's throat. "It's been a mad few days, hasn't it?"

"I thought it'd help to have her here, being American about it all." Fionn splayed a frustrated hand as both Bourke and Megan's eyebrows rose.

"You know, level-headed in an emergency, all cool and collected like John Wayne."

Megan couldn't help glancing at all five foot three of herself, more than a foot shorter than John Wayne had been, and looked up with a smile.

"A wee John Wayne," Fionn conceded. "With better hair."

"Well, that part's not hard. Is Fionn a suspect, Detective?"

Fionn flinched and went still at the question, like she'd been afraid to ask. Bourke shook his head almost imperceptibly, though he said, "No one can be ruled out just now. Can you prove your whereabouts this morning between six and nine, Ms. Canan?"

"I wasn't at Mass for all the world to see, if that's what you're asking! I was at home, sleeping," she added less defensively. "With my partner, who got up a couple times to use the loo, so he can say whether I was there or not, when he was awake to see it."

A rush of people went by, collecting some of the listening guards on their way past. Two of them, carrying a stretcher, were in paramedic uniforms. Megan sat up straighter to watch them go into the back end of the restaurant.

"Is he actually back there? Inside?"

"He's on the stairs," Fionn whispered. "It looked like somebody came up behind him on his way down and just—" She shuddered and picked up her cooling coffee to drain it again. "I stepped in the blood before I understood what I was seeing."

"Oh! That's why you're barefo—" Megan silenced herself, but Fionn gave her a weak, ill-looking smile.

"I didn't want to be tracking blood all over the restaurant. My shoes are still in the . . ." She shuddered again. "Mess. Why would anybody murder poor Martin?" Her voice rose in bewilderment. "He was a bit of a prick, but he'd done well and he donated to the boxing clubs and the youth centres and bought equipment for the GAA all where he'd grown up."

"And where was that?" Paul Bourke asked it like he knew the answer, which he probably did; even Megan knew Martin Rafferty had grown up in Bray, south of Dublin proper, because every article about him in the *Times* or the *Independent* mentioned it, making a fuss over a small-town boy done well.

Fionnuala said, "Bray" anyway, and the detective noted it down on a pad that he had, Megan realized, been taking notes on all along, even while he sipped his tea. She didn't think of note-taking as a subtle activity, but Bourke had evidently mastered it. "He went to university in Canada and came home again with a business degree that he's been turning to profit ever since."

"Where in Canada?"

Fionn looked blank for a moment. "Ontario, I think."

"Any enemies there?"

"Jesus, how would I know?" Fionn stared over Bourke's shoulder, thinking, but shook her head. "I know he had a girlfriend while he was there and it ended when he asked her to come home with him, but she didn't want to live in Ireland. He said she called it a God-plagued state and he couldn't argue, even if the Church has lost a lot of power. But otherwise . . ." She shook her head again.

"Do you know who his beneficiaries are?"

"God, no. His mum and dad, maybe? They're still out in Bray, I think, but I don't know." Tears stood in Fionnuala's eyes again and she pushed her coffee cup aside so she could put her face in her hands. "I can't even think what this will do to the restaurant," she said into her palms. "We'd the capital to keep going through the health inspection and all, I think, but we'll be closed again tonight and for how long after that, Detective?" She lifted her face. "It's a crime scene now."

"I'm afraid it'll be up to a week. You'll have insurance against this sort of thing, though. That will help ease you through."

"If we can get patrons back in after two murders on our doorstep in less than a week." Fionn thinned her lips. " 'We'. There's no 'we' anymore. Ah, God, Martin . . . !" This time emotion overwhelmed her and she lowered her head on the table, hidden in her arms, to sob. Megan put a tentative hand on her shoulder, then scooted over to pull her into a hug as she cried. After a few minutes, Fionn pushed her away, not unkindly, and mumbled something about the loo.

Megan let her go, sighed, and turned to Bourke, who had watched the entire scene with an understated sympathy. Apparently, she had a question in her eyes, because he tilted his head slightly, inviting it. "I didn't want to ask in front of her, Detective, but . . . do you think Liz and Martin's deaths are related?"

Grim consideration slid across his sharp features like he'd been holding the thought at bay and now, faced with it, didn't like the implications. "I'm afraid they almost certainly are."

CHAPTER TWELVE

The detective refused any further speculation, though truthfully, Megan was surprised he'd answered her at all. She could see for herself clearly enough that there were no surface connections between Liz Darr and Martin Rafferty, but both of them dying more or less on the Canan premises within forty-eight hours of each other pushed the bounds of coincidence beyond credulity.

Megan finally left after Fionn's boyfriend arrived and went outdoors to consider what all of those individual pieces of information meant. The bright, sunny afternoon came as a surprise after the hard light inside the restaurant, and Megan squinted her way across Suffolk Street to lean on, rather than unlock, Brian's bike and think.

The crowd had disappeared while she'd talked with Fionn and Bourke. So had most of the police, for that matter, and she supposed they'd taken the excitement with them. The bodybuilder was still there, hanging around looking somewhere between curious and distressed, and when Megan didn't leave immediately, he came up to her with a surprisingly diffident air for so big a man. "What's the story? They're saying Martin Rafferty's dead."

"Um." Megan glanced back at the restaurant. "I don't know if I'm allowed to talk about what's going on in there."

"So he's dead." At Megan's surprised glance, the big man shrugged. "Yis wouldn't be all shifty about it if he was still alive."

Megan sighed. "You're probably right. Do you know him?"

"In passing, like. I work a couple nights a week at the nightclub, after my dinner shift." He thrust a thumb toward the restaurant across the street. "And after that woman dying, Jayzus, that's hard luck. Will Canan's open again, do yis think?"

"I hope so. The owner's a friend of mine."

The big guy squinted. "I thought Rafferty was after owning the place."

"Co-owner. She's the chef."

"Oh, the one that looks like the Little Mermaid?"

Megan stared, partly because she didn't expect a guy built like this one to say something like that, and partly because Fionn's auburn hair and heart-shaped face *did* make her look a little like Ariel. She laughed. "Yeah, I guess so. I never thought about it."

"I've got kids," the bodybuilder said half-defensively, and Megan held up her hands, smiling.

"No judgement here, mate. Anyway, if you work at the club, I'm sure they'll be contacting you and everybody to let you know what's going. I really don't know, myself."

"Cheers." The big guy went back to the restaurant across the street, which wouldn't be open for an hour yet anyway. Megan unlocked Brian's bicycle and rode it home, noticing, now that she wasn't in a terrible rush, how much too big it was for her. She stopped outside her own apartment, sent him a text, found out he'd gone home, and biked the rest of the way up Rathmines Road to deliver it back to him. He met her at the front door with a book in hand—one of his own publications, something about Lucy Boston, whose novels Megan had loved as a child—and an inquisitive look in his brown eyes.

"Martin is dead," she reported as she wheeled his bike into the house. "Murdered. Fionn's not really a suspect and the cops won't say how Liz and Martin's deaths are connected, probably because they don't know. What do an Irish entrepreneur and an American food blogger have in common? Besides Canan's, I mean."

Brian, dryly, said, "You don't seem terribly distraught" and took the bike to park it in the back garden. Megan followed him through the house and out into the sunshine.

"I didn't know him very well and didn't like him very much. He had that—he always had to know the answer, you know? Even if you knew it already, he'd explain it to you. I guess it worked for him in business, but it drove me nuts. Still, it wasn't a killing offense. Especially getting his throat cut from behind in a dark stairwell. Seriously," she said, as Brian glanced at her, eyebrows elevated. "It's practically Gothic."

"You're saying that to appeal to my sense of the macabre. I'm not helping you solve a murder, Megan. Tea?" Brian locked up the bike and gestured back to the house. Megan preceded him, talking over her shoulder as they went into a kitchen that had last been updated when teal was a highly fashionable interior decorating colour.

"I'm not solving a murder myself! I just want to figure out what they had in common. And I'd like to know where Cíara O'Donnell is. I'm a little worried about her."

"Why?" Brian took down green tea, which Megan made a face at, so he made her a cup of berry tea instead while she moved books, mostly from his own press, into stacks on the small, square table tucked beneath the galley kitchen's window.

"I don't know, because she was mixed up with Liz and nobody's seen her since Friday afternoon." Books sorted, Megan sat and pulled her feet up on the straw-seated chair, putting her chin on her knees.

"You mean, no one in your very limited circle of people who know her has seen her since Friday afternoon, which was less than a full day ago, as if she is not a twentysomething whose work got closed down and left her with time to do whatever she wanted?" Brian brought the tea to the table and sat in the other chair while Megan unfolded and tried to frown at him over the edge of her teacup.

"Well, when you put it that way, it makes me

sound a little over the top. Seriously, though, I'm not going off the deep end. I'd just like to know where she is. And I'm sure the cops would, too."

"The cops, who have the actual resources to find missing—assuming she's missing at all—people? Those cops?"

"You're mocking me." Megan pointed a stern finger at her fellow American, then slid down, not very comfortably, in her chair. "I guess it's not just that. I just—I want to know what's going on and the only way I can think to do that is to find Cíara."

"All right, okay. If I can't talk you out of this, I'll try to be helpful. If you were mixed up in a murder, even tangentially, where would you hide?"

Megan grunted. "My first response is 'at home,' but then, that's where anybody would look for me, right? Not at home like where I'm living now, but home-home, where I grew up."

"And where did Miss O'Donnell grow up?"

"I have no idea and the stupid internet is no help. Cíara O'Donnell is not a usefully unique name and if she's out there under some internet alias, I don't know what it is. Because why would I?"

Brian laughed. "I don't know, why would you? Can you go get her employment history off Fionn? That might help."

"Fionn is already dealing with a suspicious death, a murder on her premises, lost her business partner, might lose her business, and had to think hard about getting me Cíara's current address. Asking her to ante up again would not be fair."

"Well, all right." Brian looked pensively into his tea, but Megan pointed a finger at him, a thought shaking loose.

"I could ask her coworkers, though, maybe. Maybe they'd know something about her. I mean, I guess I'd have to get their information from Fionn too. . . ." Megan deflated, making a face, then extracted her phone as it rang, the garage's number coming up. She muttered, "Oh, come on, Orla, it's not my fault they didn't want to stay out all day," and she looked apologetically at Brian as she answered the phone. He waved it off, settling down with his tea and a book so he could pretend he wasn't paying attention as Megan said, "Well, what is it?" into the phone.

To her astonishment, Tymon's voice came over the line. "Sorry, Megs, I know you've got the rest of the day off—"

"What? No, it's okay. Is everything all right?"

"It's grand so, but the car you drove the Darrs in was going out again and when I was wiping it down, I found a USB stick wedged in the back seat." Tymon sounded distressed. "I don't know how I missed it when I detailed the car, but—"

Megan's heart had lurched, taking up residence in her throat, and it took a moment to get past it so she could say, "Well, it's no worry, as long as Orla didn't catch you missing it."

"N-n-nooo . . ." He sing-songed the word guiltily. "I told her I found it, though, and when she realized I'd missed it on Friday, she said to throw it out straight-away. She didn't want whatever kind of trouble it would bring. I did, but—" Megan could almost hear him blushing with guilt now—"as soon as she left, I dug it out of the rubbish again and called you. It's probably nothing, but it might be important, right? It was stuck so deep in the seats it couldn't have been an accident."

"I'll be there in ten minutes. I'm just down the road. You get back to work and I'll swing by, pick it up, and we'll pretend this never happened."

A preposterously deep sigh of relief emptied the young man's lungs. "Grand. Thanks, Megs. You're a legend."

Megan said, "It's true, I am" and hung up with her heart still racing. Odds were that Tymon was wrong, that it *was* nothing, and that probably someone else entirely had lost the USB stick weeks ago, giving it time to get worked deeply into the upholstery. Except no one had contacted the company about missing it and the cars *were* thoroughly detailed every time they came in. Megan could see a wedged USB stick being missed once but not—as proven by Tymon just now—twice. She explained the whole situation to Brian and hurried off to the garage.

Tymon just happened to be taking a break, hanging out at the corner, as Megan approached. "Just happened," Megan figured, like it just happened that 2+2=4.

He handed the USB stick off to her like they were conducting a surreptitious, albeit in broad daylight, drug deal and hardly made eye contact before striding back toward the garage. Megan wanted to laugh, but even she suffered from the occasional moment of terror dealing with Orla, and she was twice Ty's age and a veteran to boot. She settled for a broad grin and took the long way home again, unashamed to admit it was to avoid Orla's gimlet eye.

Mama Dog, who had thus far shown no particular interest in going for a walk, veritably danced at the door when Megan arrived home. If a dog could cross its legs and hop desperately, she would have. Megan groaned, got the leash, and took Mama for a walk that lasted, to Megan's perception, about six hours. Mama had not previously needed to sniff everything along the way, or stop to get scratched by strangers, or have a walk all the way around the block, and after about twenty minutes, Megan said, dryly, "You're sick of puppies already, aren't you? They're only two days old. Be glad you won't have to take care of them for eighteen or twenty years, and let's go home."

Mama gave her a positively doleful look and moped along home with her head lowered, her ears down, and her stubby tail attempting to drag sadly on the ground. "Monday," Megan warned. "Monday I'm taking you to the vet to see if you have a chip. Maybe somebody will be overwhelmed with joy to get you and a bonus pair of puppies back again."

The little Jack Russell had no response to this save to walk mournfully back to her dog bed when they returned to the apartment, and to flop into the soft plush with a sigh that came from the depths of her doggy soul.

The puppies wiggled around her happily, had something to eat, and fell asleep again. Megan could feel Mama giving her tragic glances from over the bed's rim and heartlessly turned her back on the three of them so she could get her laptop and plug in the USB.

It was password protected, which Megan knew

in the abstract could be done but had never actually encountered. Flabbergasted, she stared at it a while, then, with a shrug, typed in "mollymalone," figuring the odds of that working were slim to nothing.

The memory stick opened, leaving Megan prim-mouthed with the general feeling that passwords shouldn't be that easy to guess, although upon reflection, she remembered reading somewhere that a very high percentage of passwords were simply "1234," which meant this one was better than average. "Still," she said aloud, partly to herself and partly to the dogs, before remembering she was ignoring Mama's soulful gaze.

Only after the fact did she realize that it opening with that password meant it was almost certainly Liz Darr's USB stick. Megan's hands went cold with excitement even as an embarrassed flush crawled up her face. Detecting presumably required understanding things like that *first*, instead of getting caught up in good password protocol. Still blushing and generally feeling like a sneak, she jumped about three inches when her phone rang and gave it a furious look that melted instantly when she saw Niamh's picture come up.

"Jesus, did you hear about Martin?" came Niamh's opening salvo and Megan laughed ruefully in response.

"I did, and Fionn's a wreck, and I've just—" She looked at the still-unopened files on her computer screen and decided to leave that out for the moment. "I've just been trying to figure out how everything ties together. It must somehow. What do you know about Martin Rafferty, Nee?"

"That," Niamh said in sepulchral tones, "will take a drink or two to talk out. Meet me at the Library Bar at five?"

Megan squinted at the time on her computer screen: a quarter to three. "Haven't you got a show tonight?"

"I do, but call isn't until seven. I'll see what more I can learn about Martin between now and then. There's got to be gossip. There always is, about a lad who goes away and comes back successful." She paused and said, "There's always gossip about a lass, too, for that matter" with a little less cheer.

"I can't really imagine," Megan said honestly. "The whole point of the American Dream is to go forth, better yourself, and brag about it. All right, I'll see you in a couple of hours."

Niamh said, "Mwah," and hung up, leaving Megan to her guilt about digging through a dead woman's files. It lasted long enough for her to open the first folder, after which she simply dug through them in astonishment.

Liz Darr had been a tidier soul at heart than anybody Megan knew. Her files were in folders named sensible things like "vlogs" and "blogs," and every folder within was broken down into years, then months, and finally "development" and "posted." There were no random files saved somewhere just because it was fast and convenient, and photograph files even had cross-referenced notes in their names. Megan hoped she had an assistant who did all that, because someone organized enough to blog, vlog, write books, do photography, *and* keep it all cataloged systematically . . .

She sighed. Usually, she'd finish that thought

with a hyperbolic "deserved to be killed a little bit," but in the wake of Elizabeth's actual death, that seemed neither funny nor appropriate. Probably it was never either, especially because saying what she really meant—which, in this case, was that Liz's organizational skills should be envied and admired—was more flattering than "I could kill her." She wondered briefly if other languages expressed envy and admiration in murderous terms, or if English just had a particularly violent bent to it.

A folder labeled "personal" and buried—not at all suspiciously, Megan thought—deep in the photography archives, also required a password. Megan tried "mollymalone" again, unsurprised to find it didn't work, and sat there for a few minutes, frowning at the cursor as if its steady blink would render a clue as to what would unlock it.

Obviously, Detective Bourke, or one of his coworkers, would be the key, figuratively if not literally. But the gardaí would never let Megan see the files, and while she knew perfectly well she'd be bringing the USB *to* the guards, she—selfishly, humanly—really wanted to know what was hidden in them. After a little while, feeling guilty—but not so guilty she didn't do it—she looked up "breaking folder password encryption" on the internet and, because she'd guessed the main password, was able to get past the administrative lock and open the folder. "I have a future in hacking," she announced to Mama Dog, who put her chin on the edge of her bed and blinked sadly at Megan. "Don't worry," Megan muttered. "I'll use my powers for good."

By which she meant copy the folder to her own computer and open it, apparently, although she didn't think that really fell under anybody's definition of "good." Most of the files in Liz's personal folder were equally well-organized journal pages. Megan opened several of the most recent ones, hoping to find a smoking gun of some kind—a passionate love letter to Cíara O'Donnell, or maybe a rough-draft divorce letter to Simon—and found, instead, entries about hoping to settle in Ireland, and wondering, with real concern, if Simon would be as happy at home, raising kids, as he claimed he would be. Megan said, "Hnh" aloud, wondered if she'd always talked to herself aloud or if she'd just started because Mama Dog was there to listen, and flagged the entry so she could look at it again later, since it seemed at odds with Simon's job hunting.

Nothing in Liz's journal mentioned anything *about* his job hunting either. A coil of concern tightened into dread as Megan went through more of the entries, hoping for something that at least indicated Liz had known he was interviewing at local hospitals. Instead, going farther back, she found a cryptic comment about *problems I don't even want to talk about here, you know what I mean,* which presumably Liz had, since she'd been writing to herself. Eventually, buried even deeper in the personal folder, she found another one marked "just stuff," and by that time, she didn't even feel guilty about cracking the password. Elizabeth Darr was obviously not the kind of woman to drop meaningless junk in a folder called "just stuff."

Except apparently she was, because the only file

in the folder was a plain text document that said "HD $whw3t$3&n."

Megan flung her hands in the air, noticing, as she did so, that a fierce headache had crawled up from the base of her neck to reside in the back of her skull. She diagnosed it as hunger and tension, put the laptop aside, and got up to stretch and find something to eat. It was too warm for cooked food, so she got cold cuts, cheese, crackers, and fruit—a meal she thought of as her personal variation on the commercial Lunchables—and some sweet iced tea, a drink she had to brew on her own, as it was one variation of tea the Irish simply didn't understand.

She ate sitting on the floor beside the puppies, rubbing their tummies and ears and tickling their little pink paw pads. Mama Dog squirmed around to put her chin hopefully on Megan's knee, her brown gaze focused entirely on the food, and got a slice of apple for her efforts. She crunched it down, but went back to looking greedily at the cheese and meat. Megan said, "Nope. Not unless you can tell me what 'HD whewten' means." She approximated the jumble of numbers and letters as best she could aloud. "I mean, the whewten thing is a password, but HD is what, hard drive? I don't have her hard drive. I guess the Dempseys might let me look at her computer, but I don't know, isn't that the sort of thing cops take away when they're investigating murders? Or have I just watched too much TV? I definitely didn't talk to my-self this much before adopti—*babysitting*—dogs."

She took her plate and glass from where she'd been sitting and did an "Uptown Funk" slide across the floor—at least, what she thought of as being an "Uptown Funk" slide, although it was probably from the classic movie dances video that had been set to it—and sang, "HD? Hot damn?" to herself as she did so. "HD—Hodor? HD—high def? HD—hot dog!" She slid again, amused at herself, and kept singing. "HD—hard drive. HD—hidden dir—" She stopped abruptly, turning toward her computer. "Hidden directory?" The plate and glass went on the kitchen table, halfway to their ultimate destination, and Megan climbed over the back of the couch—a dangerous proposition, because it tilted— to pick up her computer again and search on how to find hidden USB stick directories.

A moment later, she breathed, "All hail the web, purveyor of fine answers everywhere" and, with a few keystrokes, convinced the USB stick to reveal that it did, in fact, have a hidden directory. She typed in the password and the directory spilled forth dozens of financial spreadsheets, each one more recent than the last. Megan scrolled through pages of them, watching the numbers dip and rise. Mostly dip really; there were close to a decade's worth of bank statements, and Megan could see the steady fall of paying off student loans, car payments, rent, groceries, all set against monthly influxes of income. She didn't keep particularly great track of her finances herself, but it wasn't hard to tell, reading Liz's spreadsheets, that the Darrs had been spending a lot more money than had been coming in: the category "miscellaneous" had enormous dollar amounts disappear into it, and gradually, as the years went by, it also started to have questions appended to it: *misc. withdrawal, no receipts for cash spent? I* asked *him to keep receipts . . .* and *big withdrawal, said it was for gift . . . no gift came. Gift for* who *then?*

And then there were the deposits, also labeled "miscellaneous"—sometimes enormous cash deposits, with notes like *real estate sale,* and then, later, *need to get his realtor's number, ask about these sales*— that almost never made up for the amount that had been spent. One did, eventually, about three years earlier: a miscellaneous deposit of nearly seventy thousand dollars that brought their whole accounting system into the black. That, along with a large check from Liz's first book deal, had been transferred immediately into a "House!" account, and the column labeled "Rent" turned into "Mortgage" not very long after that.

After that one big deposit, their finances seemed to turn around. The "miscellaneous income" column started filling up, while the "misc. outgoing" stopped bleeding so much cash. Megan rubbed her eyes, shook herself all over, and kept looking, until one of the side notes unrolled into a passionate, frustrated document file obviously written by a deeply frightened and worried Elizabeth Darr.

Simon Darr, it appeared, had solved a gambling problem by selling drugs.

CHAPTER THIRTEEN

"There were deposits that came out of nowhere. Huge ones. Liz's notes said he claimed to have a real estate investment on the side where the money came from, and she believed him for the longest time, even when discovering the weirdest stuff, she said. Like finding prescription drugs—not a bottle, but a case—stuffed under the bed," Megan said to Niamh a few hours later, over a drink that, in retrospect, she wished was alcoholic.

Five o'clock was early enough by hours that the Library Bar hadn't yet overfilled. Its interior reminded Megan of a pool table: dark wainscoting below felt-green walls, broken by a deep, reddish-brown picture rail that matched the wainscoting as well as the glass-fronted, brass-embellished bookcases. Tall windows were framed with heavy, red-and-gold curtains that matched deeply winged chairs and Queen Anne–style couches that were crowded around low, polished wood tables that forbade more than a handful of people in any one group.

Astonishingly, no music played, which made talking much easier, or would for another few hours, until dozens or hundreds of people crowded in, shouting at one another and moving around the chairs until the whole place's librarylike ambience was lost. Apparently, long before Megan had moved to Dublin, the Library Bar had been regarded as a well-kept secret for someplace atmospheric and pleasant to meet for a pint and an actual chat, but then someone had written an article about well-kept-secret bars and ruined it for everyone. Megan liked it anyway, as long as she got there before the rush.

"How did he excuse the pills?" Niamh asked, one part genuinely fascinated and one part well-trained audience. She wore loose-legged, cream-coloured trousers that Megan suspected were actually seersucker, a puckered cotton she'd heard about but never seen anyone wear before, and a ballet-shouldered T-shirt in rose pink that made her look delicate and vulnerable. She also had on a straw hat—a cloche, Megan thought they were called, the kind that pulled down over the ears and cast a shadow with its brim—which helped hide her distinctive features. The hat exactly matched the shade of her trousers and its band went perfectly with both Niamh's shirt and, once Megan thought to check, her two-inch, heeled sandals. Megan herself was suitably and comfortably dressed in bright yellow linen capris with roomy pockets and a white tank top—*vest*, and the fact that she had to remind herself suggested she'd never use that particular Irishism naturally—but Niamh looked like she'd pulled the flawless outfit together casually, which seemed vaguely unfair. On the other hand, image was, if not everything to an actor, at least a great deal, whereas Megan didn't even have to think about what outfit to wear any day she went to work.

Megan spread her hands. "I mean, you hear about doctors getting loads of free samples from drug companies, you know?" Niamh quirked an eyebrow and Megan sighed. "Well, they do in the States, where the pharmaceutical companies are charging eye-bleeding prices for what you can get for a tenner here. So Simon just told her he'd gotten samples, or that he'd signed an exclusive for three months with some company and they'd given him a bag of product to offer his patients. Or he'd been out of the country and been able to pick up prescription drugs cheaper, so he could sell some under the table to poorer patients. It happens," she said to Niamh's dismayed expression. The actress accepted this with a nod, although Megan had the sense she was being humoured.

"Anyway, there was a long dry spell, where all the extra money seemed to vanish. Liz's notes were really relieved, like she could finally just let it go and move past it, right? Only then, when they came here, it started up again. A *lot* of money, Nee."

"And you took it to the guards, did you not?"

"I called Detective Bourke. I haven't heard back from him, but it's not like he's got nothing to do, right? So I thought instead of waiting at home like a princess in a tower, I'd come talk to you and see what you'd learned about Martin, just in case you'd turned anything up about him being crooked or something, I don't know."

Niamh managed a solemn smile. "Sure and you're only thinking of the case, not about whether you can impress the handsome detective, like?"

"Is he handsome? Charismatic. I'm not sure he's exactly good-looking. But that smile . . . anyway, no, I'm not trying to—I mean, maybe I am trying to impress him, but not to get into his pants." Megan scrunched her face and swirled the ice in her fizzy lemonade, wishing it had a shot of whiskey in it. But given that she'd had a headache from concentration earlier, she didn't really think she needed to add booze on top of that. Niamh had a glass of red wine that she held lightly in both hands, fingertips on the glass so she wouldn't warm the liquid. "Besides," she added, "he's already asked you out."

"I believe you asked me out for him."

"Oh. Right. But you didn't object. Or do you? Now that you've thought about it?"

"No, it's almost always better to date somebody a friend introduces me to, even if they've just met him, instead of some rando off the street. Can you imagine trying to use a dating site?"

"I can imagine *me* using one. In theory." Megan pulled up her feet into the big, soft chair tucked beside one of the windows and watched a few young men come in through the bar's double doors.

Niamh had taken the corner seat, her chair angled so its back blocked most of her from view, and Megan wasn't sure the cloche did much to disguise her cheekbones or jaw if someone happened to look her way. Mostly people didn't bother her, but a group of lads like the ones now at the bar might well, especially after a drink or two. "You, not so much."

"You don't need a dating site," Niamh proclaimed. "You just walk along meeting charismatic officers of the law like his own self. I, on the other hand, meet wildly attractive costars whose romantic intentions last the length of a run or a filming, and leave with me poor heartbroken."

Megan put down her lemonade and placed her hand on top of Niamh's to say, solemnly, "It's hard to be you."

Amusement sparkled in Niamh's brown eyes. "You're mocking me."

"Yes. And no. You have a weird kind of hard life." Megan picked her drink back up and breathed into the glass, watching her breath steam on its far side. "I have this horrible feeling Liz's autopsy report is going to come back with a prescription drug overdose. Except if her husband was selling prescription drugs while traveling around the world with her, he wouldn't kill his excuse to be anywhere there might be profit to be made, would he? I shouldn't jump to conclusions," she said fiercely to her drink. "I don't know that Liz Darr was murdered."

"We do know it wasn't food poisoning," Niamh said. "Or we're nearly certain, at least. And she hadn't been ill. So we suspect, don't we?"

"We suspect strongly," Megan admitted. "Detective Bourke didn't quite say they were both murders, but he thought Martin and Liz's deaths had to be connected, and a bad-luck food poisoning death wouldn't have any reason to be connected to a murder, would it? Not that we think Liz was food poisoned," she concluded hastily.

"So maybe Simon poisoned her because she'd decided to stop traveling. You said they were thinking about settling here. So if he couldn't get his drugs as cheaply here, to sell on . . ." Niamh took a sip of wine like it was rehearsed commentary on the situation.

Megan shook her head. "But honestly, if you were a doctor, would you use prescription drugs to kill someone? I'd do something horrific, like what happened to Martin, so it would seem less likely to be me."

"Except after dinner, in the middle of Dublin city centre, without anybody seeing you do it?"

"Well, obviously not. All right, I suppose if you're going for subtlety . . ."

"Maybe it's a red herring," Niamh suggested. "The obvious murder can't be the simple answer, so do the obvious thing and they'll look somewhere else. No one's arrested Simon so far."

"The gardaí don't even have the USB yet," Megan pointed out. "I wish Liz had been a little more forthcoming in her journal. 'Dear Diary, next week I'm filing for divorce from my drug-running lout of a husband,' or something like that. I never got into keeping a diary, but I thought the idea was to blurt out everything in the one private place you had access to."

"Celebrities don't have much privacy. If she—if *I*—kept a really intimate diary, when I died somebody would want to monetize it. The only way to absolutely prevent that from happening is not write it down, to just . . . remember. Even if that means the intensity of the moment fades." Niamh shrugged gracefully.

Megan studied her for a moment. "I don't think I'd want to be famous."

"I did." A rueful smile touched Niamh's lips. "God, I wanted it so much. I never thought I would be—most actors aren't, you know—but I was after wanting it from the time I can remember. I wanted to be—" She spread her hands like she was drawing a screen in the air. "I wanted to be up there, making people laugh and cry. Or in the theatre, where you *know* if you've made them laugh or cry, but to be really famous as an actor, you have to be in the movies. So that was what I wanted, wee Niamh O'Sullivan from County Clare. But that's all nonsense. Did you find out who Simon Darr was selling to?"

"It wasn't in Liz's paperwork. Why would it be? She wasn't a drug runner herself, not if she had all this secret paperwork." Megan gnawed her lower lip and drank some lemonade, dismayed at her train of thought. "Of course, if he found out she'd been tracking him—and maybe he did; maybe that's why he stopped before?—but if he'd gotten back into it and was afraid she might turn him in . . . there's more motive for murder. Niamh," she half-wailed, although not loudly, "how did I end up sitting in the Library Bar trying to figure out murder motives?"

"It's the luck of the Irish in you," Niamh said, straight-faced. Megan threatened to flick lemonade at her and she chuckled quietly. "Wrong place, wrong time. Mental things like that happen to everyone, once in a while."

"Do they, though?" Megan sighed and brushed it off. "I wonder if I could just go ask Simon all this stuff. I mean, he's busted now, right? What's the point in hiding anymore? Obviously if *I* can find this information, the guards will be asking about it."

"As you just said, the guards don't have that USB drive yet," Niamh reminded her. "But assuming you share with our attractive detective—"

"I'm *going* to *share*, Niamh! I'd get busted for obstruction of justice or something if I didn't. Wouldn't I?"

"Only if you got found out."

Megan squinted at the actress. "I think you'd be a better criminal than I would be."

"Of course I would be. Surely part of being a good criminal is being able to act. Therefore, I'm better equipped for crime than a—what were you? Field medic?"

"And driver."

"Not," Niamh said, "a combination routinely expected to lie and hide facts, as both actors and criminals are encouraged to do. And you'd better not go ask Simon if he's been selling drugs, because if he has been, I bet he'll be on the next flight out of Ireland and then Detective Bourke will have a word or two for you indeed."

"Yeah. Maybe I should—" Megan looked for a clock, though she knew it couldn't be much past half five. She caught one of the lads who'd come in earlier, now at a table on the other side of the room, looking intently their way, trying to figure out if Niamh was who he thought she was. Caught, he blushed and looked away. Megan murmured, "You've been recognized," and Niamh nodded without looking toward the group. "Anyway, maybe I should call Bourke again, though. I'd think he would see this as kind of urgent. But I guess he'd have called me back, if it was. All right, okay so, never mind Simon anymore. What's the story on Rafferty?"

"Nobody liked the man," Niamh said promptly. "Fionnuala did, maybe, but no one else. It wasn't that he cheated anyone, though his fist is as tight as me grandmother's ar—" She cleared her throat suddenly and finished with "... armpit...," making Megan laugh out loud. The lads looked over and one of them smiled, but Megan turned her attention back to Niamh as she continued. "And he never paid anybody a penny beyond what they were agreed upon. It's that he treated people badly, though. High and mighty, like, as if they were below him, and him only a boy from Bray. He must have been good at charming people, though, because he got the capital to start half a dozen businesses, including Canan's."

"Orla's like that," Megan said thoughtfully. "I wouldn't say anybody likes her after they've met her more than twice, but the first couple of times she's wonderful. She makes you laugh, and makes you feel important, and like she's trustworthy."

"Is she not trustworthy?"

"I guess she is. She's a skinflint, though. Not one red cent goes missing under her watch and she could squeeze blood from a stone."

"Like himself." Niamh nodded. "It doesn't help narrow down enemies, though, when no one liked your man."

"Well, it probably narrows it down to Canan's

employees, doesn't it? It was somebody who could get into the premises. I didn't have the impression the place had been broken in to."

Niamh grinned. "And you know so much about breaking in to places?"

"Well—"

Niamh's grin turned to a laugh. "We're only a few steps away. Shall we go have a look?"

"Sure, because that won't be suspicious at all." Megan finished her lemonade in a few teeth-achingly cold swallows. "Let's go."

They rose together, Megan making some effort to keep herself between Niamh and the lads across the room so they wouldn't get a good look at her, but the actress stood three inches taller and wore heels besides, which left her pretty well towering over Megan. A burst of noise came from the lads, indicating they'd seen her clearly, and though Niamh didn't look their way, from the activity behind them as they left, it was clear they would be followed down to the hotel lobby beneath the Library Bar. Megan ducked her head toward Niamh, breathing, "Do we make a break for it?"

"Not without interference, or it just makes it worse. I can—" She stopped at the front desk, pulling off her hat, and the young woman behind the desk went electric with excitement. Niamh gave her a disarming smile and leaned across the desk. "There's a load of lads about to come down and make a fuss. Could you ring security and ask them to be a bit in the way of the door for two minutes, just so I've a way out?"

The girl nodded, fumbling the phone in her

nervous delight. Niamh winked broadly at her, put her cloche back on, caught Megan's hand, and scurried out the door as a couple of large, black-suited men and one large, black-suited woman appeared in the lobby. The desk attendant communicated to them in what sounded like dolphin squeals, and all three of the security people rubber-necked to get a glimpse of Niamh O'Sullivan as she waved and hurried around the nearest corner. Megan would have collapsed breathlessly against the wall, but Niamh pulled her along. "We can't stop where they might see us if they come out. Come on, we'll go the long way around to Canan's."

She dragged Megan down past a pub called the Stag's Head, with a placard, now a few years old, proudly proclaiming it the best pub in Ireland, and around the corner onto Dame Lane, not to be confused with Dame Street, the Dame Tavern, or the general Dame District.

"There." Niamh let go of Megan's hand and shook herself, like a cat tidying itself after an unexpected fall. "We ought to be quick, but we can get to Canan's without crossing into their line of sight now. Acht, look at those ones. Ah, to be young, single, and prepared to get utterly car parked." She nodded down the street at a crowd of young women, one of whom, Megan thought, was the heavily eyebrowed girl from Thursday evening. She probably lived in the area, and although she appeared to have misplaced her eager young men, none of the gaggle were lacking for other admirers.

"You are young and single," Megan pointed out,

"and the only thing keeping you from being utterly car parked is your self-restraint. And the fact that you have a show in ninety minutes."

"I am the very model of a modern major . . . teetotaler, except I'm never that." They rounded the far corner, having gone around the block, and went past a gourmet doughnut shop that made Megan miss boring, old, American-style grocery store doughnuts every time she saw one. Niamh saw her longing look and laughed. "Do I need to buy you a banoffee doughnut, Megan?"

Megan shuddered. "All I want is a regular, normal apple fritter that costs a buck forty-nine, not one of these giant messes that costs four dollars."

"I thought all you ex-pats would be happy there were finally doughnut shops here."

"Those aren't doughnuts," Megan said sadly. "They're frostings and candy piled on bread. The dough isn't even right."

"It's hard to be you," Niamh said in the same tone Megan had used earlier, and Megan, equally somberly, said, "It is," before saying, "There's police tape all around Canan's, Niamh, how are we supposed to go peek and see if it looks broken-in-to? Oh, God, it's worse than that, they've got gardaí watching the place!"

Niamh took off her hat and fluffed her hair. "I'll distract them. You go around to the back and see if it looks jimmied."

Megan whispered, "I am a *terrible* criminal" at her but broke away and crossed the street before the guards had time to notice they were together. Niamh pulled out her phone, tapping idly at it as she approached Suffolk Street, and as Megan scooted out of sight, she heard somebody say, "Isn't that—?!" in a carrying stage whisper. By the time she reached the back gate of St Andrew's Church, she could hear that a small crowd had grown in front, near Molly Malone, and how Niamh's warm, welcoming laugh bounced around the square as she flirted and chatted.

Good thing, too. Megan glanced around half-heartedly to see if there were any obvious security cameras, then, gracelessly, climbed up the black, cast-iron gate and wedged her foot between its narrow spikes to give herself enough lift to clear them. She landed in a crouch, feeling somewhere between superheroic and super-idiotic, and snuck over to examine the church's back door.

It had three visible locks. One looked as old as the church itself, rusty but still formidable, and the other two were increasingly newer—one had probably been there decades and the third had likely been added sometime after the now-closed tourist office had moved into the church premises. At 6:30 p.m. on a bright June evening, there was plenty of light to see the locks by. Megan concluded immediately that she'd never know if the oldest lock had been tampered with or not; it had scratches that obviously went back nearly two centuries, just as the church did itself. None of them looked particularly new, but she didn't even know if that lock was still in use, so the age of them struck her as irrelevant.

Scrapes along the door next to the second-oldest lock, though, did look new, like they hadn't really had time to weather. The third, newest, lock, was unblemished. Megan reached for the door handle, just to try it, had a momentary skip of her heart, and, feeling like a seasoned criminal, wrapped her shirt around her hand before testing the handle, so she wouldn't leave any fingerprints.

Unsurprisingly, it didn't shift. Megan guiltily slipped back out under the police tape, went around to the front of the church, and extracted Niamh from her crowd of admirers. The actress said, "Well?" breathlessly as they made their way up Suffolk Street toward Grafton.

A little smile curved across Megan's lips. "Know what? I'd better ask Fionn how many of those locks are in use, because I think somebody *did* break in to Canan's recently."

CHAPTER FOURTEEN

Fionn replied a few minutes later, managing to sound baffled even through the medium of phone texts. **We use two locks,** she said. **Why?**

Megan started texting back an answer, then remembered that phones had the astonishing ability to allow people to communicate with their voices and called Fionn, who picked up saying, "What madness is this, calling when you could text?" She sounded tired and unhappy, but at least a thread of teasing made it through the question.

"I talk faster than I type. I was just wondering how many keys you would absolutely have to have to get into the restaurant without obviously breaking anything." Megan tapped the speaker button so she and Niamh, leaning under the awning of one of the Grafton Street banks, could both hear Fionn's answer.

"Oh, God. One, maybe. We use the two newest locks. The old one still works, but the key is so awkward, we're always after forgetting to bring it, so we stopped using it. The new one is the best of the lot, but we use the other one just the same. It's one of those you could break through with a credit card, except it's stiff as a corpse and I've never met a credit card up to the task. Why?" she asked again, voice suddenly thin with worry. "Is it about Martin's killer?"

"Yeah. We—Niamh and I—" Niamh waved, like Fionnuala could see her—"were thinking it had to be somebody who worked there. Who all has keys?"

"Me, Martin, Syzmon, Daisy—" Fionn named two of the other lead chefs, one of whom was Irishborn and one who wasn't, but not the ones suggested by their names—"Syzmon locks up most nights. And Noel, who manages the club. But only he and Martin and I had keys to the back door. Everyone else uses the kitchen door, which has the same key as the new lock, plus a couple of others, and it'd be—I guess nothing's impossible to break through, but it's a massive, new steel door and you'd have to really want to go through it."

"Did any of them really hate Martin?"

"The detective asked me that already," Fionn said wearily. "He and Noel didn't get on well because, Noel said, Martin was always sticking his fingers in how the club should be managed, when it was Noel who had the experience. I must have told him a hundred times to just let it roll off. That's what I did when Martin had an opinion about how the restaurant should be run. But Noel had a harder time of it, maybe because he's a man and—" She broke off, but Niamh snickered.

"And not as accustomed to ignoring men who don't know as much about something as he does?"

"I didn't say it." Fionn's voice turned regretful. "Are you two ladies out having fun without me?"

"If you call trying to solve a murder fun, I guess so," Megan replied. "Should we come over?"

"No, I don't think so. I know it's only half six, but Alex gave me one of his sleeping pills. He probably shouldn't have, but I've slept for shite the past couple nights and I'm utterly wrecked. Shattered. I'd be asleep if I weren't talking to you."

"Suggesting we should get off the phone and let you sleep," Megan said. "I'll call you tomorrow if we've learned anything, all right?"

"Grand so." Fionn hung up. Meg tucked her phone back into her pocket and leaned her head against the grey stone wall behind her.

"So Noel didn't like Martin but had a key to both locks, which means he wouldn't have to break in, and nobody else didn't like him enough to mention." Wherever Meg was going with that, the thought got interrupted by her phone ringing again. She pulled it back out, eyebrows lifted, and mouthed, "It's Bourke" to Niamh, as if Niamh couldn't see the screen for herself, and as if Bourke could hear Meg even though she hadn't answered the phone yet.

"I'll leave you to it," Niamh declared. "If you get caught having snuck under the police barrier, I was nowhere to be found."

Megan grinned, waved at Niamh, and watched the actress saunter off toward the Abbey Theatre as she answered the phone with a "Good evening, Detective."

"Ms. Malone." Bourke sounded like a man who hadn't slept. "I only just had time to listen to your message. It sounded important."

"I found—well, one of my coworkers found—a USB drive in the car I drove the Darrs in on Thursday. It belonged to Liz Darr, and I think it might be useful to you. Can I—is there somewhere I could drop it off safely?"

Bourke's tone sharpened. "Did you look at it?"

"Of course I looked at it. How else would I have known it was Liz's?"

A momentary silence met that irrefutable response before Bourke said, "Where are you right now?"

"On Grafton Street. I was about to head home."

"Could you stop by the station first? I'll meet you there."

"I could, but the USB is at home." She heard Bourke make a faintly impatient sound and snorted. "Well, I hadn't heard from you and I didn't want to lose it somewhere."

"No, that's fair enough. Would you mind me coming by?"

"Not as long as you're willing to take my dog for a walk."

"Dog, really? I'd have thought you a cat person."

"This may come as a surprise, Detective, but cats and dogs are not actually opposites. One can like them both. And also, it's not really my dog, but it's complicated." Megan paused. "So you're a cat person, then."

Bourke chuckled. "I am so. All right, Ms. Malone, if you'll give me your address, I'll see you in about half an hour."

* * *

Somewhat to Megan's surprise, Paul Bourke arrived at her apartment just after she did, barely twenty-five minutes later. He took in her expression, said, "O ye of little faith," and Megan, caught, shrugged as she unlocked the street-side door.

"You can't blame me. That mañana joke is real. I've learned to ask *which* Thursday if somebody says they'll be by on Thursday to install something."

"Mañana joke?" Bourke looked curiously at her, though she had the sense he was also aware of the entire street scene around them, from gym jockeys across the road to a young couple arguing about their relationship a few doors down. Megan wouldn't really have paid attention to them without his presence and wondered if being a cop tired a person out, noticing everything all the time. Bourke didn't look tired; in fact, he looked fit and interested in the warm afternoon sunlight, waiting on her to explain her comment.

"I'm starting to think only Americans tell that joke," she said under her breath. Bourke gestured, inviting it, and she sighed, inviting *him* up the stairs in turn, as she told the joke over her shoulder and unlocked her apartment door. "An American comes to visit Europe. He's just been to Spain and now he's come to Ireland, and he says to this Irishman he meets, 'One of the fascinating things I've learned about Spanish culture is that there's a sense of '*mañana*', of *tomorrow*, things can be put off until tomorrow. We really don't have that in the States. Does Ireland have anything like it?' And the Irishman thinks about it carefully and finally says—" Megan put on her best Irish accent—

" 'There is so, but . . . without that terrible sense of *urgency.*' "

Bourke laughed, surprising her again. "There's more truth to that than I might like to admit. They say there are two kinds of cultures: event-oriented and time-oriented. Ireland's event-oriented, meaning the meeting is scheduled for seven, so people start getting ready for it at seven, but America's time-oriented, which means the meeting is scheduled for seven and you're late if you show up after that. It's a culture clash that neither side deals with well."

"Huh. I wonder if remembering that will help."

The detective's smile flashed. "Probably not."

"Probably not. Welcome to my humble abode. Hey, Mama." Megan went to rub Mama Dog's ears, bemused as the little terrier's eyes narrowed when Bourke entered the room. "Nah, he's all right, girl. He won't eat your puppies or anything. You ready to go for a walk?"

Mama hunched lower in the bed and tucked the puppies closer to her, making a circular nest of her belly and paws while she glared at the detective. The puppies, visibly better at raising their heads than they had been that morning, lifted their little snoots into the air, sniffing and making interested, squeaking noises.

Bourke, his eyebrows elevated, glanced at Megan, then moved past her to hitch up his trouser legs, allowing him to crouch and offer Mama the back of his hand to sniff. "Hello, lovely girl. What's her name?"

"She doesn't have one. She's a stray. She had her puppies in Canan's the other night and I've taken them until a rescue home opens up. Fionn obviously can't have dogs in the restaurant."

"And you haven't named her yet? You're a hard soul, Megan Malone. Aww, there's a good girl," he said as Mama moved her head forward a fraction of an inch to give his hand a long-distance sniff. Then she retreated, hunkered low again. Bourke draped his hands between his knees, gazing at the protective dog. "She doesn't like men?"

"I don't know. She liked my friend Brian just fine."

"Maybe it's gingers she doesn't trust." He offered his hand again, murmuring, "I'm not going to steal your puppies, girl. I'd love to give them a rub, hm? But not this time. You wouldn't like that, would you?" This time Mama sniffed him more thoroughly but still didn't look approachable. Bourke rose, a look of mild regret on his sharp features. "I'll bet you her owner was a ginger bloke. I'll win her over, though."

"I thought you were a cat person," Megan teased.

"I've recently had it told to me that cats and dogs aren't opposites, and a body can like both."

"Hah! Fine. You want a drink or anything? Tea? Whiskey? I know you're here on business, but I have no idea what a detective's work hours are."

Bourke glanced at Mama, who watched him with wary brown eyes. "I wouldn't say no to tea of my own accord, but I seem to remember she needed a walk and I'd say she wouldn't want to go on one with me, so if you've got the USB to hand, I'll be on my way."

"Right. Sure." Embarrassment crept up Megan's

cheeks in a red stain, although she had no legitimate reason to be flustered: Bourke *was* there for work, not a social call. She hadn't meant to be flirting, but apparently her autonomic nervous system had other ideas. Megan unplugged the USB from her computer, hesitating as she handed it over. "It has hidden files."

The detective's attention sharpened on her again and her embarrassed flush turned to a guilty one. "What kinds of files? How did you find them? Are you a hacker, Ms. Malone?"

"I'm really not. I'm just the Elephant's Child, with the power of the internet at my fingertips." She looked at her hands. "Or my trunk, I guess, if I'm going to follow through on that metaphor."

"Which, perhaps, you shouldn't. Not a hacker but a Kipling fan." Bourke smiled briefly, as if intrigued, but put it away for the topic at hand. "What's in the hidden files?"

"The password for the hidden directory is buried in a folder called 'just stuff,' in another locked folder." Megan shifted her shoulders uncomfortably. "I kind of feel like I shouldn't tell you what I saw, in case I somehow interpreted it all wrong and end up sending you on a wild goose chase."

Surprise creased Bourke's forehead. "That's not a bad thought, but I'll be very interested, when all is said and done, to hear what *you* thought it was, Ms. Malone."

"Maybe I'll just have thought the same thing you'll have thought." Megan squinted. "I think my verb tenses got wrecked in there, but I'm going to pretend that didn't happen and take Mama for a walk."

"So she *does* have a name!" Bourke, eyes sparkling, let himself out.

Megan muttered, " 'Mama' is a description, not a name" after him. The little dog relaxed as soon as he'd left, but Megan sat beside her, petting her neck and rubbing her jaw, for a few minutes before getting out the leash. "This isn't some kind of secret sixth dog sense, is it, Mama? Bourke's not a bad guy, is he? He's ginger, but he can't help that. I guess we'll see if you warm up to him. *Not* that I'm keeping you," she added hastily.

Mama blew a breath through her nose, more commentary than sneeze, and, having said her piece, got up for her walk.

Even a dallying walk around Belgrave Square, one of the nearby parks, didn't keep Megan and Mama out late enough to justify going to bed. Mama settled back down with the puppies, who, approaching the end of their third day of life, were still blind and bumping around with no evident awareness of anything in the world except themselves and their mama's warm milk. Not a bad way to be, Megan thought, but she sat down with her computer and scrolled through the files she'd copied from Elizabeth Darr's USB to her desktop. Bourke hadn't *asked* if she'd kept the files after all, and she wasn't interfering with anything by having another look. And she didn't think it was illegal to look at somebody else's bank account information, at least not any more than it was to open someone else's mail, which people did all the time.

Megan sighed. Obviously Niamh was right and she would be a terrible criminal. She didn't feel like much of an investigator, either: Liz's files didn't tell her anything new as she dug through them a second time, though she kind of hoped there would be a red flag offering an obvious link between Simon's illicit drug sales and Martin Rafferty's bloody death.

Instead, her phone rang, and one of the other Leprechaun drivers, Cillian Walsh, said, "Could I get you to do a half nine airport run for me?" in the most apologetic Irish tenor possible.

As if the very idea meant she'd stayed up past bedtime, Megan yawned enormously in Cillian's ear and finished it with a kind of garbled, "Why, what's going on?"

"My sister's just after having her baby."

"What?" Megan sat bolt upright and had to snatch her computer back from falling off her lap. "I thought she wasn't due for another month!"

"She wasn't. Apparently she fell off a chair and next thing she knew . . ."

"She *fell* off a *chair*? From sitting or standing?" Megan put her computer aside and went into the bedroom, setting the phone to speaker and starting to change into her work uniform. Cillian said, "Standing," and Megan, through her shirt as she pulled it over her head, asked, "What was an eight months' pregnant woman doing standing on a chair?"

"Rearranging the fairy lights over the cot. Everything's fine. The baby's only a little small, but her lungs are strong, they've said, and they'll have her on a respirator if she needs one, but—"

"Go," Megan said, pulling on her work blouse. "Go, text me the details, I'll get the client. Go see your sister. Give her all my love and best wishes." She didn't know Cillian's sister well, but they'd met, and she would wish anyone with a new baby love anyway. "I don't usually work on Sundays, but if you need me to cover for you—"

"No, I've already sorted tomorrow. Micheál is driving for me, but thanks for asking. You're brilliant. He's on a job tonight or I'd have had him do this run."

"No worries." Megan finished changing into her work uniform and grabbed a brush to do something less catastrophic with her hair. "Text me and let me know how your sister's doing."

"I will. Thanks very much. I owe you one, Megan."

"I'll call in the marker," Meg said cheerfully. "G'night."

CHAPTER FIFTEEN

The run took Megan until nearly midnight—
the plane was late and the clients were staying
in Drogheda, forty kilometres north of Dublin—
but a picture from Cillian of his very tiny, very red,
very scrunchy-faced niece went miles toward making the night worthwhile. By the time Megan returned home, changing out of her uniform was a
nearly insurmountable effort. She managed it but
certainly didn't have another look at her computer and only fell into bed to sleep the sleep of
the just.

Mama woke her up around half five needing to
pee, and Megan staggered out with her blearily,
barely remembering to bring her keys so they
could get back in again. The morning air revived
her quite a bit, and upon getting home, she threw
on her gym clothes and ran across the street for a
quick workout. When she arrived, one of the girls
behind the counter cocked an eyebrow at her,
tapped her—watch-free—wrist and shook her head

in mock scolding for being late. Megan grinned and sulked, dramatically, around to the exercise bikes, which she regarded as the least taxing of the various cardio machines, and sat cycling with her gaze fixed on the copper dome of the Rathmines church without much of a thought in her head.

Saturday hadn't been a *long* day exactly—she was often up around six and busy until ten at night—but usually her long days consisted of driving around a lot, not running back and forth around town, and certainly not discovering acquaintances had been brutally murdered in a friend's restaurant. It turned out that kind of thing drained a person's energy, enough so—it turned out—that after twenty minutes on the exercise bike, she'd only managed about five miles of distance. Megan gave a groaning laugh and heaved herself off the bike, wiped her face with a towel, and barely avoided running into Jelena, who had stopped to greet her.

Jelena put her hands on Megan's shoulders, steadying her, and gave her a laughing smile. "You look terrible."

"It's been a completely mental few days," Megan admitted. "How are you?"

"I am well. Perhaps you could tell me about it at the coffee shop next time we both are here?"

All of Megan's fatigue fell away under a splash of delight. "That'd be great! I'd love that!"

"Let's exchange numbers."

Megan handed over her phone and Jelena put in her number, then gave it back.

"Now we can text each other and set up when we will each be at the gym for workouts and time for coffee afterward."

Megan laughed. "Look, I have to go light on the weights today because, apparently, my brain is empty, but if you don't mind spotting me, that'd be great." She texted an *It's Megan!* to Jelena's number as they headed for the weight room, and over the next forty-five minutes got a better work-out than she expected, given how poorly she'd done on the bike. By the time she got home, had a light breakfast and some coffee, and took Mama for a walk, she felt fit for the day, which she hadn't expected an hour earlier.

The puppies had leveled up again since the night before, lifting their heads more confidently and starting to realize that they each had a sibling to paw at clumsily. Megan took pictures and sent them to Fionnuala, whom Megan reckoned could use the boost when she awakened, and to Niamh, because she'd be accused of playing favourites with Fionn otherwise. She said, "Be good," to the puppies, who had gone back to sleep already, and went forth with an implausible confidence in the thought that she would accomplish a lot that day.

A brisk walk brought her back to Cíara's apart-ment and to the dismaying, but not surprising, in-formation that the neighbour still hadn't seen Cíara and furthermore thought Megan was an un-printable unprintable for having awakened them at half seven on a Sunday morning. Megan, who, having spent twenty years in the military watching coworkers who never really adjusted to a 6 a.m. reveille, generally held with not making people get up outside of their personal circadian cycle, got very quiet and stepped into the neighbour's personal space, dropping her voice to say, "You want to call me that again up close where I can hear you better."

The kid, who stood an easy six inches taller than Meg, went grey under stringy hair and stuttered an apology that Megan didn't accept. "I'm concerned about Cíara," she said in the same low voice. "I don't care what time it is. I will inconvenience you, I will inconvenience your friends, I will inconvenience anybody I have to, at any hour I have to, in order to find that young woman and make sure she's safe, and *you* will learn to have a little decency and respect for your fellow human beings. Are we *perfectly* clear?"

"Ye-yes, ma'am." The neighbour slunk back into his apartment, tail between their legs, and Megan, now riding a fresh burst of outrage, stalked back down to the street and looked up and down it for a fight. There was virtually no one up at that hour, much less belligerent and looking for a fight, though—at least, not on Rathmines Road. She could probably find plenty of people fitting that description in other parts of town; Megan took her phone out and texted Simon to check up on him.

To her surprise, he texted back less than a minute later. Megan, wincing, thought, *well, at least he hasn't been arrested yet,* and, driven by a sense of responsibility toward him, agreed to drop by when he asked if she could. She caught the Luas over to the Shelbourne and went up to his room, which smelled a little rank, and the bed still looked as if no one had slept in it.

Simon's eyes were bloodshot and his hands shaky as he offered her a seat. "I heard someone else died at Canan's."

"One of the owners was murdered. Did you know a Martin Rafferty?"

Simon's expression indicated that not only had he not known Martin, he couldn't imagine why he *might* have. Megan sighed, putting the vague—hopes?—of a conspiracy away. "I didn't think you would, but I wondered. How are you doing?"

"Terrible. I can't sleep and I—" He sniffed, as if catching his own scent. "And I probably need a shower."

Megan commented only with her eyebrows, but that was sufficient. Simon offered a small, pained smile. "Sorry. They released Liz's—Liz's body to us yesterday afternoon. I've been arranging to fly . . . to fly her home. This is all—" He shook his head, no longer even able to stumble through sentences, and put his face in his hands.

Megan sighed and stood. "How about you take a shower and I'll meet you downstairs for breakfast? You should eat. Do you know if the Dempseys are awake yet?"

"I don't think they've slept any more than I have," Simon replied hoarsely. "Ellen kept saying how grateful she was for your help. You could knock, maybe."

"It's not even eight o'clock."

As she spoke, a defeated-sounding knock, nothing like the brisk efficiency of a housekeeper, tapped at the door. Megan answered it and found the Dempseys there, both of them looking as wrung out as Simon did. She stepped out of the way and Mrs. Dempsey hugged her on their way in. Peter sat heavily on the bed and, without preamble, said, "We finally found an airline that would bring her home tomorrow afternoon. We thought we'd fly with her. We all should, Simon."

Simon closed his eyes, shoulders rounding in acceptance. "All I want to do is get home and . . ." Megan thought he wanted to say *forget this ever happened* or *move on,* but neither of those things would happen, not really, and not for a long time. "Maybe being home will help." He didn't sound as though he believed it.

Another knock on the room door, much sharper this time, made everyone jerk in surprise. Simon lifted his voice to say, "No housekeeping today, please."

"I'm afraid it's not housekeeping," a man's voice replied through the door. "This is Detective Paul Bourke."

Simon Darr jerked to his feet and went to his in-laws at the announcement of the detective's name, all of them suddenly haggard with anticipation. None of them moved toward the door, standing together in a clump instead and staring, vulturelike, as if waiting for it to open on its own.

Megan, hesitantly, rose and answered it, earning a nonplussed blink from Bourke, who clearly didn't expect a limo driver to be hanging out with a bereaved family at eight in the morning. He merely said, "Ms. Malone," though, and she said, "Detective Bourke," in response, and ushered him past her into the room. "Simon, I'm going to leave—"

"No," the doctor said sharply. "Please stay."

Meg grimaced at Bourke's shoulders and got caught as he turned, again mildly surprised, to glance at her. She made an I-don't-know face at him and said, "I think maybe I sh—"

"Please stay," Simon repeated. "You've gotten me through the last few days. I'd rather you stayed."

Detective Bourke shrugged almost imperceptibly and returned his attention to the family. "I wanted to thank you for your patience waiting for the autopsy and coroner's report. I know it must have seemed like a long time, but I have a few answers for you now. Unfortunately, the answers I have bring more questions to light. Perhaps you should all sit down."

Mrs. Dempsey gasped. Only her husband's grip kept her from falling. He and Simon helped her to the bed, then sat down on either side of her, the three of them balanced at its end like children waiting to receive a punishment. Simon made a shaking motion toward one of the chairs. "Maybe you should sit down, too, Detective."

"Thanks very much." Bourke suddenly looked all elbows and knees, his long limbs becoming more evident as he sat. "I don't know if you're aware of the usual process with an autopsy. An unexpected death like Mrs. Darr's, who was young and fit, means there's one triggered automatically. Hers was done Friday morning, as you know."

Megan hadn't, but the family all nodded. Mrs. Dempsey held her husband's arm with a white-knuckled grip. Simon's own hands were so tightly wound together, his fingertips looked red and swollen. Bourke's voice remained calm and steady. "Her autopsy showed some unusual symptoms. The truth is, I should have spoken to you about them immediately, but because of Mrs. Darr's celebrity status, the toxicology report was prioritized and I was made aware immediately after the autopsy that we'd have the report within forty-eight hours. I waited because I didn't want to distress you unnecessarily."

"How could we be any more distressed?" Mrs. Dempsey cried. "What could be worse than our daughter dying?"

Paul Bourke sighed. "Unfortunately, I've an answer for that, ma'am. I'm afraid Mrs. Darr was poisoned."

"*Poisoned?*" Mrs. Dempsey's voice shattered on the word, breaking with fear and disbelief and the terrible knowledge of what it meant. "My daughter was—" She couldn't say the word and Detective Bourke didn't make her.

"The poison used wasn't commonly available," he replied gently. "It took special access, and specialized knowledge to administer it. I'm sorry, Mrs. Dempsey. Elizabeth was murdered."

"Who—why—?" Mrs. Dempsey could go no further, losing speech to the agony of loss. Her sobs and shrieks, bordering on screams, tore the air. Mr. Dempsey pulled her against his chest, tears and rage straining his face. His every breath came through clenched teeth, deep, rasping sounds beneath his wife's uncontrolled weeping. Beside them both, Simon sat like a man emptied of his soul, his face that of someone who understood but could not comprehend what he had heard. Megan shuddered, knowing she didn't belong in the midst of that maelstrom of grief, and slipped out as quietly as she could.

She had to stop in the lobby, her heart hammering so hard she'd seen stars as she hurried down the stairs into the hotel lobby. She'd known the truth—or imagined it—on some level since the beginning; she thought Simon and the Dempseys must have, too. People didn't normally collapse of food poisoning seconds after leaving dinner. Fewer still died of it so quickly. Allergies might have killed her that fast, but Detective Bourke hadn't said Liz had died of an allergic reaction. He'd said *poisoned*.

Poisonings were almost apocryphal, in Megan's experience. Aside from the occasional rattlesnake or copperhead bite, everyone Megan knew of who'd ever been poisoned had been the victim of a political assassination or some kind of building code violation or governmental screw-up. They'd died of Russian nerve agents, or asbestos exposure, or Agent Orange. Regular people didn't get poisoned, except by accident. She went to the hotel doors and stood in front of them, not leaving the building, only staring at the impossibly bright day outside, the brilliant morning sunshine highlighting gold on the windows of the shopping centre just down the road and turning the leaves in the park across the street rich with early light.

It was only just after eight on a Sunday morning. The streets were nearly empty, only the occasional intrepid jogger or enthusiastic tourist already out, pursuing their lives like a murder hadn't happened.

The doorwoman looked at her in concern. Megan stepped back from them and fell—almost literally, like her legs couldn't hold her anymore—into one of the deep, wing-armed green chairs in the hotel lobby. Her hands shook as she took out her phone, and it took several tries to get a message mostly typo-free to send to Fionnuala: **Liz Darr was poisoned. Poison poisoned, not food poisoned. Cannon's will be okay.** She only saw the autocorrect on *Canan* after she'd sent it and didn't know if she should laugh at it or let herself cry to release some of the shock. She waited a minute, looking expectantly at the phone, then slowly realized Fionn wasn't likely to be up for hours yet.

In the meantime, there had to be something she could do: find Cíara, talk to some of Martin's coworkers, *something*, to help make the whole mess make sense. She should have tried to find the nightclub manager, Noel, the evening before, instead of—

Instead of what? Megan snorted at herself, a small sound that helped recalibrate her emotions. Instead of taking the call that let Cillian go see his sister and her new baby? Instead of walking Mama Dog and feeding herself? Instead of getting a decent night's sleep? Maybe if she was still twenty-five, running around all night trying to figure out who'd been where, doing what, would have been reasonable, but at forty, Megan appreciated her sleep. She snorted at herself again and got up, leaving the hotel behind and forming half a plan in her mind as she went.

She'd barely made it to the corner fifty metres away when a kerfuffle behind her made her turn, just in time to see Simon Darr escorted from the hotel in handcuffs.

CHAPTER SIXTEEN

Simon looked beyond anguished. His long face was drawn and deeply lined, his expression numb as Detective Bourke guided him into a police car that hadn't been there when Megan left the hotel. It had to have been around the corner, waiting. Minimizing the fuss, although hardly anyone was around to notice it anyway. Only a handful of gardaí, who, like the car, had appeared while her back was turned, and whose serious expressions would deter even the boldest of curious passers-by.

Megan, evidently counting herself above and beyond bold, sprinted back toward Bourke and Simon, though Bourke closed Simon in the car before Megan reached them. Simon sagged in the back seat, his gaze fixed somewhere low within the vehicle's interior, but Bourke looked up with a warning tweak of his head as Megan approached.

She stopped rather abruptly, suddenly aware she'd been running full tilt at a police force, albeit one that didn't habitually carry guns like American cops did. She said, "I'm sorry, he's my friend—" aware, as she often wasn't any more, of the accent that marked her as an outsider in Ireland. Then, more directly to Paul Bourke, she said, "Detective, what . . . ?"

Rue pulled at the corner of Bourke's lips. "Ms. Malone, while I appreciate your enthusiasm, I don't owe you any explanations."

"No, but—" Megan couldn't think of a weight-bearing argument to follow that up with, and besides, the situation was pretty self-explanatory. ". . . does he have a lawyer?"

Bourke shrugged, more with the tilt of his head and cant of his mouth than a broad shoulder action. "He'll be appointed one, but if you know someone daft enough to take him on, you might give them a call."

Megan stuttered over the idea, trying to think of anyone off the top of her head. What she said aloud was, "Rabbie will know," and then, to Bourke's vaguely querying glance, "My uncle, Robert Lynch. He's the Sligo harbour master and he kn—"

Incredulity filled Bourke's face. "Robert Lynch is your *uncle*?"

Despite Simon's predicament, a burble of laughter escaped Megan's throat. "As I was saying, 'and he knows everybody.' Yeah, he's actually like my second cousin once removed or something, but generationally, he's more uncle-aged, so I call him Uncle Ro . . . how do you know him?"

Bourke's exhalation went on for a while, as if pushing away a dozen improbable questions. "I worked for him a summer when I was a lad. I'd been sending her spare and she—" He broke off, paused, and finished with, "You're right. Robert Lynch will know someone. Give him a call, for Dr. Darr's sake."

Megan nodded and backed away a few steps. "Okay. I will. Don't let him say anything stupid before I find him a lawyer." Bourke raised his pale eyebrows a little and Megan sighed. "Yeah, okay, it's your job to . . . I'll call Uncle Rabbie." She pulled out her phone while Bourke got in the car and drove away with Simon.

Her uncle was as likely—more likely—than most people she knew to be up at eight in the morning, as tides and shipping containers waited for no man, but his number went straight to voice mail. Megan made an explosion in her throat while waiting for his message to finish, choked on saliva, and was still coughing when the beep sounded and she had to talk. "Hi, Rabbie. This is Megan Malone, and I know it's weird for me to call, but I need a lawyer. I mean, *I* don't need one, but a friend of mine does. He's been arrested for murder, I think, and . . . could you recommend someone? Thanks. I'll talk to you soon." She hung up, stared at the phone a moment, then went back down the street to borrow the cafe's Wi-Fi so she could make another call.

This time she used the phone's video call software—Niamh would be so proud—and gnawed her lower lip, waiting for the overseas number to pick up, if pick up was the right phrase for a video call. After a few minutes of musical tones, the screen flickered to a close-up of a man's curious, concerned face. "Megan? Is everything okay?"

"Raf." A surge of relief swept Megan and she slid down the cafe's outer wall, thumping her head lightly against it. "Hey, man."

"Hey, girl. What's wrong? Why are you calling me at midnight?" Rafael Williams got himself situated a little farther away from his computer screen, so she could see more than his brown eyes and broad nose. An entire wall of bookcases made up his background, filled with an eclectic collection of medical texts, cookbooks, and historical fiction. Megan smiled, both at her friend's familiar face and the books piled everywhere.

"Because it *is* eleven at night. It's eight in the morning here and no one is up, but I knew you'd be awake."

Relief and humor swept Raf's face. "You're never going to adapt to people getting up late, are you? Okay, but there's still something going on or you'd have used the chat group, so hang on, let me grab Sarah and you can tell us all. Sarah? Hey, babe? It's Megan and she's lost her mind! Come say hi!"

"I don't know," Megan said beneath his shouting. "I might. Except no, I really don't think I ever will. Look, thanks for taking the call even though it's stupid late."

"Well, you're right, I *am* up, although I shouldn't be, because I've got an early shift at the hospital tomorrow. Sar—oh, there you are, hey, babe." Megan's oldest friend tipped up his chin to receive a kiss from his wife, who then sat beside him at the computer and waved merrily at Megan.

Even three years after the fact, Megan still kicked herself over the fact that she'd missed their

wedding. It hadn't been her fault; she'd been overseas on assignment and just hadn't been able to
make it home, but she'd known Rafael Williams
since second grade, and missing his wedding had
been the end of her military career in every way
that mattered. She'd finished her twenty years, because it would have been stupid to walk away from
her retirement after almost nineteen years of service, but the thoughts she'd had of reupping, really
becoming career military, really pursuing advance-
ment, all of it—had vanished in the moment her
request to go home for a couple of weeks had
been denied. She still remembered being so angry
tears spilled down her face as she'd told Raf, on
the phone, that she might miss his wedding, but
the hell would she miss the birth of his first child.
She remembered, too, his big laugh, and his ad-
monishment not to rush them: Sarah had a career
to think about, and dancers only had a limited
number of peak years.

Those limited years had kept Megan from meeting her even yet, except via online chats. Both
times Megan had gotten to San Francisco since re-
tiring, Sarah had been gone, lead ballerina in the
always-touring Dancing Shoes Ballet Company.
Rafael good-naturedly accused "the two most important women in his life" of avoiding each other,
but truthfully, Megan regretted not having met
Sarah in person yet. They were gorgeous together,
Rafael a complex blend of American melting pot
that gave him medium-brown skin and black hair
that could be coaxed into waves or tight curls, depending on the humidity, and Sarah the image of
her Nigerian mother, down to a crown of braids

that Megan admired every time she chatted with the other woman.

Tonight they were down, a faintly visible cloud at the back of her head as she leaned on Raf's shoulder and said, "So how have you lost your mind?"

"She's calling at midnight, what more do you need?" Rafael asked. Sarah nudged him, smiling, and lifted round eyebrows expectantly at Megan.

"I haven't lost my mind, but I lost a client. Like, she was—" Megan hesitated, suddenly aware she was using public Wi-Fi outside of a cafe—because the cafe, of course, wouldn't be open for another two or three hours—and that the topic wasn't exactly the most reassuring. On the other hand, almost no one was around, so being circumspect seemed silly. Especially when she'd called friends in California for . . . consolation, or something. "She was murdered," Megan said more quietly.

A barrage of *holy shit!* and *oh my God, are you all right?* and *what happened?* swam over her, strangely reassuring. She promised, "I'm okay, I'm okay" a few times, finally calming them enough to relate the story of the past few days and ending with, "And I just watched Simon get arrested and I feel awful."

"Do you think he did it?" Raf asked. "What poison was used?" Sarah, beside him, reached for something off screen and bent her head as a phone's light threw her features into blue shadow.

"I don't know," Megan said to both questions. "Detective Bourke said it took special access and knowledge to administer it, and . . . I know Simon was interviewing at local hospitals. Maybe he had a chance to grab something?"

Raf grimaced. "On one hand, lethal stuff is obviously watched pretty carefully. On the other, they don't usually do a nightly check either. Does he seem like the murdering type?"

"I don't know, Raf. He seems devastated. He looked shell-shocked when Bourke took him out of the hotel this morning. I don't know if I should go talk to Liz's parents or what."

"Oh, how awful." Sarah looked up, holding her phone up to show Megan that she'd pulled up Liz Darr's website. "Those videos are so—they're so alive, so they're very sad. Even the music is sad."

"I didn't even hear the music on the second one. I barely watched it, though. Yeah, I just—why would somebody post them? I know the second one wasn't queued."

"'Queued.'" Rafael tried to hide a smile. "How Irish of you."

"Oh, pbthtlfft. I don't—" Megan stopped short, sort of horrified. "Oh my God. I don't even know how we'd say it in America anymore. Lined up? Ready to post? Oh my God. I'm Irish."

"'Queued' is fine." Sarah elbowed Rafael lightly and he laughed. "I think you should go talk to her parents, one way or another. Their daughter is dead and their son-in-law has been arrested for it. They could probably use some kind of support."

"Yeah. Yeah, I think you're right. I guess I just needed somebody to tell me it was okay."

"It's okay to go offer help," Sarah said with a smile. Megan gave her a fond look in return and Rafael pointed at the screen.

"Keep us posted, Megalodon. You can't go getting involved in a murder and then ju—"

"I'm *not* involved in a *murder*!"

"Okay, all right, in a murder *case*," Raf said in a tone that suggested Megan was spoiling all his fun. "Anyway, you can't leave us hanging. You've got to tell us what happens."

"I will, although I'll try not to call in the middle of the night again."

"Dude, under the circumstances it seems justified. But you have the power of texting. Use the group chat. And you take care, okay? Hasta la vista."

"Hasta la vista, amigo. Adios, Sarah, buenas noches."

"*Ó di àaró*, good night." Sarah waved and Megan chimed, "*Ódàáró*," best as she could, then hung up with a lightness in her heart. Their kids, if they had any, would not only be gorgeous but would speak at least three languages, and Megan made a note—as she always did when she talked to Sarah—to see if there were any Yoruban speakers in Dublin who might give her lessons. She'd be darned if Raf's kids would be able to plot behind her back by speaking a language she didn't know. Of course, she was pretty sure Sarah was fluent in French, too, but one bridge at a time.

It was less than a minute's walk back to the hotel and she went up to tap uncertainly first on Simon's, then on the Dempseys' door. A bleak-faced Peter opened the door and scowled at her for a long moment before recognizing her and stepping aside to let her in. His wife had collected herself a little in the time Megan had been gone, but Megan stopped not far inside the room, twisting her hands together in sudden, acute awareness of her intrusion. "I'm sorry. I thought—if you needed anything, if I could help in some way—I just wanted to say you could call on me. This must be—it must be impossible for you, and I'm so sorry—"

"You can do something for me." Mrs. Dempsey's voice, raw and deep with grief, scraped at Megan's ears. "I know exactly what you can do. You can prove that my son-in-law is innocent."

Megan took the deepest breath she could and promised, "I'm already trying, Mrs. Dempsey," then made her escape before mentioning that she might have gotten Simon arrested on some kind of drug charges. She almost went back, though, to ask if they *knew* anything about Simon's drug or gambling problems, but adding that burden of suspicion onto them when they'd been through so much already seemed horrible. If it came to it, if she *had* to, she'd ask about it, but if they could be left in ignorance, that seemed like it would be better.

She stopped outside the cafe again, using their Wi-Fi to call Niamh and going so far as to use the video phone app this time. It rang several times, and just as Meg was about to give up, Niamh's image came on, eyes enormously brown and sleepy, her black curls springing away from her forehead and the rest of her face hidden by a pillow. "You're making a *vone* call," she said through a yawn. "That means it must be important, and it's the only reason I'm answering. It's a *quarter* to *nine*, Megan." She sounded as though Megan had deliberately reached through time and space to call at the most appalling hour humanly possible.

Megan took a nostril-flaring moment to think of

Detective Bourke's commentary about event-based culture vs. time-based culture, then put on a perky smile. "I have a totally inappropriate question to ask you, based on stereotypes surrounding your chosen profession."

"And me still in my nightgown." Niamh sat up, though, obviously intrigued as she rearranged the pillow and the phone so she could lean on one and look into the other. She even dressed cutely to sleep, wearing a silky, notched-collar top in lemon and mint that Megan figured had matching trousers. Niamh pushed back her hair, which did no good at all—the twisty curls sprang right back into place—and said, "Talk to me. What illicit cinematic information do you need?"

"Who do actors buy drugs from?"

Niamh's large eyes widened and she laughed. "Mostly their doctors. Why, was Simon Darr supplying Ireland's finest with their fixes?"

"I don't think so. Where do their doctors get them? If it's illicit, I mean. Assuming you don't want to be seen hitting the pharmacies every three days."

"That's why we have assistants, darling. But I really don't know. I'm terribly Puritan," she said lightly, and then, more seriously, "This business is hard enough. It's obvious how easy it would be to soften some of its edges with substance abuse. I've stayed away from it, and from knowing anything about it, because like dear Oscar Wilde, I can resist anything but temptation. That said . . ." Her gaze went elsewhere in the room, clearly finding a clock. "I could ask a few people in the cast later today. I can't call at this hour—if I did, the tabloids would be screaming about Niamh O'Sullivan's desperation for a drug fix by this time tomorrow. But honestly, for the legal stuff, I don't imagine anybody knows where their doctors get it from, and for the illegal stuff . . . they're not asking their doctors."

"Ask about, I don't know, sleeping pills, then, maybe? Or pain pills. Or maybe you could introduce me to somebody who'd introduce me to his dealer. I just want to know where the theoretically legal stuff comes from, when it's sold on the streets."

"Yes," Niamh said dryly, "because no one will think that's at all suspicious."

"Oh, come on. I drive limos for a living. Tell them I'm looking to make a little extra on the side as a courier or something."

"I thought you said you'd make a terrible criminal!"

"Maybe I'm improving!"

Niamh rolled her eyes extravagantly. "All right. I'll ask around a bit before the matinee and give you a ring. This is going to look terrible for my career if anyone passes it on, Meg."

"I feel like I should say something very dramatic, like, 'A man's life is at stake, woman! Careers be damned!' Except it's too late for that; Liz is already dead, so I guess it's probably not that urgent. I'll see if I can figure out how to buy illegal drugs on my own this morning and you can call me this afternoon if you haven't heard back from me by curtain."

"Remember how yesterday I said everyone has these strange moments in their lives?"

"Yeah?"

"I'm beginning to reconsider. You might be un-usually mad." Niamh waved and Megan, shaking her head and smiling, ended the connection.

She might have to wait on Niamh's contacts, but the whole conversation had given her another idea.

A few minutes' walk took her up Rathmines Road to the Leprechaun Limos office. The door dinged as she let herself in, and Orla appeared from the back, all charm and smiles until she saw it wasn't a client. "Oh, it's your own self. You're not working today. What do you want?"

Megan threw herself into one of the big leather chairs and smiled at her pinch-faced boss. "Who are our absolute shadiest competitors?"

"What would you want to know that for?"

"Research. I want to know if I'm being under-paid."

Offense coloured two red circles on Orla's cheeks. "I'll have you know I've never underpaid a driver in me life—"

Megan actually believed that. Orla might be ready to skin every penny she could from a client, and happy to dock pay to—for example—cover the cost of an unapproved pet in a flat she was landlord of—but truthfully, Megan didn't doubt she paid fair wages. She wanted good, reliable drivers who would stay on with Leprechaun Limos for years, and cheating a driver out of their paycheck was false economy. It cost a lot more to find, hire, and train a new driver than it did to pay a good one what they were worth. "No," Megan said loudly to stop Orla's insulted rant, "no, really, I'm just won-dering how much illegal drug couriering is done by driving companies and I thought you'd know who was most likely to be involved in that kind of thing. You're too good at what you do not to have some sense of who's got a side business going."

Orla, her jaw thrust out with suspicion, stared at Megan for a long time. "Are yis messin with me?"

"No, not at all. I know we don't always get on, but honestly, I wouldn't work for you if you didn't run a tight ship, and you know more about Dublin than most of us ever will. Especially me."

"Ah, quit yer *plamásing.*"

Megan stared, then laughed. "My what? *Plah-maws?* I don't know that one."

"It means flattery," Orla said in the tone of a woman who'd won a round. "Blarneying. Butter-ing me up, so."

"Oh! No! Or, yes, maybe I am, a little, but I'm also telling the truth. You know more about this city than I ever will," Megan said. "So who's shady in the driving business?"

"Well, shite, if yis want a quick hit, it's the rick-shaws ye'd go to first." Orla Keegan's contempt for the bicycle-driven, two-person carts was legendary, though up until that moment, Megan had always thought it was because they took late-night taxi business and regarded the rules of the road as guidelines that didn't particularly apply to them. "Loads of those lads are just in the country for a few months, running drugs and making quick sales and then gone again before the guards even know who they were."

"How do they know how to meet dealers if they're new?" Megan asked, fascinated despite herself. Orla gave her a look that suggested she was both naïve and simple.

"Who d'yis think is sending them into the country to start with? And then a nice local lad says to himself, those lads are making more than I am and no one's coming after them, and so he says to them, how do I get in on this, and . . ." Orla shrugged expressively. "Next thing yis know, it's all of them."

Megan doubted that, but neither did she want to stop Orla with a discussion of veracity. "And the limo services?"

"And taxis," Orla said with a sniff. "Now, there's more guards looking out for that sort of thing, so it's riskier, see? Though they've cracked down on the rickshaws," she added with satisfaction. "I heard about it on the radio, the gardaí task forces going after those lads. About time they did something, though it's not enough. But then there's never enough guards, except when you don't want them. Last month, there were four of them after Cillian for running a red light—"

"But the CCTV showed he hadn't," Meg reminded her reassuringly. "Your drivers know better, and not because we're afraid of the guards. We know you'd skin us all alive."

Orla chortled, pleased, and got back on topic. "The point is, they track taxi drivers close like, busting them all the time, a few thousand quid of coke here, a few thousand of heroin there. The car services, they're dearer and they might run the same route for a week, but then they're not back to it for months, or never. There aren't as many patterns. I wouldn't put it past the Liffey Car Service, though, or Traveller's Wagon."

Megan sucked her cheeks in to keep herself from asking if that was a real possibility or a bias against the name; the Travellers in Ireland, known for generations as tinkers, were still looked down upon as itinerant outsiders by the larger Irish community, and a name like the Traveller's Wagon would prejudice plenty of settled Irish against a company. But, like Leprechaun Limos itself, the romance of the name drew in tourists, who were the larger part of a driving service's clientele anyway. "When you say you wouldn't put it past them . . . ?"

"Far be it from me to start rumours," Orla said with an innocence that no adult human being could legitimately lay claim to, but Megan, recognizing when she'd been shut down, smiled her thanks and went to look for some drug dealers.

CHAPTER SEVENTEEN

Ten a.m. on a Monday morning probably wasn't the best time to find drug-dealing rickshaw drivers, but, lacking a time machine to jump forward twelve or fifteen hours, Megan reckoned it was the best she could do. Grafton and O'Connell Streets usually hosted a few of the drivers at any time of day, and Grafton was only a short bus ride away.

Megan slapped her Leap Card—green, embellished with a frog, and the cheapest way to use Dublin's public transportation—onto the bus fare . . . calculator—she was sure the thing had a proper name, but she didn't know what it was—and watched the Grand Canal go by under them as they crossed a bridge. The canal still ran most of the way to the River Shannon, and thence to the Atlantic Ocean, a journey Megan wanted to take someday.

The bus left the canal behind in a moment, though, and drove through more of Georgian

Dublin, the old three- and four-storey homes, many of them now converted into businesses, and as tall as most buildings were allowed to be under Dublin's city ordinances. Megan got off on George's Street and walked past the Central Hotel, where she'd met Niamh at the Library Bar the night before, and down past Canan's.

Fionnuala's restaurant was still cordoned off by yellow police tape. Molly Malone and her sad burden of wilting flowers, testament to those who mourned Liz Darr, looked incongruently serene to Megan, knowing what lay behind the statue in the old church. Guards who looked like they'd rather be at home sleeping, or at least walking around rather than policing a quiet crime scene, nodded at Meg as she went by and answered questions from curious tourists.

Megan passed them all and went up to the corner of Grafton and Nassau, where Molly had stood for decades before road works had moved her to Suffolk Street.

A couple of rickshaws idled where she'd once stood. Megan tapped on one of their shells—red and white, emblazoned with a local food delivery company—and got the attention of the driver. He, like every other rickshaw driver as far as Megan could tell, was a young man in his twenties, with a ready grin and a pitch about where he could drive her already on his lips. She interrupted with, "Hi. I'm not a cop."

The driver, skinny, around twenty-two, and made primarily of a beard and sunglasses, pulled the glasses down to look at her. "A cop would say so, wouldn't she? You look kind of like a cop."

"Probably because I was in the US military for twenty years."

"Yeh?" Distrustful hope came into the kid's eyes. "You looking to hook up or something? 'Cause you're fit."

"Ha. Thanks, but no. I do have some weird questions and will pay you the equivalent of a ten-kilometre lift to answer them."

A predatory gleam replaced the lad's hope. "We work for tips. I could use a solid one."

"Tips for tips, then, assuming you give me some useful information."

"Deal."

Megan sat in the rickshaw. The kid turned in his seat, hanging his arm over its back to look at her curiously. Megan took a ten out of her wallet, held it up, then folded it into her palm. "If a person were—theoretically—interested in purchasing certain illegal substances, where would she source them from?"

Suspicion warred with curiosity on the rickshaw driver's face. "Are you sure you're not a cop?"

"Positive. Even if I was, I'd be out of my jurisdiction, wouldn't I? I'm obviously not Irish." She laid on her Texan twang there, and the driver relaxed a little.

"*Theoretically*, I might know a lad or two."

"Brilliant." Megan took out another ten, held it up, and folded it into her palm with the first. "*Theoretically*, if a person was looking for something specific—let's say sleeping pills—would your lads know where to find them?"

"That shite's easy. How much is this theoretical buyer looking for?"

Another tenner brought the euro amount Megan was laying out to well over what a ten-klick lift would cost. "The theoretical buyer is interested in the theoretical supply line, not the actual product. I'm trying to understand where someone who was himself a dealer would get prescription drugs in large enough numbers to sell."

Suspicion arose in the driver's face again. "Are you a reporter?"

"Honestly, I'm just a busybody." Megan took out a twenty this time and wished she could expense it to somebody. "So let's say I'm a well-off white American—"

"I dunno, that seems like a stretch."

Megan laughed. "Yeah. Use your imagination. So, I'm a well-off white American—a doctor, let's say—and I've dealt prescription drugs in the States. Now I'm looking to set up shop in Ireland. What do I do?"

By now, the driver had the same expression Orla had worn earlier, one implying Megan had a remarkable combination of naivety and stupidity. "You mean theoretical, don't you," he said slowly, as if talking to a child. "You're no dealer. You should go home and stick to what's safe."

"Probably, but let's assume I'm not going to."

"*Theoretically*, if you weren't an absolute eejit, you would figure out that there's pharmacists and chemists who'll skim a little off the top, or miscount their product, or claim a shipment got lost, and sell out the back door. *Theoretically*, if you're a doctor, you might have mates at a pharmaceutical company anywhere in the world who'd ship you what you need in exchange for a cut of the profits."

"How would I get that past customs?"

"You'd have another mate on the ship, or in customs, or both, or ye'd drop it in the ocean and send some young, dumb gobshite out for it. D'ye not even read the papers, then?"

"The papers," Megan pointed out, "mention the big busts off the coast, not the ones that get through. It'd be easy to think—if you were an eejit—that they catch it all."

"If you were an absolute muppet," the driver agreed. Megan tried, as she always did, not to laugh at the term, which, broadly, meant fool in Irish parlance, and invariably brought puppetry to her American mind. The kid, seeing nothing funny about the word, rolled his eyes and went on. "But if they caught it all, there wouldn't be any busts on land, would there? Look, lady, you seem nice, so lemme suggest something. Don't do crime. It won't end well for yis."

Megan laughed again and handed him the fifty euros. "I think I'll take that advice. Thanks for your help." She climbed out of the rickshaw, then stopped, leaning on its shell. "Wait, one more thing. If I wanted to talk to one of those pharmacists who can't count, where would you suggest I go?"

"I'd never say." The driver shook his head violently. "That gets into territory I'm not going near. You'll get yourself in trouble."

"It was worth a shot." Megan whacked the rickshaw shell in farewell and meandered north, toward the river, with the vague supposition that a less wealthy part of town would be the best place to find drug dealers. Then again, rich people had money for drugs, so she might be barking up the

wrong tree. Her phone rang in her butt pocket—
she'd tried on the knee-length shorts in the store
to make certain the pockets were deep enough to
hold the phone—and she took it out, glancing at
the time before she answered the local, but unknown, number. "This is Megan."

"Ms. Malone." An American woman's shaky voice
came over the line. "This is Ellen Dempsey, Liz's
mother."

Megan stopped short at the corner of College
Green, a space that hadn't actually been green for
at least a century but did front Trinity College, a
glorious old university founded by Elizabeth I.
Traffic beeped and rumbled past, suddenly loud
in Megan's ears. She pressed her finger to her
open ear, hearing her heartbeat rush. "Mrs.
Dempsey? Is everything all right?"

"No," Mrs. Dempsey wailed. "Liz has posted another blog!"

It took Megan, almost running, less than five
minutes to backtrack up Grafton Street and over
to the Shelbourne Hotel. She took the stairs up to
the Dempseys' room two at a time, her heart burst-
ing in her chest as she knocked and, gasping, was
given access.

Simon's laptop computer—or Liz's, more likely,
because it was the one she'd used, the one that
had the passwords to Liz's blog saved—sat open
on their desk. Mr. Dempsey slumped in front of it,
his skin tones so grey, Megan feared for his heart.
He lifted his gaze dully to Megan, then rose and

moved away from the computer, but speech was apparently beyond him; it was Mrs. Dempsey, voice still quaking, who said, "We were reading the comments. So many of them are so lovely. She touched so many lives. But then—then—" She made a tremulous gesture at the computer and the chair. Megan sat down.

There had only been two vlogs from the USB stick left unpublished: this was one, the one from Newgrange, filmed the morning before she'd died. Vibrant and laughing, she looked into the camera, her voice full of cheer as she said, "We're here for the wrong solstice—smile for the camera, Si!—" and turned it on her husband, who, embarrassed, waved and ducked his head, moving himself out of the lens's view. It swung back around to Liz, who said, "Such a handsome guy shouldn't be so shy about cameras. Anyway, this is Newgrange, one of the world's oldest Neolithic—that means 'stone age,' aren't I fancy?—sites, older than the pyramids or Stonehenge! And at the winter solstice, the sun spills right into what's called the birthing chamb—oh, wait, did I make that up? I made that up. It's a passage tomb, that's what it is, that's why it reminds me of a birthing chamber; anyway, it lights it up and apparently it's simply amazing, buuuuuuuut you have to win a lottery to be here for the winter solstice. So it's almost the summer solstice now, the other half of the year, and I'm just going to take you right in. . . ."

She did, too, going in with the camera ahead of her, so her viewers would see what she saw. It was the same video Megan had watched before—the same video, in fact, that she had stored on her own hard drive at home, not that she'd mentioned as much to Detective Bourke.

The same video save for one thing.

This one had a sweet rendition of "Molly Malone" mixed over it, thin tones of an unsupported soprano singing in the background.

Megan closed the laptop and steepled her fingers in front of her mouth, trying to absorb—to *imagine*—what that meant. After a moment, she turned to the Dempseys, who huddled forlornly on the bed. "I have a copy of this video without the music. One of my company's valets found a USB drive with backups of Liz's files on it, this included."

"Then who put the music on it? Why would they do that? And that awful song again—" Mrs. Dempsey shrank at her husband's side. He put his arm around her but seemed unable to speak.

"I don't know," Megan said with quiet determination. "I don't know, Mrs. Dempsey, but I'm going to find out. You're still leaving tomorrow?"

"We're supposed to," Mrs. Dempsey whispered. "They released her body. We can fly her home, have a funeral . . . we didn't want to wait. Even though Simon is . . . is . . ."

"Simon is in trouble." Megan's voice sounded hard to her own ears and she struggled to soften it. "Even if he's innocent of Liz's murder, it appears he's been dealing prescription drugs illegally. And not just in the States but here, too."

Mr. Dempsey's face tightened with anger. "I knew it. I *knew* it!" Mrs. Dempsey only collapsed farther, her face in her hands. Peter continued above the soft sounds of her crying. "He always had either too much or too little money. Even before they got married he admitted to Liz that he'd had a gambling problem in college. He said he'd worked through it, but I'm sure he didn't. I'm sure he kept it up, because Liz would sometimes mention that money had gone missing, but he'd always have an answer and she always wanted to believe him. Those real estate investments? He didn't come from money. Those were a front. New doctors aren't paid *that* well, not enough to throw around cash like he did, and I told Liz—she came to us worried about his finances, wondering how he could afford—I *told* her—but she didn't want to believe me . . ."

"But she did," Megan said quietly. "She's been tracking his finances for years. I think she might have confronted him about it last year, because it stopped. But then, when they came here, it started up again. I don't know if he knew someone, or if there was just an easy market he couldn't resist . . ."

"Is that why she's dead?" Mrs. Dempsey gasped around a sob. "Did he kill her because he knew she'd take him to the police this time?"

"I don't know," Megan said again. "I want to find out. You—I think it would be all right if you went home. Laid your daughter to rest. You've had an impossibly hard few days. I just wonder if you could leave the laptop here? I'll ship it back to you, but I want to figure out who's posting those blogs, and it'd be easier with—well, with Liz's password, but I don't know what that is, and the account is already logged in on this computer."

Mrs. Dempsey's violent nods answered Megan long before she'd finished asking. "Take it. Take it, I don't care if I never see it again. She loved this job so much, but all I know now is it took her away from me forever." Her husband pulled a card from his wallet, offering it to Meg. Not a business card but a personal one: It had their home address and phone number on it. Megan nodded and tucked it into her phone case, then she packed up the computer, and hesitated before she left the room.

"What you said about the real estate being a front, Mr. Dempsey. Do you mean, like, money laundering?"

"I never believed he was investing with the money he took from their accounts," Liz's father said bitterly. "I couldn't prove it, but I always thought he was gambling it away. I'd believe that he started selling drugs to cover it, when he got in too deep. And I doubt that was the half of it. All the traveling they did? He could have been buying diamonds and smuggling them back to clean his filthy money, or meeting with offshore accounts lawyers . . . Liz never wanted to believe the worst of him."

"No," Megan murmured. "I suppose she didn't."

CHAPTER EIGHTEEN

Megan rarely carried a bag—her phone and cards fit into her jeans pockets—so she headed home on the Luas with Liz's laptop tucked under her arm, and the power cord with its converter scrunched in her hand. It felt like she'd already stuffed a full day's activity into the four hours she'd been up. The morning had warmed up nicely, and though almost three years living in rainy Ireland wasn't quite enough to beat the Texas out of Megan, she admitted privately that the locally outrageous twenty-eight degree weather felt pretty darn hot. The sunshine warmed her unprotected hair until she smelled hints of coconut and jasmine from her shampoo as she walked from the tram station to her apartment.

She was struggling with the laptop and her keys, trying to get her front door open, when her phone set her butt to humming and buzzing. Key in the door, she turned it, grabbed her phone, and said, "Yeah?" without looking to see who it was.

"My fairest American cousin!" replied a jovial voice. "It's Rabbie, Megan. What's this nonsense about you needing a solicitor?"

"Oh, thanks for ringing me back, Rabbie. *I* don't need a lawyer," Megan stressed. She got in the door, bumping it closed behind her as two inept puppies struggled to lift their comparatively massive heads and figure out where the breeze was coming from. Mama knocked them over, licking them thoroughly, and Megan, who had been looking "puppies and peeing" up on the internet, dropped the laptop on the couch and hurried to get all three of the dogs onto the pee mat. "Someone I know, another American, does, though. A criminal lawyer? He's just been arrested for murdering his wife. Or maybe just drug running, I don't know."

"Jesus, Megan." The good humor didn't exactly drop from Rabbie's voice—he always sounded cheerful, as if putting on a performance to sell the quintessential Irishman to the world—but he became considerably more serious. "You're after not calling around for months and then you ring me with this? Are you well?"

"Honestly, I'm fine." Mama Dog had licked her babies into bowel movements, an act that Megan regarded as unsanitary in the extreme, and had collected them again to drop them back into their bed. The entire activity had apparently worked up an appetite and they whined and yipped and sniveled as they worked their way around to nursing properly. Megan, mesmerized by them, said, "Do you remember a Paul Bourke, ginger with blond eyebrows, who worked for you one summer?" to her uncle.

"Sure, skinny as the day was long, but strong," Rabbie said immediately. "He was driving his mam spare, getting into trouble with the guards, nothing serious, but it could have been, and she sent him to her sister's best friend for the summer to straighten him out. They were strictly Catholic, so they were, and Paulie was after getting himself out of the house however he could, even if it meant sweating and sunburning on the docks all summer. I never thought he was much to look at, but the girls would get giggly over yer man's smile."

A grin worked itself across Megan's face. "Well, I never. He's the arresting detective on my friend's case. Really, he was in trouble with the guards as a kid?"

"Nothing serious," Rabbie said again. "Just being a gobshite, as lads are. I'd heard he grew up to be a guard. Good on him, that's a good lad. I can ring and tell him there's all been a mistake—"

"No!" Megan laughed. "God, no, Rabbie, let the man do his job. But even he said to get Simon a lawyer, and when I said you were my uncle, he said you'd know someone. Ugh." The last was to the pee pad, which really wasn't all that disgusting, because all the babies had to expel was liquid, but an *ugh* still seemed in order as she collected it for the rubbish. Rabbie, somewhat distantly due to her phone having slipped, inquired as to her well-being, and she got the phone again to say, "No, I'm fine, I'm just . . . babysitting . . . some dogs. Puppies."

"Send me a picture so," Rabbie demanded, and

when they were off the phone, promises of a lawyer ringing her, she did. Rabbie responded with an **aww ADORBS are you keeping them!?** that reminded her of teenage girls, not dock workers in their sixties. His next text was a more sedate **I'll have Gareth ring you about your friend**, as if they hadn't established that in conversation. She sent an **absolutely NOT!** about keeping them and a series of love hearts for his help, and fell onto her couch to open Liz's laptop.

Her phone rang again immediately and she stared at it accusingly, but then answered, because it was Fionnuala, who sounded tired and stunned. "Oh my God, Megan, I'm just after waking up and seeing your texts. Liz was poisoned?"

"Murdered, yeah. So, I mean, the good news is it definitely wasn't Canan's. I don't know how it all ties in with Martin, though."

"I've been wracking my mind, trying to think—who do they suspect did it?"

"They arrested Simon Darr this morning, after I texted you."

"What? Oh no! Do you think he did it? He seemed so nice!"

"I don't know. His in-laws—well, they wanted me to prove him innocent, but he's been selling drugs, too—"

"*What?*"

". . . it's been busy since I talked to you last." Actually, Megan supposed, she'd known about the drugs before she'd last spoken to Fionn, but they'd had breaking and entering to discuss at the time, and it hadn't come up. Caught between amusement and horror at what the past few days

twice, then to the new vlog, and sat back, lips smashed together in thought while Liz did kissy-faces and hand hearts at the shellfish.

The vocals on the new vlog were Liz's own. In fact—Megan leaned forward again, scrolling down Liz's blog page to find and listen to the other two posthumous vlogs. She held her breath, listening, head tilted so her ear was nearer to the speaker, as if an extra centimetre or two would make all the difference.

And maybe it did, because after listening to them, Megan felt confident that the same record-ing had been used for all three vlogs. Liz, like a ghost, sang in the background of all three vlogs, and she obviously hadn't done that postproduc-tion work herself.

Neither, though, had Simon. Although—Megan shook her head, muttering, "No jumping to con-clusions," either to herself or the dogs, who didn't care. Just because Simon Darr currently resided within Dublin's penal system didn't mean he hadn't produced the videos and set them to upload. "Ex-cept I *looked*," she said, definitely to the dogs this time. Mama thumped her tail once, as if tolerating Megan's commentary without paying attention to it. "I looked, and they weren't . . ."

Feeling like she might be losing her mind, Megan checked the blogging software's dashboard again, as she'd done a couple of days earlier with Simon watching. As before, there were definitely no posts pending, though the most recent one, she saw with a shock that ran chills into her finger-tips, had come from a different IP address than the last several.

Her phone rang, startling her badly enough that Mama Dog lifted her head to eye her in astonishment. She whispered, "Sorry," picked up the phone, saw Fionnuala's name, and answered with a little laugh. "I think I've half-convinced myself there are ghosts, Fionn."

"You're in Ireland, Meg. Of course there are."

Megan waited a moment for the laugh or vocal shrug that would indicate Fionnuala was kidding, but none came. Eyebrow lifted, a shiver running down her spine, she said, "That wasn't the reassurance I was looking for."

"Is it Liz Darr haunting you? She's got every reason to be, doesn't she? Haunting all of us, not just you. *I* had a loan out from the bank for Canan's, but Martin had investors. That was his side of the business and I never asked much about it. I'm thinking that was a mistake, now. There are loads of people I have to talk to, and—it's not that it's all a foreign language." Fionnuala sighed heavily. "There's classes, you know. Part of the culinary school I did taught you how to run a business and all of it. But it was so much easier to let Martin deal with the financial side. He loved money. I just love to cook."

"You said you'd thought the business was doing well but that the books said it was much closer to the margin than you'd thought, right?"

"I've been over them a hundred times since Thursday night. I thought—I'd seen the numbers before, Meg. A thirty percent intake over costs is doing really well for a restaurant, and Martin had been so damn pleased we'd been making more like forty, forty-five percent. But the books say we're operating at eighteen or twenty percent now, and I don't understand. That's just for the restaurant. The nightclub was taking in barrel loads, it turns out." Fionn made a bitter sound. "I shouldn't have bothered learning to cook and just practiced mixing drinks."

"You've lost a *twenty-five percent* profit margin?" Megan's voice sharpened so much that Mama Dog shook herself loose of the puppies, climbed out of their bed, and crawled into Meg's lap, a warm, comforting lump. Megan felt her heart grow three sizes and rubbed the little dog's head until she put her chin on Megan's thigh and relaxed.

"I don't know how!" Fionn wailed. "Meg, the restaurant does steady business. Two seatings a night, between the early birds and the late diners. We average eighty percent full from Wednesday through Saturday, and fifty to sixty percent capacity the rest of the week, with the specials we run and all. The Monday Mollycoddle is a huge success—"

Megan laughed quietly, as she always did at the name. Monday nights were notoriously slow in the restaurant business, and Fionn had, with the opening of Canan's, introduced Mollycoddle Mondays, where prebooked reservations got diners 15 percent off their meals and a bottle of wine at half-price. Groups of women, especially, would come in together, calling it Mollycoddle Mammy, and have an evening away from their families and responsibilities. It had started out popular and had grown so successful that people booked weeks and months in advance. Fionnuala, thinking of that, cried, "And I've got to rebook everyone who won't be able to come in tonight, ah, *shite*—!"

"Up the discount by five percent and throw in an extra bottle of half-price wine," Megan suggested. "And invite them to reschedule for Tuesdays or Wednesdays in the next six weeks, so if you get the restaurant open again by Monday next you won't have two times as many customers trying to come in as will fit."

"You're very sensible." Fionnuala didn't sound pleased.

"It's so much easier to be sensible about other peoples' crises. If it was my own, I'd be in a useless panic."

Some of Fionn's irritation faded in a sigh. "Then I need you to come over and be sensible for me, as I'm a wreck without a thought in my head. I wish I could get hold of Cíara. She's got a sweet voice for talking people into things and she'd charm them all into the Tuesdays and Wednesdays."

"You haven't heard from her?" Megan's tone sharpened again and Mama performed a very large, dramatic sigh, as if asking what all her hard work was for if Megan was just going to keep getting upset about things.

"Not a word, and she was supposed to work today if we were able to open. How am I to run a business with that sort of thing going on?"

"I don't know." For a moment, Megan was grateful that Orla, and not she, handled the operations of Leprechaun Limos. She'd never had any urge to own a business herself, and watching the tribulations of those who did would put paid to any notions that came creeping along. "Do you know where Cíara's from? I mean, where she grew up?"

"I haven't the faintest, sorry. She wasn't at home, then?"

"No, but her neighbour is now equal parts furious at and terrified of me."

"Sounds about right."

"Hey!"

Fionnuala laughed. "That didn't come out the way I meant it. Look, Megan, I've got to go. I've an accountant coming to look at the books to see if she can figure out the discrepancies—"

"Right, hey, um, look, did Martin have any, um. Unsavory acquaintances?"

She heard a world of prejudices and snarky comments about the wrong-side-of-the-tracks area where Martin Rafferty had grown up in the silence before Fionnuala sighed and said, "No, not that I know of. Why?"

"I just—I'm trying to put together why Liz and he were both killed. What they could possibly have had in common besides Canan's. And I've been finding out some stuff about Simon Darr that could . . . I don't know. It might explain those differences in the books that you're seeing."

"You think Simon and Martin knew each other? Can't you just go ask Simon?"

"I don't see how they could have. It's just that Simon—well, even if he didn't murder Liz, apparently he sold prescription drugs under the table, and his father-in-law thinks he might have been into money laundering."

This time Fionn's silence carried thunderous horror. Her voice sounded thin when she finally spoke. "You think Martin was using Canan's to launder drug money?"

"I have literally zero reason to think that except the discrepancy you mentioned." Megan folded herself over Mama Dog, who remained a comforting bundle in her lap. "I didn't think anything of it at all until I found out about Simon," she said, almost into the dog's short fur. "I want to say I'm sure I'm wrong, but obviously I'm not sure."

"All right." Fionnuala's voice strengthened. "All right, look. I'll get you his girlfriend's number somehow, and a couple of the lads he's known from way back. His funeral's not until Wednesday, so you've a little time to talk to them. Meg, I'm not going to mention money laundering to the accountant, but if she brings it up . . ."

Megan nodded. "If she brings it up, I'll call Detective Bourke about it all. In the meantime, I'll just see what the heck *I* can figure out."

CHAPTER NINETEEN

She'd just woken up the computers and started working on them when her phone rang again. Megan closed her eyes, speaking, she supposed, to the dogs. "Don't people know this is the twenty-first century and we use texts to communicate instead of actually calling people?" Mama Dog sighed heavily and Megan, agreeing, turned over the phone to see an unknown number. "I hate answering calls when I don't know who it is." She answered it anyway, with, "Hi, this is Megan Malone."

A male voice said, "Good morning, Ms. Malone," which made Megan look for a clock, although she already knew it had to be after noon. Morning oftened continued until after lunchtime—one or even two o'clock in Ireland—but she hadn't quite gotten used to that. "This is Gareth McGrath with Hearlihy and Co Solicitors. I'm a defense lawyer. Your cousin Rabbie asked me to call you."

"Oh! Oh, *deadly*, thank you so much. I've got a friend who's in trouble, an American friend who's been arrested for murder, and he needs legal representation."

"Who," McGrath asked, "will be paying the solicitor fees?"

As he was speaking, the doorbell rang. Megan rose to buzz the visitor in, and a few seconds later Brian Showers bounded up the stairs to her apartment. Megan wobbled the end of the phone at him, indicating she was having a conversation, and invited him in silently while she tried to remember what question McGrath had asked. "Oh. Uh. I'm pretty sure Simon can afford a lawyer." Megan made an *eegh* face at Brian, who returned a *what?* face of his own. "It's not pro bono anyway. And that exhausts my knowledge of legal terminology, just so you know."

"Is he guilty?"

Megan said, "God!" explosively. "God, I hope not. I don't know."

"Who is he accused of having murdered?"

"His wife, also an American."

"Oh." Interest came into McGrath's voice. "Is this the food critic? Elizabeth Darr? I follow her blog. Followed, I suppose. They've arrested the husband, have they? That'll cause a fuss. Where are they holding him?"

"Uh, I don't know. Detective Paul Bourke is the investigating detective, if that's any help. I can call him and find out. Or I guess you could?"

"Why don't you," McGrath said decisively. "Text me the location and I'll meet you there."

"Me? Why me? I'm not a lawyer."

"But you are, I trust, Mr. Darr's fri—"

"Doctor."

"Doctor? Brilliant, you're right, he should be able to afford the legal fees. I trust you're Dr. Darr's friend, and while it's a rare fool who turns down counsel, particularly non-Legal-Aid counsel, when it arrives, it never hurts to have an explanatory presence alongside you. When was the arrest?"

Megan, feeling like her head must be spinning, said, "Around eight this morning?"

McGrath, sounding more like a gossipy aunt than a defense lawyer, said, "Five hours ago. Let's hope he's had the sense to keep his gob shut," and hung up, leaving Megan with the phone to her ear and astonishment on her face.

Then she hung up and turned to Brian's inquisitive look. "Uncle Rabbie strikes again. He got Simon a lawyer, and I have to—" She waved the phone in the air, trying to encompass all the things she needed to say.

"Go on then," Brian said cheerfully. "Text me when you have something juicy."

"I will." Megan kissed his cheek, then scurried for the front door, texting Paul Bourke as she went. It took a few minutes for him to respond that Simon Darr was being held at Pearse Street Garda Station. She forwarded that on to McGrath, ran home to walk Mama Dog, and hurried off to the garda station.

The Pearse Street Garda Station was an intimidating grey edifice that Megan had passed dozens of times without realizing its significance. It ran the length of the block, three stories tall with steeply sloping attics and tremendous old chimneys rising higher yet. One end of the building was curved into a tower, showing off nine white-framed windows. The whole thing looked alarmingly forbidding. Megan breathed, "Jeez" as she approached its main entrance, the centremost of three featured arches at the middle of the building. As she went through the heavy doors, two stone-sculpted police officer faces looked sternly down at her from a hundred years in the past.

A guard who looked about thirteen lifted his gaze from behind the front desk as Megan entered. She gave him a perfunctory smile. "I'm here to see Simon Darr. He was arrested this morning."

"Ah," said a big voice, "you'd be Megan Malone, then. Gareth McGrath." McGrath was a generously proportioned man—big jowls, big shoulders, big belly—in his fifties. He had a deep voice, soft hands, an even softer handshake, and could have, Megan thought, taken the wall's place and held up the ceiling with ease, if necessary. He gave the young garda a nod, and the kid, sighing like this kind of work was beneath him, escorted them through the station to the holding cells.

Simon Darr sat alone in his holding cell, head lowered and shoulders slumped. He looked up at the sounds of their arrival, and his baffled gaze went from Megan to McGrath and back again.

"You need a lawyer," she said simply. Simon's expression began to clear a little, as if she'd provided an unexpected life buoy and he couldn't imagine why. "I told you I'd help if I could. This is Gareth McGrath, a friend of my uncle's. But Simon, I have to ask—"

"You don't," McGrath said, his deep voice sour. "You've nothing to ask my client, Ms. Malone, though I appreciate the introduction." He gave her a hard look through his big eyebrows until she left, wondering if she could have said anything that would have allowed her to stay. Probably not, because she was pretty certain that even in Ireland, there was a such thing as attorney-client privilege, which could presumably be rendered null by a third party in the room. Not that she really knew if it worked that way in the States, but it sounded reasonable. *She* wouldn't be protected by that privilege, so could presumably be induced to report whatever she'd overheard discussed between them. Shaking her head, she left the garda station and met Detective Bourke just in front of the building.

His eyebrows lifted marginally in greeting. "Ms. Malone." It sounded remarkably like *what are you doing here*, and she tilted her head and nodded toward the station's interior. Because perfectly normal people did things like that, she thought with a sigh, and said, "I was visiting Simon" aloud. "He's got a lawyer now. Uncle Rabbie says well done on growing up to be a guard, by the way."

Bourke's quicksilver smile rode on the end of a laugh. "Does he, now. Tell him I'm sure it was the hard work that summer that set me on the path."

Megan, curious, said, "Was it?"

"It certainly impressed upon me that I'd prefer not to lift fish totes for a living. It taught me I'm not one for the smell of the salt sea or the brisk wind off the Atlantic, and left in me a lifelong admiration for those who do that kind of hard physical labor year in and year out. I've friends in the guards who have never worked that hard in their lives and think themselves clever for it, but I think they're wrong. I think there's not many of us who wouldn't be better for a summer or a year learning how much effort goes into getting the things we expect on our tables *on* our tables."

"Tote that barge," Megan half-sang quietly and, more clearly, said, "How egalitarian of you, Detective."

Bourke inclined his head. "All thanks to Uncle Rabbie."

"He'd be pleased. Is Simon going to be okay in there? I don't know anything about Irish jails," Megan said apologetically.

"He'll be as well as any man accused of murder," Bourke replied, not at all reassuringly. "I'm not eager to condemn the man, Ms. Malone, but all the early evidence points his way."

Megan sighed. "Yeah, I get that. How do you—" She broke off, feeling foolish, then continued at Bourke's small motion of encouragement. "How do you figure out if he's really guilty or innocent, though? I mean, you have to find Cíara, right? And see if Liz was actually having an affair. And you have to figure out if there's any connection between Simon and Martin Rafferty, but how do you even do that?"

Bourke chuckled. "We ask loads of questions loads of times, in as many ways as we can to see if the story stays the same. And we look into their pasts, to check if they ever crossed paths. We talk to friends, and to enemies if we can find them, to figure out if there's anybody who would want a man—or a woman—dead. Sometimes," he said with a sparkle in his blue eyes, "we ask Google, and it tells us all the craic. Not often, though. Mostly. it's boring desk work, if you want to know the truth of it. Tracking financials and travel patterns and security cameras. Most criminals aren't as clever as they think they are."

"Some of them must be, though. Clever enough that even if you know they're trouble, you can't pin anything big on them."

"And the trouble with nabbing them on something small is, then they go to prison, learn how to be a better criminal, and return to the streets better prepared than they were before. But neither Simon Darr nor Martin Rafferty have a criminal record, so whatever they've got in common, it's not that."

Megan said, "Well, there's the money laundering," without thinking, and Bourke's attention focused on her like a sunbeam in the hot summer afternoon.

"The what?"

"I'm—oh, God, I shouldn't have said anything. Look, let me ask you something. How would a person go about money laundering anyway?"

Bourke stared down at her for several long seconds. "Why is it you're asking?"

"Liz's parents think Simon might have been involved in it, and there's a lot of money missing from Canan's books, apparently. Seriously, though, how do you even do it? I have no clue." Megan looked around, as if the garda station stairs might offer her somewhere to hide in mortification for even bringing up the topic. They didn't, and she returned her squirming gaze to Bourke, whose pale eyes were incredulous.

"That's because it's illegal, Ms. Malone, and law-abiding people don't ask how to do illegal things."

"Sure, but do you know?"

The detective sighed deeply. "Take your cash to a casino, or find a junket who will give you casino chips in exchange for your cash. At a fee, of course."

"Of course." Megan squinted her eyes at him, trying to indicate he wasn't actually being very helpful. "What's a junket? I thought that was what film stars did to promote their movies, like a press junket."

"Ms. Malone," Bourke said, sternly, "I'm not about to tell you everything you need to know to enter a life of crime. If you're only asking so you can sort out what Dr. Darr has been up to, the general idea of it should be enough, and I'll remind you this is my investigation, not yours."

"Well, yeah, but he's my—" "Friend" overstated the relationship, but she'd stuck her neck out a long way for an acquaintance. "I just want to know what happened," she muttered. "So 'junket' has to do with gambling? Because of the casino chips? Gambling is legal in Ireland, right?"

Pieces were starting to fall into place, as satisfying as putting a puzzle together, or solving a crossword, except she couldn't quite see the picture yet. Or the theme, if she wanted to keep with the crossword metaphor.

"It is," Bourke replied warily. "What are you up to, Megan?"

"You know, you just called me 'Ms. Malone'

twice in a row when you were reprimanding me, and now that you're trying to figure out what I'm doing, you went with 'Megan,' probably because people respond well to hearing their names. Try a more subtle tact next time, maybe, huh? I don't know what I'm up to, but if I figure it out, I'll tell you."

Bourke, dryly, said, "Lovely," and looked beyond her at the station. "I'd best be getting back to it."

"Of course." They both stepped to their rights, the smooth creation of distance reminding Megan of Regency dances in movies. It evidently reminded Detective Bourke of the same thing, because he offered a small, precise bow that Megan answered with a curtsy her jeans shorts and T-shirt didn't do justice to. They went their separate ways, both smiling, and with Megan considering just who *she* could ask questions of, to find both Liz Darr and Martin Rafferty's killers.

Instead, a minute later, she got a phone call from an unknown number, which, when she answered it, proved to be Gareth McGrath. Megan tried to put him into her contacts while talking and ended up hanging up on him.

Embarrassed, she added him and waited an extra few seconds to make sure he'd realized they'd lost connection before calling back. He didn't give her time for an apology, only said what he'd been trying to say when she hung up, which was a weary, "Am I understanding correctly that last night you gave the police evidence of my client dealing drugs without first informing me?"

"Um. I didn't think of it that way, but . . . yes?" Megan turned back toward College Green and

Dame Street, where she'd be able to catch a bus back home but found a building entrance to lean in so she'd be out of the way of passers-by while talking on the phone.

"Megan," McGrath said in tones both fatigued and thunderous, "whose side are you on here?"

"*Elizabeth's!*" Megan surprised herself with the force of her cry. "I mean, Jesus, Gareth, I don't want Simon to be a drug dealer or a murderer, but I want justice for his wife! I want to know why a man with everything would deal drugs, and I want to know why someone would murder a food critic and an entrepreneur, and I want to know how they're connected! I want to know where Cíara O'Donnell is, and why Liz Darr is posting vlogs from beyond the grave, and what I'm supposed to do with the three stray dogs living in my apartment!"

"Em, what dogs?"

Megan sagged against the building's glass door and sighed. "Nothing. Never mind about the dogs. So Simon *was* dealing drugs? That's what I thought the paperwork meant, but I'm not exactly a forensic detective, or whoever it is who figures out that kind of thing."

"Your police detective came in with proof of it and he confessed, having been caught red-handed," Gareth said. "He swears to God he didn't kill his wife, though."

"Who was he dealing to? Did you believe him?"

"That kind of man? Desperate housewives and stupid students. He's not the type to get himself in deeper with gangs or major drug runners. He deals prescription drugs, not the hard shite."

"Prescription drugs are hard enough. Aren't something like over half of all drug deaths from prescription drugs, not—" Megan's vernacular failed her. "Not street drugs? Like, illegal ones. You know what I mean. What's his source here? He wasn't employed in Ireland, right? Even if he was, I don't think the drug companies here go around handing out bucket-loads of samples like they do in the States, do they? And what about that quiet period in the paperwork, where Liz thought whatever he was in to had ended? Why did he start up again?"

Gareth's chuckle broke up over the phone connection. "Rabbie says you drive rich people around in fancy cars. I think you missed your calling. You've got a detective's instinct for asking the right questions."

"Well, what are the answers? He can't just be shipping stuff in from the States, can he?" Megan thought guiltily of the large bottles of ibuprofen and aspirin *she* had brought back from America the last time she'd visited, after discovering the latter, especially, couldn't be bought in packs of more than twenty-four in Ireland. But aspirin didn't fall under the same drug class as opioids or stimulants, and she'd still expected some hypervigilant TSA agent to confiscate it all. "He's got to have a local source. What hospitals did he say he's been interviewing at . . . ?"

"Whose side are you on?" McGrath asked again. "These are questions for the gardaí to ask, Megan, not you."

"I know that, and I'm sure they will. It's just that they won't *tell* me, and I want to know."

"It'll all get written up in the *Independent*," Mc-Grath said. "When it's all done and over with. You'll get your answers then."

"Have you no God-given curiosity, man?"

"It's my job to only be as curious as absolutely necessary and no more. And you've made me more curious than I like, so you and Rabbie will owe me for this."

"You're getting paid," Megan retorted. "We won't owe you anything."

"Just keep your nose out of Dr. Darr's business," Gareth replied sourly. "I've got enough of a job already, thanks to you."

CHAPTER TWENTY

Niamh would be onstage by now and hadn't called to enlighten Megan on the topic of where theatrical types got illicit drugs. "Actors," Megan said aloud to the building, in a tone that indicated their lack of reliability, then laughed. Mama Dog wasn't even there and she was still talking to herself. Maybe she needed a dog after all. Or maybe she *didn't*, she told herself firmly. *Maybe* she needed a real, live human person around to talk to, although with the amount of time she'd spent on the phone the past few days, Megan didn't really think she suffered badly from a lack of people to talk to.

She pulled earphones out of her pocket—she had long since decided she would never buy anything that didn't have large enough pockets to carry her credit cards, phone, keys, and earbuds—and marched up to Dame Street to the beat of an Irish pop duo called Jedward. They were twins and she'd been seated next to one of them—she had no idea which—on a short-hop flight, during which he'd scrolled through a truly astonishing number of selfies on his phone and sung along to music he had on his headset. He'd had far too much cologne but a rather nice voice, and Megan had looked up their stuff afterward. They weren't bad, and most pop music was good to walk to anyway, so she bopped along happily enough until she got to a bus stop, where the timetable sign informed her the bus wouldn't arrive for another twelve minutes.

She could be halfway home by then, walking, and she always preferred to keep moving than to wait for a bus that, like Godot, might never come.

She turned Jedward off, though, and pulled up Liz's website instead, listening to all three of the vlogs again, hoping to isolate the music enough to recognize the recording of "Molly Malone." Nothing sounded familiar as she stopped into the George's Street Arcade, a Victorian construction purpose-built as a shopping centre a hundred and fifty years before, and got a frozen yogurt from a shop at its far end. The Arcade was probably her favourite shopping mall in Dublin, even though she couldn't get much practical there, not unless she wanted to buy old books, wigs, hats, or retro-style clothes, which she loved but could never convince herself to wear casually.

Someone joined in singing "Molly Malone" as she worked her way back through the Arcade's narrow halls, toward George's Street, and realized she'd been whistling the tune the whole time she'd been shopping. She waved at her accompanist, went back out into the sunshine, and got on the bus when it caught up with her halfway up Camden Street—literally halfway home, just as she'd expected.

The bus was sweltering—air conditioning was not a thing in Irish vehicles—and she was grateful to disembark near her apartment, where she went upstairs and searched on "Elizabeth Liz Darr Molly Malone" while tickling puppy tummies. The babies were getting visibly stronger by the hour, although according to the internet, they wouldn't even have opened their eyes by the time somebody from a rescue centre was able to pick them up. A tragic little pang shot through Megan's belly at the thought and she shut it down fiercely.

There were an absurd number of hits on the combination of Liz and Molly Malone. Most of them were magazine interviews, but the one from the *RTÉ Lifestyle Show* had a video. Megan lay on her tummy, put a puppy on each hand, and hit *play* on the computer's touchscreen with a wet puppy nose.

It didn't work. She giggled and stretched her neck until she touched it with her own nose. It started to play and she backed up again, shaking her head to uncross her eyes.

Liz Darr, dressed in a Peter Pan–collared blue dress with a retro cut, sat across the couch from a well-dressed blonde and a balding RTÉ presenter, both of whom Megan had seen before in various news clips and neither of whose name she knew. The first few minutes were the usual sort of inanities talk shows generally opened with: introducing and lauding their guest, a dumb joke that everyone laughed a little too hard at, and praise from the guest for the hosts and the area in general. Then they got down to the really incisive, hard-hitting questions, like, "What brought you to Ireland?" and "Have you a favourite town?" which Liz answered with grace and obvious pleasure. Megan whispered, "When are they gonna get to Molly?" to the puppies, who had fallen asleep on her hands and had no opinion on or interest in the matter.

They got to Molly near the end of the ten-minute segment, with the blonde host saying, "Now, Liz, I understand you sing, and that you've a favourite song about Ireland?"

For all that Megan knew the whole thing was planned, she still admired Liz's laughing, "Oh, no. I mean, yes, I do, but no!" before, after a few seconds of persuasion, she put her shoulders back and sang the opening verse of "Molly Malone" quite beautifully.

An actual chill raised hairs on Megan's nape and sluiced cold ripples down her spine. Liz's RTÉ performance was unquestionably the same rendition of the song used in the posthumous vlogs.

Megan sat up carefully and very gently put the puppies back in their bed with Mama, then pulled the laptop onto her crossed legs and hunched over it, listening to Liz's lovely voice sing what had become her dirge. She backed it up when the song ended, listening again, trying to figure out if there was anything in it—a changed word, a dropped verse—that might indicate why someone had laid the song, this *version* of the song, over a dead woman's video blogs. No matter how many times she listened, she ended up shaking her head, unable to hear anything amiss.

"Put a pin in it," she said aloud, for once actually giving herself advice she wanted to listen to, rather than just filling the quiet air. She mimed doing that very thing, sticking a pin in the thought, and got up to stretch, walk around the flat, and think.

Mama Dog sighed heartily at her antics and Megan waggled a finger at her. "Moving helps me think. You know who I need to talk to? Noel. I wonder if Fionn's got his number." She texted Fionn, who responded a couple of minutes later with the nightclub manager's mobile number and a warning that he tended to sleep until four in the afternoon. Megan wrote **it *is* 4 in the afternoon** back to her and called him.

His voice mail said, "This is Noel Duffy and I will never, ever check my voice mail. Please send a text" and ended. Megan muttered, "Fair enough," and sent a text asking if she could meet up with him.

He wrote back immediately with **sure, im at the club** and Megan promised to be there within half an hour. She took Mama for a quick walk, got her home again, and on the way out the door got a photo text from Cillian, showing him sitting on the edge of a hospital bed with his sister and her itty-bitty baby. The two adults were smiling like tired fools. The baby had been caught in midyawn, and her mouth was a great, gaping, black hole in her tiny red face. Megan turned back, took a picture of the puppies squirming around on their bellies, and sent it back with **does the young lady need a friend to grow up with**? She was still chortling over Cillian's explosive **NO!!!** when she got to

Canan's and found Noel outside, sitting on the Molly statue's platform and looking unhappily at the cordoned-off church building. "Noel?"

He looked around, his gaze landing on her with a vague degree of recognition. They'd met a few times, mostly in the busy restaurant—enough so that Meg could pick his compact frame and fashionably faded brown hair out of a line-up, if she had to. She wasn't sure he could do the same, though he stood and offered his hand with a polite, "Howza, Meg, what's the story."

"Hey, Noel. They still won't let you in, huh?"

"No idea when they will, either." Noel sat on the statue's pedestal again, shoulders hunched with tension beneath a snugly fitted pink dress shirt. He wore *extremely* well-fitted dress slacks in dark grey, too—Megan wouldn't have minded if he'd remained standing—and his shiny leather shoes looked like they cost a month's take-home pay. "Turns out the guards can close off a crime scene for up to six days. Who feckin knew? They say it probably won't be that long, but they're keeping it closed until tomorrow, at least."

"Fionn's in bits." Megan sat beside Noel, looking up at the church, too. "She said all the numbers she'd seen were great, but now they're not. Do you think Martin kept two sets of books?"

Noel gave a sharp, ugly laugh. "If he didn't, he's the only honest club owner I've ever known. Yeh, of course he did. I'd make the deposits, yeh? Martin was in every night to count down the tills, and I'd make the deposits. And I can tell yis, I was putting more money into the bank than the club took in. I've worked in a club since I was eighteen, like. I can tell how much a nightly take ought to be, just from seeing how many people are in and out. The club here, it does good business, but not that good." His glance slid toward her cautiously and away again. "'Course, I could be wrong."

"I'm not a guard," Megan said. "It's no business of mine what you knew or didn't know. I just wonder how a guy like that—successful businessman, educated in Canada, all of that—gets involved in money laundering. There've been a lot of laudatory media articles about him, you know? None of them say he grew up in trouble, and all of Ireland is kind of a small town, in its way. If he'd run with the wrong crowd as a kid, there'd be rumours about his success now, wouldn't there?"

"'Run with the wrong crowd.' You're sure a Yank, so you are."

Megan laughed. "God, I'm not, though. It's like—" She laughed again. "To everybody outside of the States, yeah, we're all Yanks. But to Americans, Yankees are Northerners. North*easterners*, from the New England colonies, the Unionists in the Civil War." She laughed again, this time at Noel's baffled expression. "I'm from Texas. Calling me a Yank, to my ears, is like calling a Dublin-born lad like yourself a Rebel," which, in Irish parlance, meant from County Cork. Dismay, nearly offense, flew across Noel's face, and Megan laughed a third time. "Now you get it. But yes," she finally agreed. "Yeah, I'm a Yank, and I don't even know what the Irish version of 'ran with the wrong crowd' would be."

"'Fell in with the wrong lot,'" Noel offered. "And you're right, Martin didn't. He might not have gotten into this fix if he had. There's loads of good in finding local investors, all the community-building like, but the reason people use banks is, they're regulated thugs. Martin . . . look, I'd say he didn't know who he was getting in bed with until it was too late."

"Who?"

"It's worth my life to answer that."

Surprise shot through Megan, making her hands cold despite the afternoon's warmth. She wet her lips, trying to figure out how to respond, then, cautiously, said, "So I'm guessing you didn't, and won't, tell the guards any of this." Noel's gaze shifted away and didn't return to Megan's face. She was quiet a moment before dropping her voice to make a guess. "The guards will be looking in to money laundering. They've reason to. But I know that if a few quid of those oversized deposits didn't make it into the club's bank account, that's not any business of mine."

Noel's shoulders relaxed incrementally.

Megan turned a thoughtful gaze on the old church building, with its handsome, vaulted entry at the side and the more usual, broad wooden doors at the front. A second building of the same stone and style sat beyond it, presumably the rectory, and a parking lot too small for the size of the place abutted the restaurant next door. "I never thought about the risks of borrowing from individuals or local investors instead of banks, at least, not beyond, like, risking pissing your folks off for not paying them back on a car loan or something. That's, um, enlightening. Thanks for the insight, which I totally came up with on my own."

A breath of humor escaped Noel's lips and he

produced half a smile, aimed at the church. "Sure you did so. Somebody needed to know," he said very quietly. "But I couldn't be telling the guards. Not just because a few quid might have gone missing. There are other things."

Megan nodded. "Like I said, it's no business of mine. But if you ever want to talk to somebody who's a total outsider and knows nothing of the details, you've got my number, and . . . yeah. No business of mine." She stood, then hesitated. "I've got what's probably one more stupid question." Noel flickered an eyebrow, invitation to continue, and she said, "Did—do—drugs get sold in the club? Street drugs, or illegal prescription drugs?"

"We've got security cameras everywhere to make sure that doesn't happen." The line sounded sharp, rehearsed. Noel slid another glance at her, then turned his attention elsewhere, as if, by not looking at her, what he said next actually came from someone else. "There might be a few blind spots, if you know where to stand."

"Did you ever see Simon Darr in any of those blind spots?"

Noel looked straight at her. "You'll never find a bit of footage with Simon Darr at the club."

Megan whispered, "Right," and then, almost as quietly, "Thanks, Noel," as she left.

CHAPTER TWENTY-ONE

She ended up back at the Library Bar, only a five-minute walk away, whirling unconnected bits of information around in her mind like a tornado looking for somewhere to touch down. The bemused bartender there gave her the fizzy drink she ordered, and a pen and several napkins to write on, asking, "Don't you have a phone to take notes on?" as she did so.

"Ah, yeah, but I'm old and writing things down is faster than thumb-typing them out." Megan gave the woman an absent smile and took her drink and her napkins to a table, where she ignored the drink in favor of scribbling down what she knew.

Simon's gambling problems had led—she suspected—to selling drugs to cover his debts. He'd given it up for a while, but had begun again when he'd come to Ireland, for reasons she still didn't know. Detective Bourke probably did by now, but Megan could just imagine his face—or tone of voice—if she called up and asked. And Noel had

implied that Simon *had* sold drugs in the St. Andrew's nightclub, but that no one would ever
prove it.

On top of that, he'd needed somewhere to launder his drug money . . . and Martin Rafferty, it appeared, had been eyeball-deep in money laundering
through Fionnuala's restaurant. They might have
crossed paths, but when or where Megan had no
idea. And how *Liz*, instead of Simon, had ended
up dead because of it—Megan shook her head,
took a sip of her soda, and blinked away tears as intense carbonation went up her nose. She had to be
missing something. Something to do with Molly
Malone, as unlikely as that seemed.

After another nose-burning sip of soda, Megan
put her headphones back on and listened to Liz's
RTÉ interview again, all the while moving around
napkins that said *Liz* and *Simon* and *Martin* or had
drug and money laundering notes on them. Liz's
tuneful "Molly Malone" ended and the woman host
pressed her about what, particularly, appealed to
her about that song.

"There are so many layers to it," Liz Darr explained. "To begin with, it's simply about a working woman, someone who's up at dawn every day
to do her job, and I think we can all relate to that.
But there's more to it than that, to me. Poor Molly
dies of a fever—"

"'And no one could save her,'" sang the host, as
well as Liz herself had done, and Liz's laughter
bubbled in Megan's ears for a moment.

"Right. And, you know, to me, there's a terrible
reflection of the world we're still living in, when I
hear that. Healthcare, especially healthcare for

women, is so precarious, so underserved, in so much of the world, and to hear a centuries-old song speaking to that same problem—I mean, I know how far we've come in that time, don't get me wrong, but it still resonates for me. And then you add into it the question of Molly's . . . other job, shall we say? The oldest profession, one that women today are still driven to in order to make ends meet, or to escape abusive relationships . . . I don't know. To me, Molly's story is a story of the female condition, and what we do to get by in the world. And wow, that really kind of brought the whole thing down, didn't it? Invite me on to talk about the Irish tour and a new book and you get a quick dissertation on domestic abuse. . . ."

"Well, in fact, it makes the transition to our next segment very nice, as next up I have Janet Ní Shuilleabháin from Women's Aid, and we'll be talking about how women—and men—*do* escape those scenarios. But first, Liz Darr, internationally renowned food critic and author, thank you for your time!"

Liz's "My pleasure" was drowned beneath audience applause, but Megan almost didn't hear it anyway. She'd written down an astonished *DV? Domestic violence* beside Simon's name and turned off her headset to stare in silence at the pieces of paper she had before her.

Paul Bourke would never tell her if she called up to ask whether Elizabeth Darr's autopsy report had shown any signs of domestic violence. Liz's parents *might*, but Megan couldn't imagine calling to ask such a question. She couldn't really imagine asking it at all, but the link felt real somehow.

Maybe that was the notorious gut instinct police officers in film and TV were always counting on, although Megan noticed someone usually told them they needed facts to back up their guts with.

She folded her napkins into a pocket, finished her soda—its carbonation had faded some and didn't render her teary-eyed with bubbles—and left the bar to walk over to the Shelbourne Hotel.

The Dempseys were still in their room. Megan was grateful that they invited her up when she called from the front desk. Even so, she hung back, not coming farther than the end of the hall beside the bathroom, when she entered. Mrs. Dempsey, jaw set tightly, said, "What is it?"

"I have an awful question to ask," Megan said quietly. "I'm trying to understand—to find out—what happened to Liz—"

"We know what you're trying to do." The words, although sharp, didn't feel cruel; they only felt like a grieving parent struggling to push through the worst days of her life as functionally as possible. "Just ask."

"Did Liz's autopsy report show any signs of domestic abuse? New or old?"

Mr. Dempsey said, "Jesus" in a grief-torn voice. His wife sat down hard on the bed, fists clenched in the covers, as if trying to keep herself from falling off the face of the world. It took several seconds before she could answer—Peter didn't even try to—and when she did, it was just with the shake of her head. Megan nodded, but Mrs. Dempsey gathered herself to speak and finally managed, "No. No, they asked about two accidents, and now that *you're* asking, I understand why. She fell off a horse a few years ago and broke her upper arm, but Simon was actually filming her at the time, so he clearly wasn't at fault. And she tripped on the hem of a long dress, going upstairs, a while ago, and broke her . . ." She touched her upper lip, just below the nose.

"The maxilla," her husband said roughly. "It's called the maxilla. That was at a friend's wedding. She ended up being a bridesmaid in a borrowed dress and an ice pack, but she refused to go to the hospital until they were married. There are pictures of her with her entire face swollen up." He laughed, though it fell apart into tears. "Those are the only two bones she's broken as an adult. She fell out of a tree when she was seven and broke her arm then, too, but . . ." He shook his head. "Why?"

"Because—I don't exactly know yet. There's something I think I'm missing. I'll tell you when I've figured it out, all right? I'm so sorry for asking." Megan retreated, feeling like an utter heel, and worse, not knowing what to do with what she'd learned. It had to fit together somehow, the puzzle pieces all laid out before her but their edges blurring and shifting instead of creating reliable shapes.

She walked the hundred metres up to the Luas and tagged on, taking a seat and pulling her crumpled notes from her pocket to spread on her lap. *Simon* and *Liz* and *Martin, money laundering* and *drugs* and— "Shoot."

She'd forgotten to write down the blog posts, and tore one of the napkins in half so she could do that. Blog posts and Cíara, who probably wasn't really missing but also hadn't been seen in two days, which was missing enough for Megan's tastes, just then. If Liz and Cíara *hadn't* been having an affair, or at least a friendship, there had to be some other connection, unless Niamh's gossip was all wrong. In Megan's experience, Nee's gossip was often exaggerated but rarely entirely mistaken.

She took out her phone and tried "O'Donnell Liz Darr" as a search combination and, for the first time, got a hit.

Four months ago, just weeks in to the Darrs' Irish tour, Elizabeth Darr had written a scathing review of the Sea & Sky restaurant in Bray, owned and operated by Joseph O'Donnell. In May, just over a month ago, the restaurant had closed permanently, citing poor reviews and declining clientele as its reason for closure.

Megan, heart rate accelerating until she felt like she'd been running, gathered her notes and lurched to her feet as the tram reached her stop. The sunshine pounding on the sidewalk radiated heat that made her realize her trembling hands were so cold, she was having trouble holding her belongings. She shuffled under the tram stop's glass-and-metal shelter to sit on a narrow, slanted bench long enough to get her notes back into her pockets, and to grip her phone in both hands while she read the article again.

There were no pictures of Joseph O'Donnell or his family, nor any mention of their names, just an estate agent's photo of a beautiful little building on the Bray waterfront, white paint and blue shutters making it look rustic and welcoming.

Hair stood up on Megan's arms, chilling her despite the heat. Shivering against it, she walked home with her attention on the phone as she read more about the restaurant. It had opened late in Ireland's Celtic Tiger years, barely long enough to establish itself before the boom collapsed and Ireland's economy fell to pieces. Since then, it seemed to have been touch-and-go until Liz's review put the final nail in its coffin.

Reading the articles over the years, Megan wondered at the fortitude of anyone willing to try running a restaurant as a business. Fionnuala deserved an evening out and heaps of admiration, particularly if she pulled Canan's through its current mess.

Everyone, Mama and puppies alike, was asleep when Megan arrived home; Mama didn't even twitch an ear in response to the door opening and closing. Megan tiptoed to Liz's computer and went into her blogging software, copying the IP address that the last vlog had posted from, and pasting it into a search window.

The IP came back as a Bray address, and all the breath rushed from Megan's lungs.

Cíara O'Donnell might not come up on an internet search, but Joseph O'Donnell, proprietor of the Sea & Sky restaurant, did. Megan didn't have the resources to nail down whether the IP address correlated to the O'Donnells' home, but they were both in Bray, which was a lot more than she'd had half an hour earlier.

And Martin Rafferty was from Bray. Knowing that made her fingers twitch. There had to be a way to connect him to the O'Donnells, though for a few long moments of staring at her computer screen,

Megan couldn't figure out how. Then she opened a new search window and started typing, more as if her twitching fingers had plans of their own than through any really conscious thought. She'd typed in "canan's restaurant investors" and opened yet another window for "sea & sky restaurant investors" before she fully understood what she was doing. Once she did, a thrill of nerves zinged through her and she had to take a couple of deep breaths before checking the search results.

Most of them were predictable: different banks, mostly Irish but one in Canada on Canan's behalf, some family money, some personal savings—it astonished Megan, what detail could be found in news articles and financial reports—and a general variety of angel investors, none of whom meant anything to her as names. Both restaurants did have an investor in Bray, but the company names weren't the same. Megan sank back in the couch, glowering at the computer screen, then, arms stretched so she could type, she put in both the Bray companies to see what there was to learn about them.

Nothing helpful: one had been established in the '90s; the other was much newer, part of the late teens economic recovery that mostly seemed to be rich people getting richer. The older company was run by a man whose picture indicated he'd been middle-aged then and was presumably old by now; the newer, by a young-ish woman. Megan put both their names into the search and wasn't surprised to come up with hits, since she figured investors usually had internet presences. The man had been in business for decades and the woman had inherited some family money she'd decided to put to good use.

Megan, skimming both of their biographies, felt like hitting her head on a wall. Investigations— even real-life investigations—looked exciting on TV, but she supposed they'd been edited to remove all the tedious bits, or at least had been given voice-overs to add some drama to the moment. She clicked the woman's bio shut, eyes flickering over something that twitched in her mind as she did, and had to open it back up again to figure out what had set off a warning.

Nothing really: a connection to a Lynch, was all. Megan had connections like that of her own, which was probably what had made her notice. Then, out loud, not caring that the dogs were asleep, she said, "Oh, *dang*, Meg, come on already," and called Rabbie.

"Don't tell me you need another lawyer," Rabbie said sternly upon answering the phone. "I've sorted one out for you already, and he's none too happy with being handed a confessed drug dealer as a client."

"He'll still get paid," Megan replied. "No, I don't need a lawyer. I just wondered if you know anything about, uh . . . Cora Kelly, in Bray? Or Micheál Hayes? He's about your age."

"Micheál Hayes is a man you want to stay away from," Rabbie said without hesitation. "If he his own self wasn't involved in the Troubles, you can bet his father was, and there's not a penny that family's got that wasn't made off the blood and heartache of others. Even today, you'd tug your cap if you saw the man in the street and never breathe a word of where the money they made went."

Megan, fascinated, said, "Where *did* it go?"

"You never heard it from me, but between you, me, and the wall, I'd say you can look to the cocaine and heroin on the streets and see a path leading straight back to Micheál Hayes."

"Straight back? Really? Then why isn't he in jail?"

"Well, it might be a twisty path, at that. Nobody's proven anything, though they've been looking to for decades. After the Good Friday Agreement, all that gun-running money got cleaned up somehow, but you don't stop knowing how to smuggle just because peace has broken out. Watch what you say, though, Megan." Rabbie's voice was as serious as it could be. "There's slander laws here like you haven't got in America. Now, that girl, what did you say her name was? Cora Byrne?"

"Kelly."

"No, that's wrong," Rabbie said decisively. "Cora Byrne was Micheál's niece who went off to America in the eighties when she was just a wee thing. Her mother was his wife's sister and her husband died in the Troubles. Nelly Byrne wouldn't have a thing to do with Ireland after that, said the whole lot could murder each other in the streets and she'd never say a prayer for any of them, and her sister, Micheál's wife, Anne that she was, died in 1993 without ever having heard from Nelly again."

Megan, both incredulous and delighted, said, "How do you *know* so much?" and Rabbie gave a deep chuckle.

"It's not such a big country as all that, my love,

and when you see the wee girl and her mother off at the port and watch them looking their last on the auld country, it's not a thing you forget."

"I think you've got a heart as big as the world, to remember everything like that. So Hayes's niece, Cora Byrne, left as a little girl, and Cora Kelly is running an investment company out of Bray now. It's probably coincidence."

"Probably," said Rabbie cheerfully, "unless it's not. What *are* you after, Megan?"

Megan said, "Answers," absently, typing a search query into her computer. "I'll give you a ring back later. Thanks, Rabbie."

"Be good," Rabbie admonished, and Megan hung up to read a Wikipedia variation on Cora Kelly's biography. *Born in Ireland and educated in America.* Well, that could mean almost anything. Megan snapped her computer shut and decided she'd go figure it out for herself.

CHAPTER TWENTY-TWO

God—or more to the point, Orla—forbid Megan should *borrow* a car from the car service. She hired it, paperwork and all, and got on the road to Bray at about a quarter past five, which was a terrible time, even on a weekday, to look for an investor. Ireland's white-collar businesses tended to close at five on the dot, or six at the latest.

There were two roads down to Bray: the scenic route along the water, which Megan much preferred, and the M50, which was as close as Ireland got to a freeway system. The latter took less than half the time, and—not being Irish-born, and unable to embrace the mañana-but-without-such-a-terrible-sense-of-urgency aspect of Irish life, Megan took that, getting into the south-Dublin town just before six.

Bray's waterfront still had the seaside resort air it had developed almost two centuries earlier, with pretty Victorian buildings dominating the entire shore from the northerly end all the way down to the hill called Bray Head at its southerly end. She parked at the DART station and, after a longer walk than expected, found the O'Donnells' restaurant just on the south side of Bray Head, both the mountain and the derelict hotel of the same name. The restaurant was a comparatively new building, probably from the 1970s, before it was decided that the waterfront's Victorian charm had more tourist-trapping value than new builds. Consequently, it looked badly out of place, especially with its blue-shuttered windows boarded up and a heavy, steel security door in front of the original front door. An estate agent's information hung on a board outside the building, and Megan took a picture of it in case she needed the number later.

Then, with her phone's mapping software turned on, she walked up into the town proper. Literally up—Bray itself was set above the waterfront—and she slowly found her way to Cora Kelly's office. She spent the entire walk trying to remember what "estate agents" were called in the States, struggling with it even though she knew she'd known it as recently as yesterday. The word *realtors* finally dropped into her head, awakening a bloom of triumph and amusement. She'd had friends in school and the military whose first language wasn't English and who would occasionally find themselves unable to remember a word in their native tongues. Doing the same thing with words *in* her native language fell somewhere between embarrassing and laughable.

Aware there was no way someone would be in the office at 6:15 on a Sunday evening, Megan knocked anyway, waited a few seconds, and backed up to look regretfully at the building. Once upon a time it had been a standard "two up two down" Victorian home but had clearly undergone extensive changes since.

All investigative curiosity aside, Megan always liked seeing the insides of old buildings, even when they'd been completely refurbished with modern interiors. She liked it better still when they hadn't been modernized, or when they'd been "renovated sympathetically," as the housing shows said, with the high ceilings and cornicing and old window sashes left in place.

A little regretful, she paused on the sidewalk, trying to decide which way to go, and to her surprise, a woman's voice behind her said, "Sorry, did you knock?"

Cora Kelly looked very like her website picture, if a few years older: nicely highlighted auburn hair that probably didn't grow out of her head that colour, an intelligent brown gaze, and a carefully calculated smile that spoke of both curiosity and caution.

Megan, genuinely surprised, said, "Oh!" and came back up the walk to stand a comfortable distance away. "I did, yes, hi. I'm sorry, I figured no one would be at work. It's a Sunday and such a long shot, but—" She stopped herself, cleared her throat, and said, "Sorry. My name is Megan Malone. I'm looking for some information on an acquaintance of mine." She offered her hand, and Cora, after a moment's hesitation, shook it.

"Cora Kelly. I actually live above the offices, so you caught me somewhere between home and work." Cora sounded like Megan's friend Brian

Showers but more so: her accent was a complete mess of Irish and American, as if it had no idea where to settle. "What can I help you with?"

"A friend of mine—an acquaintance—has gone—" Megan wrinkled her face. "I don't know if she's gone missing or if I just can't get hold of her, if that makes sense. I've only just met her, so I don't have her number, but there were a couple of deaths recently and I'm just . . ." Cora's eyes had widened progressively as Megan spoke, and she ended up finishing, "I'm just making a mess of this, aren't I?"

Cora lifted one hand to hold her thumb and middle finger an inch apart, mouthing, "Maybe just a little," with obvious humor. "Want to try again?"

"I'm looking for a girl named Cíara O'Donnell," Megan tried, and Cora's expression cleared.

"Oh. Joe and Edna's daughter?"

"Oh my God, you know her?" Megan's voice shot up and she tried to claw it back down into its normal register. "Yes, that's her. Her father ran the Sea & Sky restaurant?"

"Well." Another pinch of humor darted across Cora's face. "I'd say it was Edna who ran it, but yes, I know them." Concern replaced the humor. "Wait, what's happened to Cíara? Why don't you come in for a moment?" She stepped out of the doorway, inviting Megan into a clean, fresh, modern office off a hall that emphasized Megan's impression of the original two-up-two-down layout of the house: stairs to one side, a hall along them, two rooms front and back, though the back had long since been extended, and extended again. Megan counted two more doorways leading into what had probably been a large garden, 150 years ago and were now more office space and probably a toilet.

The initial office, fronted by an old, curved bay window, was lit by filtered sunlight through a lace privacy curtain over the bay window, and retained a number of its period features, including the fireplace that would have once warmed the room. A sofa, probably custom-built to fit the curve of the bay window, sat in front of a radiator that did half of the heating job now; another radiator sat in the space beside the fireplace, nearer to the back wall. Cora's desk, with a computer and phone on it, had a couple of nice-quality chairs facing it, and two framed pictures, one of which was presumably her family, and another that Megan couldn't see at a glance.

The walls and the fireplace mantel displayed a dozen or more photographs of businesses on their opening days: ribbon-cutting ceremonies, corner-stones being laid, someone smashing a bottle of champagne on a building's front steps. Cora was in a few of them, alongside beaming business own-ers, and—judging from a mid-range-quality Nikon DSLR camera half-hidden by the computer screen on her desk—Megan bet she'd taken a number of the others. There were art prints as well, pho-tographs taken around Bray, and Megan paused to ask, "Are these yours? They're beautiful."

"Oh, thank you. Yes, it's a hobby. But what's wrong with Cíara?" Cora gestured to the sofa and sat at one end of it herself, a frown wrinkling her forehead.

Megan, sighing, sat as well. "Maybe nothing. It's just—did you read about the food critic's death? Elizabeth Darr?"

Cora's face went solemn. "I did."

"Well, Ciara knew her, and it turned out that Liz's review had been the—"

"The final nail in the Sea and Sky restaurant's coffin," Cora said with a sigh. "Yes. That was an investment that paid off. I was sorry to see it close."

"Right," Megan said, relieved she didn't have to explain it all. "But I haven't seen Ciara since right after Liz's death, and then yesterday the owner of Canan's, the restaurant Liz died at, was murdered."

"Jesus!"

"I know. So it's probably nothing, but I'm worried about Ciara. And—I'm sorry, it seems a little stalker-ish now, but—I looked up people who might have been involved in the restaurants and found your name and hoped you might be willing to tell me where Ciara lived, or where her parents lived, so I could check on her."

"Sea and Sky is the only restaurant I've invested in. You said restaurants," Cora said to Megan's confused blink.

"Oh. Yeah, I'd looked up people in Bray who invested in Martin's restaurant, too. In Bray, because this is where he was from, and I thought—you know, the hometown thing? I thought maybe people here would know more than some random investor in Canada or something. And I could drive to Bray," Megan admitted with a quick smile. "If I hadn't been able to find you, I guess I would have tried the other guy—Michael Hayes, I think his name was."

"Mee-hall," Cora said, correcting Megan's pronunciation to *Micheál*, the Irish version of *Michael*, almost absently. Megan's stomach tightened, but she only nodded, brushing it off as Cora went on. "It would be a little unorthodox of me to give you the O'Donnells' address or contact details, but . . . I hate to think of anything happening to Cíara, too."

"It's almost certainly nothing." Megan scrubbed her hands over her face. "It's just bothering me, you know? With two people dead, I just . . . I can't even imagine how she might be caught up in it all, but I just want to make sure she's okay."

Cora smiled suddenly. "Americans, huh? Always trying to fix other people's business."

"Oh, God. Not necessarily one of our better traits, honestly."

"And yet also one of your—our—most charming. I grew up there, though I've been back in Ireland almost fifteen years. I got a business degree in the States and the Celtic Tiger was booming, so I thought, why not come home and make my mark?"

Cora smiled, as if suddenly embarrassed at bragging, and Megan shook her head, admiration in her voice as she said, "That's a big change, a big risk. That's amazing. Good for you!"

Delight fought with shyness in Cora's face at the praise. "Thank you. My mother was furious with me, actually. She never wanted anything to do with Ireland again, and she didn't care much that I'd done well. Coming home to a country that had done badly by her was unforgivable."

"Ireland's been a hard country for women for a

long time," Megan said quietly. "It's getting better."

"Everywhere's getting better. Not fast enough, but nothing ever does, does it?" Cora moved her hands like she might wipe away tears, though none had fallen or even shone heavily in her eyes. "Well. Enough of that. Tell you what, I'll give the O'Donnells a call and see if Cíara's home."

"Oh, you're brilliant. Thanks very much." Megan politely looked away as Cora got up to use the phone, as if by turning her attention out the window, she had magically turned her hearing off, too. Cora's brief conversation ended with a thanks, and she came back to the couch frowning.

"Her da says she's not home, which I wouldn't normally think anything of, but now you've got me worried too."

"I'm sorry," Megan said, meaning it sincerely. "What a thing for me to do, just turn up on your doorstep to make you worry about someone else."

"Americans," Cora said dryly.

"Yeah. Look, I'll give you a call when I find her, okay? Just so you don't have to be fussed about it. I'm sure she'll turn up soon."

"Ah, you're very good. Thanks—it's Megan, right? Thanks very much, Megan."

"No worries. Thank *you* for your time. I know this was a weird thing to have fall into your lap."

"Not at all." Cora escorted her to the door and Megan waved as she trotted down the steps and struck off back toward the boardwalk.

The minute she was certain she was out of sight—and an overblown sense of paranoia meant she'd gone three blocks and around two corners to achieve that certainty—Megan stopped to lean against a wall and press her hands against her stomach.

Cora Kelly had known who Micheál Hayes was. Known well enough that she'd corrected Megan's American pronunciation of the name—*Mykul*—to the Irish *Mee-hall*—without even thinking about it. Everything else she'd said—details Megan bet she wouldn't have given an Irish-born person—lined up with what Uncle Rabbie had remembered of Cora Byrne and the mother who had left Ireland decades earlier. Whether Cora had a finger in the family pie or not, Megan would lay money on the Hayes family being the connection between Martin and Liz's deaths.

When she trusted her voice, she took out her phone and called Paul Bourke. His voice mail picked up immediately and she stomped her foot like a three-year-old, then held her breath behind her teeth until his message stopped and hers could begin. "Hi, Detective Bourke, this is Megan Malone. I'm out in Bray looking for Cíara O'Donnell and I just—look, it's probably nothing, except I just spoke with a woman named Cora Kelly, one of the investors in—ah, jeez, this takes a lot of explaining. Look, can you give me a call as soon as you get this? I'll explain then."

She hung up, but, phone still in hand, she put "joseph edna o'donnell bray" into the search engine and spent a minute swearing at the European Union privacy laws that meant that, unlike in the US, she didn't get a hit on a home address—or, more likely, an option to buy a pass to a website that would give it to her—immediately. Normally, she approved heartily of making it more difficult to find people online, but without the resources of an actual police department, at the moment she found it a real bother. The internet generally agreed that, yes, indeed, Joseph and Edna O'Donnell lived in Bray, but wouldn't go any farther than that. Finally, exasperated, Meg stomped back down to the boardwalk near the closed-down restaurant and started waylaying passers-by with an embarrassed laugh. "I'm looking for Joe and Edna, who used to own the Sea and Sky? I was supposed to visit, but I wrote their address down wrong . . ."

The second person she stopped laughed, patted her shoulder, and said, "You're not far wrong. They're just down the street there, d'you see the red door? Two doors past that."

Megan, in her most American accent, said, "Oh my God, thank you so much," and got another laugh that sent her on her way.

Three minutes later, holding her breath, she knocked on their door.

CHAPTER TWENTY-THREE

Joseph O'Donnell looked very like his daughter, with the same broad face and strong jaw beneath a headful of thinning but enthusiastic blonde curls. His hair was worn much shorter than Cíara's and made the paleness of his blue eyes that much more startling in a tanned face bruised with weariness and defeat. He looked like he'd be at home in a business suit, though at the moment he wore jeans and a T-shirt that emphasized he was still graced with a youthful build, but with its strength chipped away until the very act of opening the front door took a mustering he hardly had left in him. He simply waited for Megan to speak with no particular curiosity or interest on his face.

Megan's heart twisted in sympathy: losing a business he'd poured his life into must have been devastating to leave a man not yet fifty in this condition.

Megan said, "Hi," gently. "Mr. O'Donnell? My

name is Megan. I wondered if you had a minute to talk?"

Mr. O'Donnell shrugged one shoulder, not much of an invitation, but not, at least, an outright rejection. Megan nodded her thanks and took a breath, expecting to engender anger with her next words. "I have a few questions about your relationship with Elizabeth Darr."

To her utter surprise, O'Donnell slumped with absolute despair, obviously using the doorframe for support. "God, I wish she hadn't died. I knew someone would come, after she did. What are you, a guard? A reporter?"

"No, neither. Liz was a friend of mine. I'm trying to figure out what happened to her." Megan hesitated, lip caught in her teeth, then plunged ahead. "You're sorry she died?"

"Jesus, yes, what kind of monster do you think I am? Oh." A bitter note came into his voice. "Oh, you thought ah, sure, the O'Donnells, they'd want her dead for ruining their restaurant. All I wanted was the place back. We might have opened again under a new name, if we could scrape the capital together. But with her death? No. No, that finishes us. There's too many people like you, who'll put it together that she died after the place closed, and they'll decide we had something to do with it, whether we did or not. Nobody can make a go of it with that kind of rumour dogging them."

Megan nodded. "A friend of mine runs the restaurant she died outside of and said something similar."

"Canan's at St Andrew's?" Joe O'Donnell nodded heavily. "And the owner died yesterday, didn't he? They're fucked," he said bluntly. "I'm sorry for them, but they are."

"I hope you're wrong. I think—" Megan looked for the words. "I know Martin was the money man for Canan's. It must be just about impossible to find financing these days, with everyone wanting a sure thing. I'm afraid my friend, Fionn, the woman who runs the place—I'm afraid she'll end up taking money from the wrong people, to keep the restaurant afloat."

"I wouldn't know anything about that. My wife handled the money. Said I had no head for numbers. My job was to be good-looking and cook, is what she said. Said they were the only things I was good at."

Megan offered a little smile. "I don't know, you must have been a pretty good dad. I only know Cíara a little, but she's a lovely young woman."

Surprise filtered through Joseph O'Donnell's blue eyes and he cracked a smile that looked lost and uncertain on his lips. "Thanks. She's my good girl. She worked at the restaurant while she went to university, got her degree. I thought she'd take over. Not cooking, but like her mam, running the place." Whatever pleasure he'd had in the thought faded. "But that's all gone now."

"I'm really sorry." Megan meant it. "Cora Kelly said Sea and Sky was a good investment and she'd been sorry to see it close. Maybe she could be convinced to invest again."

O'Donnell's expression turned quizzical, shoulders rising and chest caving, as if he was asking a question. Megan frowned. "Cora Kelly? She called a few minutes ago—well, maybe half an hour now—to ask if Cíara was home?"

If he heard her, Joe O'Donnell didn't show it, his attention going beyond Megan to someone on the street. Megan followed his gaze to a woman of about his age with a mothering face and a cloud of soft curls unlike either Joe or Cíara's corkscrews. By the time she looked back to Joseph, he'd shrunk back into the doorway, shoulders hunched. "I'd best be getting back inside. Dinner's not ready, and herself likes it to be on the table when she gets home."

As he spoke, the woman called down the street, her voice light and teasing. "What are you doing out here, talking to pretty women, Joe? Is my tea ready? Get inside wit' yis, and let me sort this out." Though she sounded cheery, a few more steps brought her close enough for Megan to see that she looked weary and walked like every step ached. She had on a coat despite the evening's warmth, and heavy white shoes with serious support, the kind worn by people who had to spend all day on their feet.

Megan offered a smile. "Mrs. O'Donnell? My name is Megan. It's nice to meet you."

"You too, chicken. What can I do for you?"

"I was just here to ask after Cíara. Work's been closed, but I hadn't heard from her in a few days, and I wondered if she'd come home after all the fuss."

Joe O'Donnell stopped in the doorway, his whole big body going still. His wife took her coat off and handed it to him; his hand snaked out, took it, and came back in as if he was afraid of the sunshine touching him, though his tan, bearing deep shadows in the sunlight, said he spent plenty of time outside. Edna wore a tired-looking nurse's uniform that explained her heavy-duty shoes, and glanced down the road toward the restaurant. "Cíara? No, love, she hasn't been home in days. Joe, is my tea ready?"

"Almost." Joseph cast Megan a startlingly desperate look, then disappeared into the darkness of the house.

"You know how girls are," Edna O'Donnell said to Megan. "Once they've grown up a bit, there's no coming home, or calling, or any of it, for fear they'll have their wings clipped."

"I suppose all kids are like that." Megan smiled at Mrs. O'Donnell and tilted her head toward the house. "I'll let you get your tea. Sorry for the intrusion."

"Not at all, love. Tell Cíara to call home, when you see her."

"Of course." Megan waved and wandered off down the road, away from the O'Donnells' house and the restaurant alike.

Half a block later, at the next corner, she turned toward the seaside and took the next block back, the strains of "Molly Malone" playing loudly in her mind, and the segue between Liz Darr's segment on the *Lifestyle Show* and the following section about domestic abuse filling her vision.

Joe O'Donnell's strong arms had not been shadowed by evening sunlight but by fading yellow and green bruises.

* * *

One side of the boarded-up Sea & Sky restaurant faced the beach, where dozens of sunburned Irish families were splashing in the cold seawater and playing on the rocks and the brief stretch of sand. At this southerly end of the beach, there were fewer families, but more hikers on the road and path leading up to Bray Head. The other long side of the building faced the hill where the train ran by, and the two shorter sides of the building faced, respectively, an open parking lot and a derelict hotel with houses, including the O'Donnells', overlooking it. It left nowhere Megan could conceivably break in at seven in the evening without someone being likely to notice. But Edna O'Donnell had looked at the restaurant when Megan asked where Cíara was, and Edna O'Donnell worked at a hospital, where she could have gotten the slow-acting poison that had killed Liz Darr.

Breaking in to private property, she would explain to Detective Bourke later, seemed like a good idea at the time.

She had to go back to the car for a crowbar and—given that the walk back was nearly a mile in length—she drove it down to park near the restaurant, instead of walking back along the waterfront with a crowbar in hand. She parked on the road, rather than draw attention to herself by using the otherwise-empty car park, and had nearly left the car behind when she thought of the footmats and went back to get one.

A minute later, she found that nobody seemed to notice, or care, that she was striding up to the restaurant with a crowbar in hand. She'd learned in the military that acting as if she knew what she was doing, and as if she was supposed to be doing it, went a long way, but it always surprised her when it worked. She stopped at the windows on the restaurant's far end, as far as possible from the O'Donnells' house, and partially blocked from a view of the beach by the restaurant itself.

Cranking the plywood off the bottom of the window wasn't very hard, but she ended up climbing onto the sill, precariously, to get the top free. It came loose with a screech that stood her hair on end, and too late, she realized she was holding the plywood for balance. It, and she, fell backward and crashed to the asphalt, Megan barely cushioning her own head from cracking against the ground.

The crowbar clanged as it fell beside her, but, lying breathless and in pain beneath the sheet of plywood, she thought that at least the board had fallen on her and hadn't clattered to the hard ground. On a personal scale, she would have preferred it hit the ground, but in so far as she was trying to be sneaky, it landing quietly on her comparatively soft self was better.

She squirmed out from under the board and stood—staggered—to sit on the roadside kerb for a couple of minutes, trying to catch her breath and waiting for the body-wide pain to fade. Nothing had broken, but her whole spine ached, and her tailbone hurt a lot more than just an ache. She didn't feel at all ready to get up, but she made herself do so anyway, and levered the blue shutters open with the crowbar. Then, seeing no other option, she shattered the window with it and cleared as much glass as she could with the crowbar.

The thick, rubber footmat went over the jagged

edge. Megan chopped a couple of rough holes into the plywood with the crowbar's business end and leaned the wood up against the building's wall to give herself something to climb. She propped the crowbar by the wall and, a few seconds later, flung herself into the restaurant's cool, dark interior like a seasoned criminal.

She landed on glass, most of which, fortunately, lay flat, and came away mostly unscathed but cursing, then called, "Cíara?" in a soft voice that still carried through the silent building.

No answer except a faint, electronic hum. Megan got up, teeth gritted against aches and cuts, and—unheroically, she felt—went and washed her hands in the enormous kitchen sink, getting bits of glass out of them before finding some bandages in the first aid kit situated above the sink. Blood welled through them, but it was better, and more sanitary, than bleeding all over the building. Megan flexed her hands a couple of times to be sure of her ability to use them, then returned to the restaurant's patron area, searching behind counters and under tables, and down a set of stairs that led to the toilets and rooms marked "private." They were locked, and Megan banged on them, raising her voice to say, "Cíara?" loudly enough, she hoped, to be heard inside, but not outside, of the building.

The back of her mind told her she was being absurd. Aside from the window she'd just shattered, the restaurant didn't look like anyone else had broken in, and presumably only the estate agent would have keys to the massive steel door that had

been installed. The logic of that didn't do anything to soothe the worry in Megan's belly, or the
instinct that said Edna O'Donnell hadn't glanced
toward their old restaurant coincidentally. Feeling
less heroic and more criminal, Megan found a fire
extinguisher and used its blunt end to smash the
knobs off all the downstairs doors, breaking the
locks so she could get in.

There were paper towels and cleaning supplies,
from bucket and mops to window squeegees, and
the toilets had an old, musty, sewage scent, but
Cíara O'Donnell wasn't tied up dramatically, like a
damsel in distress, behind any of the doors. Megan
put the fire extinguisher back and, as an after-
thought, gave it a half-hearted wipe to remove fingerprints. As if Detective Bourke wouldn't figure out
she'd done all this herself, after the message she'd
left him.

She prowled through the rest of the restaurant
upstairs, finally returning to the kitchen to lean
against the sink and frown across pot racks at the
enormous steel wall taking up half of the kitchen's
back side. A rankling sensation said she was missing something, but she'd explored the whole of
the restaurant, finding nothing out of place.

It took an embarrassingly long time to realize
the wall across from her was a tremendous freezer
door, and that the freezer's engine was the source
of the quiet hum that sat in the bones of her ears.
Megan lurched forward, banging against the pots
and pans, and found the door handle, hidden behind another of the tall kitchen racks. A heavy
kitchen ladle was stuck through the handle, effec-

tively locking it. Megan threw the ladle away, yanked the door open, and gasped as a cloud of frost whooshed from the opened door. *"Cíara?"*

A thin, exhausted voice whimpered, "Hello?" and Megan ran into the freezer.

Cíara O'Donnell sat in a ball, only her feet and bum on the frozen floor, with her arms wrapped around her legs and her long, bouncy hair loose so it fell over her shoulders as a shield against the cold. She could barely lift her head as Megan fell to her knees beside her, though she let out a cry of pained relief as Megan's warm arms went around her. The girl wore shorts, sandals, and a thin, strappy cotton top, the worst outfit possible to be wearing in such cold. "Come on," Megan whispered. "Come on, I know it's impossible, but come on, honey. You have to get up. We have to get you out of here."

Cíara's nod was barely a tremble against Megan's shoulder, and it was Megan's strength alone that got Cíara to her feet. Not upright: the girl couldn't make herself unhunch, and Megan didn't try to force it. She hunched with Cíara instead, helping her to the door, and kicked it shut behind them so it wouldn't freeze the whole restaurant. Cíara was too cold to cry and made awful little mewling sounds instead, a mingle of pain and relief and fear and cold. Megan kept whispering, "It's okay, it's okay," as she guided Cíara into the restaurant, where there was carpet, at least, to sit on. Cíara's legs gave out as soon as they left the kitchen.

Megan went down with her, literally wrapping her legs around Cíara to offer some body warmth while she stripped off her own shirt to drape it over Cíara's shoulders.

"I'm going to call the hospital and the guards," she said, getting out her phone. "Then I'll lie down with you and hold you, to help you start warming up again. You know about hypothermia?" Cíara gave another shuddering nod, her whole body already starting to shiver, great, twitching shivers that came from her core out. Megan bit back tears. It was an amazingly good sign, because when people couldn't shiver at all, they were truly dangerously cold.

She dialed the emergency number, her voice sharp with relief as someone answered and she could say, "Hi, I'm at the old Sea and Sky restaurant in Bray with a young woman suffering from hypothermia. She's been locked in a freezer for a while, I don't know how long."

Her gaze went to Cíara, seeing if the girl could provide an answer, but Cíara's head was down again and she'd fallen over sideways on the floor, curled into the tightest foetal position possible as she convulsed with shivers. Megan said, "The front door is steel-bolted. Please get an ambulance here as quickly as you can," and hung up to call Paul Bourke.

He'd just picked up with a brisk, "Ms. Malone?" when a steel bar smashed across Megan's shoulders and threw her on top of Cíara's half-frozen body.

CHAPTER TWENTY-FOUR

Cíara grunted with pain, or maybe relief, at Megan's warm body making a blanket on top of her. Megan didn't think she herself had cried out, although all the air seemed to be gone from her lungs and it might have made a pained sound as it left. Red and black filled her vision, bursts of agony that left no room for trying to make sense of anything. She tried to inhale and found she could. It cleared her sight and her mind and, as if it took unusual insight to reach the conclusion, she realized if someone had hit her, it seemed very likely they would try to hit her again.

In the movies, she would have done some kind of amazing flip that got her back on her feet and in fighting condition. Even in the moment, she could almost see the cinematic thrill of it all, its grace and power and confidence. It would have been great, but what Megan really did was roll over on poor Cíara like the girl was just a lumpy part of the floor.

She was still on top of her, in fact, when she drew up her legs and snapped them out again at a half-seen opponent, catching a glancing blow on the thigh and disrupting the hammering blow with a—a *crowbar*, with Megan's *own* crowbar—that was swinging down. The crowbar slammed into the floor a few inches from Ciara's head. Ciara screamed, trying to scramble out from underneath Megan, away from their assailant. Megan rolled forward, toward their attacker, and saw, in the corner of her vision, the crowbar rise again. She snatched at it, catching it with only her fingertips, but like the kick, it was enough to throw off the assailant, and gave both Ciara and Megan a precious heartbeat of time.

Megan didn't know, honestly, what Ciara did with it. She jumped to her own feet, adrenaline burning away the worst of the pain across her shoulders, throwing the world around her into sharp enough focus that she could finally see what was going on.

Edna O'Donnell, flush-faced and furious, stood just out of arm's reach with the crowbar held low, like a baseball bat or, Megan thought, a sword she knew how to use. The older woman snarled, "Interfering *cow!*" and ran forward, swinging the crowbar in an upward arc. Megan took one step back at the last possible second, stuck out her foot, and tripped the older woman, who lost her grip on the crowbar as her hands splayed to catch herself. She hit the floor hard, her teeth cracking together, and Megan sat on her butt, seized her hands, and twisted them into the small of her back.

Edna, screaming with both pain and outrage,

let loose a string of invective that Megan's old
Army squad would have appreciated for creativity
and length, while Megan looked around for something to tie up the other woman with. A sinking
feeling in her belly started to say it would have to
be Megan's own bra until a thought struck her and
she twisted far enough around to look at Edna's
feet.

She was still wearing the sturdy nurse's shoes,
with their thick, heavy laces. Megan changed her
weight on Edna's back until she could push off a
shoe with one foot, then planted her knee between
Edna's shoulders while she unlaced it. The furious
older woman tried with all her strength to push up
beneath Megan, or reach back and scratch her,
and largely ended up beating her fists on the floor
like an enraged toddler. Megan leaned harder
into her spine until she got the lace loose, and
then hog-tied the other woman with a certain degree of satisfied ruthlessness.

Cíara had crawled halfway behind the cashier's
counter and lay shivering against its cool wood.
Megan, buzzing with energy, left Edna and went to
put herself between Cíara and the counter, wrapping the girl in as much warmth as she could.
Cíara, stuttering with cold, whispered, "I never saw
anybody take down my mam like that."

Megan tightened her embrace around the
younger woman. "Tell me what happened."

"She's m-mea-mean," Cíara whispered. "Grew up
mean. She used to—she'd have been a fighter, a
boxer, if they'd have let her, like. But they wouldn't,
back then. So she'd hit us when she got mad, 'cause
she didn't have anywhere else to send the mad.

And she got fiercer and fiercer when the restaurant started doing badly, and she'd tell Da he'd be worth more to her dead and don't think she didn't know how to do it."

"You shut up!" Edna shrieked. "You shut up, you little slut!"

Cíara turned her face against Megan's shoulder, shivering harder now. "She showed me the poison ages ago, to scare me into behaving right. Said she'd kill Da with it and there was nothing I could do. She told me how it'd take hours and she'd be nowhere near him when he died, so they'd never think it was herself, and then I'd have her alone to answer to. So when Liz died—when Liz died—" She began crying, tears hot against Megan's skin and probably scalding against her own. Meg finally heard ambulance sirens, and a little relief dripped through her.

"That cow ruined us!" Mrs. O'Donnell screeched. "She deserved to die and I'm only sorry I wasn't there to see it! But you don't know. You don't know." Her rage turned to broken sobs inside a breath, short, ugly sounds that Megan thought were real, and born of fear. "You don't know what I did to keep that place afloat, how hard I worked."

"Liz w-was my friend. I w-went to t-t-talk to her after the restaurant closed, I hoped she would maybe change her review, like. I thought it might help us open again. She wanted to help. She didn't mean for it to close. We went—" Ciara shivered from her bones out and fell into tired whimpers that punctuated her explanation. "We went around together a few times, when she wasn't busy, just to talk about what we could do to help Sea and

Sky reopen, or get a new start. She didn't want to tell her husband. She said they had troubles of their own and I didn't need to come into it, and then she died and I didn't know what to *do*. I knew it was Mam, because of what she'd showed me. I knew it, but I—" Cíara whispered. "I was too s-scared to tell the police. I'm sorry. I hoped if I left a clue someone would figure it out. And you did, you— but Mam figured it out, too. She threw me in there. She said a day in the cold would teach me not to snitch."

"I'm surprised it didn't kill you," Megan said, probably too honestly. The sirens had stopped, voices audible outside.

Cíara gave a wet, hiccuping laugh. "She had to turn it on this morning to get it cold. If it had been all the way cold when I went in . . ." She gave up trying to talk and just shivered against Megan.

"What *did* you do?" Megan lifted her voice a little, speaking to Edna again. "How much money did you clean for your investors? For Cora Kelly, or her uncle Micheál?"

Terror spiked through Edna's tears and she shook her head violently. "I wouldn't know what you're talking about."

"Sure you don't." Megan closed her eyes and lowered her head over Cíara's. Someone outdoors had bolt cutters. She heard the harsh clang and snap of the steel door opening and finally relaxed. "Tell it to the guards."

An angry sneer came into Edna's voice. "There's nothing to tell, I'll tell them—"

"You've told us loads already," said Paul Bourke from the door. All three of the women, even Cíara, looked toward his slim frame silhouetted by the evening sunlight, and he raised his phone, which had an open connection on it. Megan gave a startled, shuddering laugh and looked for her own phone, which lay faceup under a table. She'd forgotten about it, but it had evidently survived the fall when she'd been hit.

Suddenly there were paramedics and police officers in the room, swooping in to take Cíara from Megan's embrace, surrounding Edna, examining the broken window and spilling through the restaurant to see, Megan supposed, what damage she had done.

Detective Bourke stopped in front of her, a hand extended to help her up. Megan took it, letting him pull her to her feet. He looked her up and down, eyebrows rising quizzically. Megan looked down at herself, saw she wore only a bra and jeans shorts, and discovered she was too tired to blush. "I gave Cíara my shirt."

"The very shirt off your back. We can ask little more of each other." Bourke slid his own suit jacket off and offered it to Megan, who accepted it gratefully. As she shifted her shoulders, putting it on, Bourke hissed and didn't quite touch her arm, but made a motion like he'd turn her.

Megan turned, looking over her own shoulder as she did so. Even from the awkward vantage, she saw a swollen, purpling mark that had only just barely failed to break the skin running across her entire upper back. "Ah. Uh. I got hit with a crowbar." She pulled the jacket on, sighing at its warmth and wincing as the lining brushed the huge bruise across her shoulders.

"A crowbar." Bourke's gaze skipped away from her, found the crowbar and its proximity to the now-handcuffed, still-enraged Edna O'Donnell, and looked back at Megan. "You've had quite a day, Ms. Malone. I'm not absolutely sure if I should thank you or arrest you."

"Yeah, I know. I figured. I'll, uh, I'll pay for the damage I did here." Megan felt as though her brain was thickening, slowing down as the adrenaline burned off. "It'd be nice to not get arrested. What are you doing here?"

"Your somewhat scattered message regarding Cora Kelly offered enough detail for a detective to deduce that he might be needed in Bray," Bourke said a little dryly. "Ms. Malone, did it occur to you to contact the *Bray* gardaí?"

Megan frowned up at him, feeling increasingly dim. "No. No, I didn't have any proof, and I thought if Ciara was in here, if she'd been poisoned, someone needed to get to her right away. I didn't know about the freezer." She shuddered suddenly, cold rushing over her. "Sorry. I'm sorry. I'm not half as cold as Ciara, but I was trying to keep her warm and the excitement is wearing off. I'm . . . you heard Edna confess? On the phone?"

Bourke sighed explosively, watching a couple of other guards escort Mrs. O'Donnell off the premises. "I did," he said when she was gone. "I don't think you intended for that to happen, but I thank you for it anyway. And I shouldn't tell you this, but the money-laundering tip played out very nicely. I arrested Martin Rafferty's killer while you were leaving that peculiar message. He was one of the nightclub's bouncers, a man with known low-level gang connections."

Megan said, "Oh my God" faintly. "The big bald guy? Bodybuilder?" At Bourke's askance look, she said, "I talked to him. He seemed nice." She shivered again and Bourke frowned.

"Will you come this way with me, Ms. Malone?" Again, he didn't quite touch her but, with a gesture, encouraged her into motion. After her first wobbly steps, he offered his arm, and Megan took it gratefully. Her entire body felt thick, nothing responding as well as it should. "I have the feeling that right now you might know more about the connections between Liz and Martin's deaths than I do," Bourke said as they crossed the threshold into the evening sunshine. Its warmth melted right into Megan and she sighed, eyes closed, as Bourke guided her. "Or might suspect more, at least. I don't want you to get your hopes up, though, Ms. Malone. You're not going to have single-handedly broken down a money-laundering ring. Martin Rafferty was definitely involved in one, but even if Mrs. O'Donnell was, neither she nor our bodybuilding friend are going to give us any additional information. They're far more afraid of the gangs than the guards."

"I don't think . . ." Megan sat where Bourke directed her to, no longer really able to focus on anything except trying to talk to him. "This restaurant never did very well, according to the reviews and papers, but it stayed afloat until Liz's review. I think Mrs. O'Donnell killed her partly because she's a hateful person but also because she'd been laundering money for somebody for a long time. Maybe Cora Kelly."

"*Who*," Bourke said, mystified, "is Cora Kelly?"

"I think she's Micheál Hayes's niece. Uncle Rabbie told me," Megan said to Bourke's astonished expression. "I don't know if you can even prove it, or if they're working together in any way, because she left Ireland as a toddler and I didn't have enough time to do real research, to try to link them . . . but that would be your job anyway, wouldn't it?"

Her back hurt so much now she could hardly breathe, and for a moment she just focused on Bourke's shirt buttons. Silvery-white, on a light pink shirt. She'd always heard redheads weren't supposed to wear pink, but also thought people should wear whatever they wanted. She raised her eyes to study the contrast of his shirt and his hair in the evening sunlight and thought, overall, it was a rather nice combination. And the pink looked good with his pale skin. His expression grew increasingly quizzical as she stared blankly at him, and finally, she remembered she was spelling out her theories for him.

"Right. Anyway. I found old articles mentioning Micheál Hayes had invested in Canan's, or at least in Club Heaven, and that Cora Kelly was an investor in Sky and Sea. It's the only link I've got between them besides Rabbie's gossip, but Rabbie's gossip . . ." She made an explanatory gesture, and Bourke chuckled.

"Robert Lynch's gossip is more reliable than most people's sworn testimony. It's mad that you're his cousin."

"Remind me to tell you about the truck driver

sometime." Bourke twitched his eyebrows in a silent promise that he would as Megan took a breath that sent searing pain across her shoulders. Dizzy, she planted her hands firmly on either side of her hips and focused on her deductions. "So his gossip about Micheál's niece Cora fit the right age for Cora Kelly, and they're both investors in companies that look like they've been money laundering. I don't even know—I think Simon's drug running is incidental. I don't think he was washing money through Canan's or anything. He just got caught, because Edna O'Donnell was furious at losing her business and killed Liz for it."

"And Martin Rafferty?"

Megan sighed, then wished she hadn't. Her back felt hot everywhere and a deep breath sent chills through her so violently that she shuddered. "There was too much money going through Canan's, and through Club Heaven. I don't know how Martin got mixed up laundering, except maybe by taking investment money from the wrong people." She looked up at Bourke, who swam a little in her pain-edged vision. "That's how it happens, isn't it? You owe somebody, or you're grateful, so you do a little favor, and then another one, and then you're in so deep you can't get out. I think Martin got in too deep, and when Canan's and the club closed down because of Liz's death, their laundering scheme dried up and he couldn't pay, so they killed him."

"Killing people," Bourke said thoughtfully, "is a bad way to get the money they owe you."

"Not if you can get insurance paid out. And not if what you really want to do is scare other people into not falling behind on their payments, or . . . whatever." Megan swayed, and Bourke nodded at someone behind her. They crouched and said, "Ms. Malone? I think we should take you to the hospital."

Only then did she realize she'd sat on an ambulance's back bumper. She gave Bourke a vaguely accusatory look that he answered with a brief shrug. "You don't look so well, Ms. Malone."

"Honestly, I don't feel so great either. But I can't stay overnight. I have puppies. Can I . . . Where's my phone?" To Megan's surprise, Bourke produced it. She took it like it was a talisman and gave him the sternest look she had at her disposal, which wasn't, she feared, very intimidating. "I'll go get checked out and make sure nothing's broken, but I'm calling somebody to come pick me up and take me home after that."

"All right, Ms. Malone." Bourke smiled and stepped back, but she reached for his hand without imagining she would catch it. Nor did she, but he stopped, and she said, "What's going to happen to Simon?"

"He'll probably do time for drug running, unless you're wrong about him being only tangentially involved with the laundering mess. If he knows anything, he might be able to make a deal. He wouldn't be like our local lads, too afraid of the gangs to say what he knows. I'll stop by the hotel and tell the Dempseys what's happened," Bourke promised. "Your friend Fionnuala already knows that Mr. Rafferty's killer has been arrested."

"Oh, deadly. That means Nee knows, too." Megan hadn't realized, until she spoke, that she'd been subconsciously trying to figure out how to explain everything to Niamh and Fionnuala and also get sleep that night. Learning she didn't have to was an unexpected relief.

The paramedic touched her shoulder. "We should go now, Ms. Malone."

"Right. Okay." Megan, stiff with pain, climbed into the ambulance and waggled her fingers in adieu as the doors closed on Detective Bourke. The paramedic checked her reflexes and reactions while she phoned Cillian from work, and he promised to pick up the company's car from Bray Head and collect her as soon as possible.

An X-ray at the local hospital proved her back was bruised and swollen but nothing was broken, and Megan was waiting at the door when Cillian arrived ninety minutes later. With his curling black hair and blue eyes, he looked the part of a superhero as he strode up to get her, and Megan, amused, told him so. He said, "Up, up, and away," and instead of expecting her to tell him everything that had happened, he kept up a cheerful chatter about his new niece the entire drive back into Dublin. He even took Mama Dog for a walk when they got to Megan's apartment, while Megan, rather mechanically, found herself a pint of ice cream to eat, because it was easier than anything else available in her flat.

Cillian dropped Mama off and told Megan to take care, although, she thought, he could just as easily have been talking to the dog. It seemed like good advice, though, so against all good sense, Megan gathered Mama and the two puppies up and put them onto her bed before crawling into it herself. Only after she was in it did she remember she hadn't changed into pyjamas and that, in fact, she was still wearing Paul Bourke's suit jacket.

Megan, smiling, whispered, "I'm definitely not keeping you" and fell asleep to the comfort of three warm bodies curled against hers.

Megan & the rest of her lot
will return in more Dublin Driver Mysteries soon!
Watch for DEATH ON THE GREEN
by
Catie Murphy
coming your way in
September 2020.

Please turn the page for a quick peek at
DEATH ON THE GREEN!

CHAPTER ONE

L ou MacDonald lay facedown in the hazard pond, his pink shirt billowing and puffing with air as the water dragged him under.

A baffled silence rolled over the little group who crested the small hill to find him there. They were mostly fans, men and women who had braved a soft, not-quite-raining September morning for the chance to watch aging PGA champion Martin Walsh play a casual game across the green. The soft-voiced, good-natured murmuring that had come with watching a world-class golfer—even one past his prime—couldn't stand up to the shock of a death on the green. The entire gathering stood rigid with shock, no one able to even imagine what they should do.

Goosebumps shivered over Megan Malone's spine and arms. She didn't even *belong* there really. She was just Martin Walsh's employee, hired to drive him and his wife around for the ten days they were in Dublin. She knew almost nothing about

golf, but Martin had invited her to walk along the
course after dropping his wife, Heather, off at *her*
golf course, farther north on the little flat island in
Dublin Bay. Megan, always preferring to go for a
walk than sit idly in the car for hours at a time, had
come along willingly. She felt her black-and-white
chauffeur's uniform marked her as the help, but
as far as Walsh's fans were concerned, being in his
employ meant she belonged to some secret league
they couldn't hope to aspire to and they kept a re-
spectful distance.

His caddie, a man half again as large as Walsh
himself, was pleasant, especially after Megan offered to help lug clubs. That got her into his good
books, but he'd turned down the offer, and since
his job was being at Walsh's side, he didn't have
much else to say to her.

So Megan had trailed along with the group,
watching them from the outside rather than being
a part of it. Not that she minded. Getting a
glimpse of people's lives from the outside was part
of why she loved her job as a driver.

Usually, though, those glimpses didn't end with
a dead man floating in the middle of one of Ireland's trickiest water hazards.

Lou MacDonald, a big, friendly man, had been
less impressed than the fans, and more open than
the caddies. He'd chatted her up at the clubhouse,
fascinated to hear how an American had come to
be driving limousines and town cars in Ireland.
The short version, Megan had told him, was that
she had citizenship through her grandfather, so
they couldn't keep her out. He'd laughed and
she'd offered to tell him the long version as they

walked around the greens, but MacDonald waved her off with a promise that he might join the group on the last few holes, if the weather warmed up a little. Otherwise, he was more content to sit with a tumbler of whiskey than tromp across the damp greens on a misty Irish morning.

It seemed absolutely impossible that he could be drowned in a pond at the fifteenth, when they'd left him in the cozy clubhouse less than two hours earlier. And yet there he was, sinking lower into the pond while everyone stared in dismay.

Megan finally jolted toward the water, jumping over the low bank into the pond with her knees well bent, to keep from landing hard in unexpected shallows. Freezing water splashed up as she landed deeper than she expected, soaking her all the way to her bra.

She straightened, gasping, and lurched forward, struggling through hip-deep reeds that were nearly invisible from the surface. She heard splashing behind her, as if she'd shaken the others into motion by acting herself. Someone was on a cell phone, calling for help, but Megan reached Lou's prone form and turned him over, fearing it was too late.

His face was flaccid, his skin cold to the touch. She checked for a pulse anyway, finding none, and still lowered her ear to his chest, just in case she might catch some last, promising thump of his heart.

Martin sloshed to her side, his face a grimace of distress. "He's—he can't be—" Like Megan, he felt for a pulse, checking Lou's wrist, though unlike Megan, he dropped the dead man's hand almost instantly, looking queasy. He wasn't a large man, was Martin Walsh, but neither was he so small that he couldn't hit a golf ball what looked like miles to Megan's untrained eyes. He was fit, dressed for casual warmth on the course, and trembling like a frightened animal. The whites of his eyes glared around their brown pupils, and his lips were already going blue. "It hasn't been an hour since we left him! He can't be this cold!"

"It's the water." Irish lakes might be nearly at their warmest in mid-September, but the pond still had a bone-chilling heaviness. It had already penetrated Megan's thigh muscles and was draining the heat from within her. Standing waist-deep in numbing wetness, she felt the muck on the bottom of the pond seeping over her shoes and slowly offering a false sense of warmth.

She gnawed her lower lip, staring at Lou's body, then made a decision and seized his arm, wading back toward the shore.

"Megan, what are you doing? What are you doing?" Martin splashed after her, wake from his movement rolling ahead of them both. "He's dead! Shouldn't we leave the body where it is for the police?"

"He might not be dead. Cold-water shock can slow the metabolism way down. I want to try CPR, but it's a lot easier on shore. Get something warm. Take everybody's coats. There's a—" She got to shallower water and had to turn, grab Lou by the armpits, and drag him the rest of the way to land.

Lou MacDonald hadn't been a small man in life. Now, weighed down by pond water and the boneless relaxation of unconsciousness, Megan would have sworn he weighed about a quarter ton.

Her foot slipped on the pond lip, sandy soil breaking off to splash into the water, and she nearly lost her grip on Lou's body.

Teeth bared and breath short with concentration, Megan tried again, taking a large, awkward step back and straining to haul Lou up. She staggered, back aching, heart pounding so hard it blurred her vision, and shook her head a little in denial, although whether she was saying *no, I can't do it,* or *no, I won't fail,* even she didn't know.

Martin, nearly green with horror, grabbed the dead man's legs and heaved him upward as Megan scrambled backward with the bulk of his weight. A second heave got him all the way onto shore. Martin all but ran from the water as Megan fell onto her bum, then righted herself to hands and knees so she could turn Lou's head to the side. She fished in his mouth with a finger, pulling his tongue straight so it wouldn't choke him. Water dribbled from his mouth and Megan heard Martin throwing up on the grass a few feet away.

"Here." One of the onlookers came forward with his coat. Other people came with him, offering help in increasingly loud, chaotic tones, until a matronly sounding woman snapped, "Put them on top of each other on the ground and smooth them out. You and you, help this woman move the body onto the coats." Even in the midst of a crisis, a tiny spark of humor blossomed in Megan's chest when everyone fell in to helping, unable to deny the Irish Mammy Voice.

A few seconds later, Lou had been moved to the pile of coats. Megan crawled on them, too, putting weight on his sternum in hopes of forcing water from his lungs. The coats were enough warmer than the damp ground that she became aware, very abruptly, of just how cold *she* was. Someone— a woman, from the scent and the glimpse of long, polished nails—touched Megan's shoulder and spoke quietly. "Let me get this wet coat off you."

Megan, still trying to force water from Lou's lungs, nodded. Between one push and the next, the woman stripped Megan's chauffeur's jacket away, then dropped a warm, puffy winter coat over Megan's shoulders. A violent shiver started in Megan's gut and shuddered its way out. She shoved her arms through the coat's sleeves, wishing she dared stop to strip her wet shirt from beneath the coat, but except for that first mouthful, no water had come out of Lou yet. Megan didn't want to risk a hesitation that could cost the man his life.

It felt like forever, although it surely wasn't really more than a minute or two before someone said, "There's no water coming out."

Megan snarled, "I *know*," and only then, slowly, upon hearing someone else say it, began to realize what that actually *meant*.

Lou had only expelled a mouthful of water when she'd turned his head. She hadn't been able to force any more water out of him since, although she was both strong and trained to do that sort of thing correctly.

Suddenly spent, she fell back from Lou's body, only then seeing that blood had pooled beneath his head, staining the light-blue lining of some-one's coat.

Megan clenched her teeth and reached into her inner chest pocket for her phone. For a heartbeat she panicked: the phone wasn't there. Neither was the pocket, for that matter, because she was wearing somebody else's warm winter coat, not her black uniform jacket. She looked around, realizing there were a couple of dozen, maybe more, worried, frightened people looking down at her and the body. One of them was the nail-painted woman who'd taken her jacket and still held it, clutched against her chest.

Megan waved her hand at it and the woman, startled, hugged it closer as she looked around as if wondering what Megan wanted, then visibly realized she was holding what Megan wanted. She handed the jacket back, and even in the grey morning light, even with the fabric black and hiding water well, Megan could see that, despite her splashing entrance to the pond, it wasn't wet much past the ribs. Her phone was probably safe. She still breathed a sigh of relief when the phone turned on without complaint. Megan closed her eyes as she touched the name she needed and put the phone to her ear.

"Detective Bourke? This is Megan Malone. I've just found a dead body."

Author's Note

I've taken as few liberties as possible with Dublin's geography and sites for *Dead in Dublin*, but I'd like to confess to the few places where I've gone properly awry. I'm sure readers won't be surprised to hear that there is not, in fact, a driving service garage of any sort on Rathmines Road, much less one called Leprechaun Limos. Most of the other sites, including the magnificent Stella Theatre, are real, and the copper-domed Church of Mary Immaculate really is a stunning landmark used by everyone in the area. On the other hand, the mortuary at St. James's Hospital has been re-imagined to suit my needs.

Furthermore, with all due apologies to several nineteenth-century architects, I've rearranged the interior of St. Andrew's Church on Suffolk Street to my liking. At the time of writing this, the 150 year old building is under redevelopment and by the time *Dead in Dublin* is published, it's expected to hold a modern food hall, so readers of the Dublin Driver Mysteries will be able to stop by and imagine Fionnuala has cooked up a bit of a meal for them.

My most egregious departure from reality lies in Bray, where the site of the Sea & Sky Restaurant is actually a parking lot. The rest of the boardwalk, however, is very real, and a genuinely gorgeous way to spend an afternoon if you're visiting the Dublin area.

Readers who would like to work their way through Dublin along with Megan can do so at mizkit.com/DublinDriverPhotography, where I'll be posting a series of exploring-Dublin images to go along with each book in the series. I hope to see you there, and on my newsletter, tinyletter.com/ce_murphy!

Catie